The City of Antra has existed through all the ages of Man, every imaginable iteration at one time or another. Majik has come and gone, come and gone again, and *changed*. But always the landmarks are there to be found... the nine Maj Towers, the Great Library, the Tall Troll Tavern, the Bazaar in Yellow Zirkot, the Merkezi Guild, Jalazani's Bathing House. Oh, and Morvedraz' wine shop, of course...

Sometimes called the Arbiter, the presence of the Dwarv Morvedraz has been a constant in the City for many years now...

Tales of Morvedraz

as told

by

L.H. Brady

TALES OF MORVEDRAZ

A Canopic Games book.
Published by arrangement with the author.

PRINTING HISTORY
First Canopic Games edition/September 2022

For information, address
Canopic Games, 5211 10th St SE, Salem, OR 97306

ISBN: 979-8-218-06135-7

PRINTED IN THE UNITED STATES OF AMERICA

1

"*Nore...*" Morvedraz murmured as he lay facing upward to gaze at the velvet blue of the Kwamadan night sky.

"*Nore, what am I to do with you? Impudent child. Ambitious and keen beyond your years. Foolish in your bravery... Perhaps I should have left you to the barbarians. You'd be some rich Lethani's slave by now.*"

The image made him shudder: to think of his darling girl, sleeping on cold stone, eating raw grain and sipping at sponges soaked in sour wine. She was not far from this when he'd found her, bound and barefoot, face swollen and purplish from beatings. Even then, barely a woman, she would not check her resistance under the most severe treatment. It was this resolve that had attracted the barbarian chief, believing that his master would find the girl's energy a refreshing if contradictory change from the throng of pliant slaves he kept. It had been the chief's charge, to find "a challenge," something that would not give itself so readily, that needed taming and discipline. When the chief found the girl, hair shorn like a boy's and clothed in kind, yet with a mature, round figure that belied her disguise, he wondered if her demeanor would match her image. He'd walked toward her as she leaned over a small fire and pulled her from her crouch. When he forced his huge, rough palm underneath her shirt she landed a swift, solid knee to his groin. He doubled over only slightly, protected by an iron cup, knowing he'd found the one.

Morvedraz marveled at the coincidence of encountering this particular band of raiders with this particular girl. Or *was* it coincidence? Who but he could have bartered successfully for her? True, he was no wizard, and, though a hardened trader and merchant, he fought his battles over a counter and goblet of wine—no match for a band of trophy-hungry thieves.

But I have a secret.

He smiled when the dusty band approached on horseback and reached beneath his cloak, wrapping his hand around the object that hung heavily from his neck. Once given to him, Morvedraz had never removed the large, rounded ellipse of a strange, unfamiliar stone. Its weight had become part of him, the sway of it when he moved like the weight of a fifth and vital limb. Perhaps that was why he used it so effectively. And when he murmured the ancient words etched onto its surface, the murderous hoard seemed to sway in mid stride, grow listless and pliant. Within a quarter hour the barbarian chief and Morvedraz sat around a campfire swapping stories while smiling through sips of *blakwine*.

The chief had heard of the *blakwine* of Antra, but had always considered its attributes myth: how its power could rejuvenate and sharpen, give a tired army a distinct advantage over an equally beleaguered foe. He'd heard also of the *kororah*, the long, near-black sticks rolled of a mystical *tabak* that filled the mind with pleasure and heightened the senses. The barbarian sat around the fire with the strange old Dwarv, sipping at a great cup of the bitter liquid, puffing at the oily, smoldering stick, and felt a transcendent pleasure.

The exotic substances, blended with the stone's *majik*, gave Morvedraz just enough power over the chief to coax the unwilling girl from his bond. They stood in the Kwamadan dawn, having remained awake all night, the stimulation of the *blakwine* and *kororah* that had held the barbarian in rapture fast receding. Morvedraz felt his ability to charge the amulet's power waning, and he pressed the chief for a trade.

"Come now. Surely a keg of the *blakwine* and cabinet of *kororah* are well worth the price of a little wench." His stomach clenched at the thought of the harm the girl had already felt at the hands of these brutes. True, he'd seen the same potential in her that the barbarian had seen, but with a different end. He felt a strong essence when near her, the sign of an ancient and confident spirit. She exuded a natural power, one of which she had no awareness.

Yet.

It was also his weakness for the outcast, the exiled, that drew Morvedraz to the girl. For was not he himself an outcast, welcome in many circles of power and wealth, in different lands and in the company of so many races, yet belonging to none of them? And how would he be treated if not for his wares and the power of the stone he wore?

Weary of the girl's relentless struggling, the chief pulled up the stake that held the rope around her neck and handed it to Morvedraz—for three kegs of *blakwine*, and three cabinets of *kororah*...one hundred fifty gallons and one hundred fifty sticks. These riches would have brought the barer ten thousand *zekzi* in the markets of the great City of Antra. Morvedraz had traded them for a dirty, mute girl. All on the prospect of a feeling.

The irascible barbarian had encouraged Morvedraz to beat her to prove his worthiness as a master, but he used the last waves of the amulet's influence to beg off the challenge, assuring the barbarian that such unnecessary harm would only serve to diminish the value of Morvedraz' new asset, to which the chief assented. It would have made no difference to the girl, who possessed no more energy to resist, no saliva left in her parched mouth with which to spit at her new captor.

After the barbarians shrank to only a distant line of dust on the horizon, Morvedraz dropped to his knees in front of the girl, his own tears wetting the warming dust in front of her bare feet. He looked up to see her ellipse-shaped eyes, golden hued and squinted with a look of utter contempt. He tried several common dialects to

communicate with her, to explain his motives, to give reason to his methods. She stood in stony silence. He cut the
ropes from her neck, hands, and ankles, and watched her
run—perhaps fifty feet—before collapsing in the dust. He
covered her with a blanket and waited while she slept,
and when she awoke, handed her hot *blakwine*, bread and
cheese.

His attempt to communicate had transformed into his
own solitary supplications to ancient gods. He'd worked
himself into a trance-like state with his meditation, rock-
ing back and forth to summon guidance from some unknown source. When his prayer subsided and he found
himself sitting cross-legged, staring at the setting Daystar,
the girl nowhere in sight, he leapt to his feet, shouldered
a pack and sniffed the air around him. He could make out
her scent clearly, and he hurried in that direction. Soon he
found the tiny indented footprints in the dust leading to
an outcropping of large boulders at the bank of the great
river, climbed over and saw, cradled by a ring of stones, a
deep, black pool hidden within, the water collected from
the steady current running just a few feet beyond the rocks.
The girl crouched waist deep in the cold water, scrubbing
her naked body with only the river sand she held in her
palms. Morvedraz cleared his throat and the girl immediately sank to her neck, then looked around wide-eyed at
the old Dwarv standing on the high rock. He opened the
pack and lifted from it a clean tunic and leather pants and
a pair of soft leather boots. He held them up so that she
could see, laid them all out on a rock to collect some of the
warmth of the dying light, then turned and picked his way
over the rocks back to his small camp. He llit a fire, sat
sipping *blakwine* and smoking a glistening stick of *kororah*
until the girl returned. The Daystar had long set, and he
had wondered what choice she would make. Yes, he could
use the stone to influence her, direct her will. But he chose
not to.

She walked slowly toward the fire and stopped above it, gazing into the warming flame, then in one weary motion dropped cross-legged onto the dirt. He offered her a cup, and she took it.

"There is bread, cheese, meat." He repeated the phrase in as many languages as he knew. She stared blankly at his face. Then he pointed to the food and her face followed the direction of his hand. She picked up the hard loaf and bit greedily into it, did the same with the other fare. Morvedraz shook his head as he watched her stuff herself. He took a long draw on the *kororah* stick and inhaled deeply, against custom, allowing the potent, spicy smoke to saturate his lungs before releasing it billowing cloud-like into the night sky.

"Ah!" he cried, then cursed a few words in the ancient language shared with him by an old wizard, the one who'd bequeathed to Morvedraz the precious stone. He still kept the tablets onto which the language had been etched—the same tongue that awoke the power of the amulet—but had never heard anyone beside himself and his old mentor speak the strange tones. Then he turned to the girl who sat staring back at him with wide, fascinated eyes.

"*What are you called?*" he rasped at her in the dead language, and watched amazed as her eyes widened even more. She chewed the last of her food and swallowed, then cleared her throat before allowing her small voice to speak.

"*Leonora.*"

Koloran had stayed up late, well after closing the wine shop doors and extinguishing the candle in the window, to prepare for Morvedraz' return from Kwamada. The boy arranged tables, dusted counters, chose the wines to be offered for the next day's tasting, doing so with a grudging urgency. Leonora—"Nore," as she preferred—had been less than ambitious in her efforts with the menial labor while their father journeyed to Kwamada for wares. While the older, reticent Koloran proved a tireless provider, his stepsister took as much advantage of the old man's absence as opportunity offered.

It was not only this behavior that maddened Koloran. Perhaps if she were only lazy... But, rather, it was *how* she treated him, coupled with her apathy, that drove his resentment. He remembered when Morvedraz had brought her home, her hair shorn like his own, wearing a baggy tunic and pants, head bowed toward the floor but her wide, amber eyes scanning everything in her path. He thought she looked like a common beggar from Hilo Street, and at first wasn't quite sure if she were even female. But when she straightened herself and stood with her shoulders back, he caught himself staring at the outline of her breasts pressed behind the tunic's coarse cloth. Koloran was nineteen years old and had never lain with a woman, had never even asked one to share a moment with him in the evening, though Morvedraz had encouraged him to. Koloran's anxiety would always overshadow his desire, and he could only speak in his dreams to the pretty young women who strolled Long Street on warm afternoons, their hair flowing, smiles bright.

He stood, awkwardly staring at the curious stranger whom his father had brought home, and he felt his desire and had to shift his stance. Then Morvedraz walked toward him, placed a hand on his shoulder.

"Koloran, I want you to meet Leonora. From now on, she will be as your sister, and you her brother. Treat her in like honor."

His desire shrank immediately and his face grew hot, embarrassed by his body's reaction to the mysterious young female.

"Clear the storeroom in the basement. Go to Valera's and buy furniture, take her to Karnas and have her fitted for a proper wardrobe. Then return, and we will begin her lessons."

It took Nore only a scant few months to master the entire Antran language, even the most obscure, colloquial expressions, and as her verbal skills grew so did her confidence. Her obstinacy remained, and she and her new brother fought heatedly and often. But as she began to work the counter at the wine shop, her combative nature gave way to a puckish demeanor that enchanted clients. Soon the tasting room counter stood five deep each day with wealthy citizens all clambering for a pour and a few moments conversation with the lovely Leonora.

The wealthy clients thought her at first a fine pleasure slave whom the crafty Morvedraz had procured to expand his shop's services. But when they approached him on the price of "an evening in the girl's company," he refused them gracefully yet resolutely, explaining that she was no servant, but equal apprentice to Koloran, and family as well. Some customers' cheeks flushed with embarrassment and they begged the proprietor's forgiveness, which he gave magnanimously; others simply chuckled and patted the old Dwarv on the back, certain that he kept her to warm his own bed.

While Leonora's status grew in the eyes of those who frequented Morvedraz', Koloran could never manage to elevate his persona above the role of "help." When the wealthy citizens and regents of the *Maj* came to their private booths to enter into bargains or discuss matters of state, it was Koloran they looked to for service. And he obliged them tirelessly, filling goblets of wine and mugs of steaming *blakwine*, lighting *kororah* sticks, arranging special meals: seeing to their every comfort. But it was Nore whom they asked to join them in a hand of *kare*—a popular card game—or simply to sit with them for a few moments and chat of the events of the day. By then her beauty was known throughout the City, and she managed it to her distinct advantage. Nore still looked very young—perhaps eighteen—for she had no memory of when she'd been born, nor even where. But she played her role with the skill of a *grand dame*.

Koloran would often grow infuriated with his cohort, who looked at him with the same haughty expression as did the dignitaries who sat basking in her charm. At night, after the shop had been cleared and closed, and he approached her, she would simply say, "Koloran, I could never keep the shop with the same care you do. It's just not *me*. And besides, what do you expect? For me to lift fifty gallon barrels into racks?"

"No. But it would be nice if you'd pick up a broom or clear a table once in a while—"

"Brother! I keep the conversation flowing. I entertain the crowd. If not for that there wouldn't *be* as many tables to clear. Don't you see? That *is* my work." She'd say these things with a deft certainty and a coquettish smile, then turn and leave her brother to mop floors, take inventory of casks, while Nore fled into the warm Antran night.

Koloran's retiring nature and bookkeeping acumen proved no disadvantage to the daily business of running a wine shop. But his demeanor and basic skills would not serve to continue the shop's more private enterprise. The venue's underlying purpose remained its most vital, and its most profitable. To call his title "unofficial" would be such a grand understatement as to bring a furtive chuckle from the Regent of the *Maj* himself, for the humble, self-deprecating—if well-fed and obviously comfortable—merchant, Morvedraz, was known widely, yet most covertly, as The Great Arbiter of Antra.

This service had grown from humble beginnings when he was a young, struggling vendor, attempting to gain an economic foothold with his new wine business. He had come into possession—by not the safest means—of a large shipment of prized but, at the time, illegal Kwamadan wine. The political struggles between the Regency and Red *Maj* had rendered the verdant vineyards of Kwamada on the axis side, its fruit contraband. Yet it remained the highest quality wine in the known world, and the wealthy and powerful still thirsted for it with the same zeal with which they supported the ruler who'd banned its purchase. Morvedraz had carefully, quietly made known the availability of his supply. Two rival families, both prominent in local society and wealthy beyond comprehension, sought to procure it and had made arrangements to meet at the shop to barter for the entire lot: fifty tuns, some bottled, much still in barrels, enough to keep the family and their honored guests sated for at least several years: enough time for political currents to ebb and revive more common means of procuring a treasured commodity.

The families sent their representatives to Morvedraz' in the Hour of the Basilisk, long before the Daystar would pierce the horizon. They came in parties of six, and they came armed. Morvedraz had indicated in writing his prohibition of weapons, but yielded as the arrivals showed no sign of heeding his protest.

"At least unsheathe your swords. Leave them downstairs on the tables. Then we may sit quietly and have our discussion like the gentlemen we all are."

He smiled when he spoke and exuded a calm confidence, though his stomach churned and his brow dampened. Slowly, grudgingly, the twelve men unstrapped their belts before Morvedraz ushered them upstairs.

He could have merely taken a written offer and awarded the precious wine to the highest bidder. But he knew that the transaction would mean far more than the procurement of a pleasing libation; it would mean status to the family who served it; respect, honor, the envy of those lucky enough to partake of it. He knew also of the chance that bequeathing such prestige to one party could foment hostility between the winning and losing families, which might channel toward himself, and he had long ago resolved that his business, no matter what it may be, would make no enemies, would serve all equally, and profit from all in kind.

When he guided the representatives to the large booth, he purposely ushered them into their seats so that no man sat next to more than one of his own family. None sat at the thick, massive wood of the circular table having any more physical presence over another than did his neighbor.

"Gentlemen," Morvedraz began, "let me say that I sincerely thank each of you, and the honored families whom you represent, for indulging this process of my choosing. I'm sure that our efforts will produce an outcome pleasing to all who have come to share in this wonderful and rare wine."

"What's this meeting all about, Morvedraz?" The huge Lethani from the Trialek Family interrupted, freezing Morvedraz in his place. "Let each side make its offer and allow the better to leave with its rightful merchandise."

"Yes," echoed a dark-skinned Za-Zhirazani from the Family Lor. "Why prolong this 'process,' as you call it? I see no need for a discussion. Let us present our bids."

"Gentlemen!" Morvedraz smiled, regaining the floor for a moment. "I beg your indulgence. I believe that I have a far more pleasing way to determine who will go away from this table with the merchandise. One that will, in fact, leave no one without a portion of that which he desires."

"Do you mean to divide the wine?" the Lethani shot. "My instructions are clear. I am to leave this room only having secured the entire shipment of—"

"What do you mean, *only*," the Za-Zhirazani interrupted, his words dropped slowly from his moist lips. "Are you implying that our presence here is futile? That our offering will be unworthy? Perhaps you should let the proceedings begin before your tongue utters any other misplaced sentiments."

"How could your meager family hope to outbid the Trialeki? We know something of the City's commerce, and it is no secret that the coffers which once brimmed in your treasury are depleted from the many foolish ventures of your family."

"Gentlemen, please! If I may have your attention for only a few moments, I believe that I can convince you that this discussion is most—"

"I need no convincing, Dwarv." The Lethani stood. "I am already certain of the outcome of this 'discussion.' Our bid is one thousand *zeks*." The Lethani held his grinning face high.

"Perhaps you should be more open to our guest, good friend. My family bids two thousand *zekzi*."

"Three thousand," the Lethani added blithely.

"Four thousand *zekzi*," the Za-Zhirazani countered, but hesitantly.

"Ah, does your purse grow light already? Did you think my family would stand to be outbid by the likes of yours? Five thousand *zekzi*."

Morvedraz looked unpleasantly on as the Za-Zhirazani took a deep breath, his dark brow glistening in the candlelight.

"Five thousand five—no, wait... Five thousand seven hundred *zekzi*!"

"Ha! Do you really think a few hundred would make us falter? Cheer up, friend. At least you will leave tonight with your purses still full of what little they hold. And I'm sure we'll be glad to toss you a few bottles to ease your pain." The Lethani said this and turned to Morvedraz, looked him sternly in the eye. "It is late, and I am tired. So let me end this pitiful exchange at once. We will deliver to you, for the entire five tuns, seven thousand *zekzi*."

Those present sat in silence, but for each man's breathing. Morvedraz' mind whirled with the thought of the offer. He had never in his few years of business even let his hopes wander to thoughts of this kind of profit. Such a sum would allow him to expand his inventory, build onto the shop, create a thriving enterprise that would ensure his wealth for life.

"Well, Dwarv? What do you say?"

But he could not bring himself to contradict his original intent. While the sheer magnitude of the offer played at his desire, something within him still echoed the belief that he could be more, far more, than yet another well-to-do merchant.

"Good Lethani, gentle friends all. This offer is most generous and, quite frankly, beyond anything I'd have hoped for—"

"Then it's done!" The Lethani bellowed, and his party cheered along with him. "We came prepared to transport the wine tonight. Here is a token of our honor." He hefted a large, heavy bag onto the table. "One thousand zekzi. We will have an emissary transport the remainder to you over the next fortnight. And I must say that it has been a pleasure—"

"Eight thousand zekzi!" The Za-Zhirazani rose above the jubilant Lethani, who turned toward his adversary.

"Reprobate! You have no means to honor such an offer! Do you think we'd have come here knowing otherwise?"

"What did you call me?"

"Watch your tone, friend. Besides, this deal has already been done. The merchant has his down payment." And saying this, the Lethani thrust the heavy purse so that it slid across the table, landing solidly in Morvedraz lap.

Whether it was from the humiliation of losing, or whether the Za-Zhirazani mistook the Lethani's sudden movement for an advance, Morvedraz did not know. But he could only watch as from between the fold of his robes, the Za-Zhirazani drew a secreted slim dagger, grabbed the hair of the representative to his right—the Lethani's own nephew—and pressed the blade to his throat. The next few moments played out in agonizing slow motion as Morvedraz froze amid the struggle. Bodies thrust at one another over the round table, enraged voices mingled in the haze, a thin spray of blood dotted the varnished wood. Morvedraz sat paralyzed and trembling, sure that his botched plan would not only render the downfall of his business, but in all likelihood his life. He clutched the heavy bag of coin hard against his chest, and as he did so felt a pain against his breastbone.

It was the amulet he'd worn for the past many years, given to him by the Humani wizard who'd taken the orphaned Dwarv and raised him as a son. The wizard had taught Morvedraz sparingly of the amulet's power, and equally warned him that its use should be held sacred; the ability to bend the will of a subject could so easily corrupt the user. His innate Dwarvani mistrust of *majik* well intact, Morvedraz had had no intention of ever actually using the amulet and wore it merely as a good luck token and a memento of his adopted father. But now, chaos and violence erupting all around him, he reached inside his robe and held the stone tightly, then, trembling, uttered the words he'd memorized so long ago but had never, never voiced, the words that would bring the amulet to life.

When he finished the almost silent incantation the cold surface of the stone heated, so suddenly that he quickly released it, and he felt a warmth emanate outward and a wave of energy wash over his body. He wiped the sweat from his brow and peered over the purse still clutched to his chest and saw that all the men sat calmly, if breathless, and stared at one another, their bewildered and distraught faces relaxed of the strained lines of conflict. The Za-Zhirazani's dagger slipped from his hand and landed squarely on the table, startling several of the men, who jumped at the sudden noise. Morvedraz had no idea what effect the amulet would actually produce nor, if it worked at all, how long it would last. But the men appeared at least quiet now, if confused, and he took advantage of the momentary chance.

"Now, gentlemen, I see that you have come to your senses and determined that no arguing or other such distraction is necessary." When he said this he slowly reached for the dagger, not picking it up but merely placing his open hand on it and sliding it toward himself until it rested out of reach of any of the men.

"Let us regain the business of determining how we should share this wonderful wine."

Morvedraz produced from a hidden compartment under the table two bottled samples of the precious wine and a box of lush, oily *kororah*. He filled a goblet and passed it to the man on his right. The Lethani stared at the gleaming ruby liquid, then turned to face his adversary and handed the goblet to him. The Za-Zhirazani bowed his head in thanks and accepted the cup, but passed it in kind to his neighbor. One by one, the men repeated the gesture until each sat sipping his own goblet. Morvedraz clipped the closed end of each stick and handed them to the men. The first Lethani took a candle from the wall sconce and held it for his neighbor who puffed until his stick burned with a bright, orange ember. The men did this with such civility, such patience, that Morvedraz seemed suddenly surrounded by an entirely different group than the one who'd held each other at knife-point only moments before.

Slowly, quietly, Morvedraz explained his plan, explicated a brilliant and rebuttal-proof argument: each faction should have their due share of the wine. The Za-Zhirazani family, it was discovered, had nowhere near the price they'd offered in attempting to outbid the Lethani. They had only hoped to dupe their adversary into relenting, purchase a fraction of the wine after the fact, and have the bragging rights that they had successfully outbid the wealthy and powerful Trialeki of Leth, news that would race throughout Antran commerce and allow the Lor to recoup some of their lost reputation. The Lethani, while possessing every copper of the seven thousand *zeks*, had no intention of paying such a sum to a fledgling merchant, no matter how precious the commodity. Instead they'd have left after presenting him with the down payment and a promise of the balance sometime soon—of course it was difficult moving such large amounts of currency undetected—and then simply leave Morvedraz waiting for a final installment that would never arrive. What could the Dwarv have done? Run to the *gardzi* and demand justice for being cheated of his illegal goods?

When the true nature of each faction's plan unfolded so did their willingness to come to an alternate arrangement. Where they had sat roiled moments before in utter conflict, paying their host nothing but contempt, each family now agreed to what they could reasonably afford, and, even more marvelously, that the other had a right to share in the purchase. In the end, the Lethani left with 35 tuns of Kwamadan wine, for which they agreed to pay 5000 *zekzi*. They produced another bag containing 2000, leaving Morvedraz with sixty percent of the amount owed with the original 1000, with a deeply sincere vow to have the balance delivered to him before sunset the next day. The Za-Zhirazani took away the remaining 15 tuns for 2500 *zeks*, the entire sum presented to Morvedraz before their departure.

When each party disappeared into the pale, pre-dawn Hour of the Jewel, Morvedraz took a long sip from his goblet and pressed his hand against the dangling amulet, gazing at the table on which the bargain had taken place, now covered in coin. And Morvedraz rested with not only a small fortune at his fingers, but certain that his skillful efforts as intermediary would be rewarded in far greater ways.

When word was told of his skill diffusing hostility between the rival families spread throughout the City's circles of influence, Morvedraz found himself in greater demand, not merely for rare, difficult-to-find merchandise, but merely for his counsel. They came hesitantly at first, not sure how a Dwarvani shopkeeper could possess such powers of persuasion and diplomacy, but still they came, and as his abilities grew in reknown, so did the caliber of his clientele. Soon they sought Morvedraz not merely to arbitrate purchases, but simply to ask his interdiction in disputes, matters which would not be "suitable" to bring to the attention of the official courts, and certainly not in the interests of any parties involved to do so. Morvedraz honored their requests—for a generous yet equitable fee—always concocting an arrangement suitable to all. For those who clamored for his service yet lacked the means, the Arbiter asked only for their understanding that perhaps at a time in the future Morvedraz might avail himself of some indulgence that would fall within their ability. This alone grew his reputation far beyond one of simply a high-priced advocate, but as a Dwarv of empathy and honor.

Morvedraz opened the shop early for normal business, before the dawning of the Daystar, so that the wealthy merchants and emissaries of government could stop for a steaming mug of *blakwine*. He always closed the shop at nightfall to normal traffic but kept a large candle burning brightly in a high window, a sign that the Arbiter sat ready to render service into the small hours of the morning, if necessary.

During midday Morvedraz enjoyed taking long walks around the city, accepting offers of fruit, cheese, and bread from street vendors, always with the understanding that these wares required no payment. He would stroll, nibbling a crust, the evidence of his own efforts alive all around him in the city's bustling economy. One day, several years into his growing reputation, he wandered through a side street, a mere alley, to take a shortcut to his favorite antique shop. There he saw a Humani boy, dirty and gaunt-looking, barefoot and clothed only in a man's torn tunic, a length of twine tied tightly around his waist, rummaging through a pile of trash. The boy sensed the Dwarv's presence and turned to face Morvedraz, then shrank into a crouch and pushed himself fearfully away with his feet into the darkened corner.

"There's no need to be frightened." Morvedraz squatted so that he could see the boy at eye level. "Come closer." He beckoned the child forward with an outreached hand. The boy slid into the light, and Morvedraz could see the terror in his eyes.

"It's all right. I won't hurt you. I am Morvedraz. What's your name?"

The boy swallowed and took a deep, wheezing breath. "Koloran."

"Koloran. That's a fine name. Where do you live, Koloran?"

"Nowhere."

"Nowhere? Everyone lives somewhere. Come now. Where is your mother?"

"Dead."

"Oh." Morvedraz spoke, feigning disinterest, struck by the abject dispassion of the boy's tone. "I'm sorry. Then, your father...?"

The boy remained quiet and merely shook his head.

"I see. Well, where is it that you sleep, Koloran?"

"Wherever it's warm."

Morvedraz knew that the waning winter sun would soon sink into still, cold night, the streets icy and landscape blanketed in frost. He thought of the boy huddled amid the frozen garbage.

"Koloran, are you hungry?"

The boy nodded.

"Here. Take something to eat. Go ahead." Morvedraz held out a crusty roll and small wheel of cheese. The boy stared skeptically at the food.

"Well, then, share it with me, will you?"

Morvedraz lowered himself to sit on the cold stones of the alley. He broke the bread and handed one half to the boy, then tore off a hunk in his own mouth and chewed. Seeing the man eat, the boy bit ravenously into the roll, chewing it loudly while breathing through his mouth. Morvedraz halved the wheel of cheese, and the two sat silently eating until each had finished. As he sat watching the ragged boy devour his meal, Morvedraz noticed how his pale brow beaded in sweat and his body shuddered in small tremors.

"Koloran, you look ill. May I touch your forehead?"

The boy hesitated, then relented, nodding and sliding forward on the damp stones within reach of the Dwarv. Morvedraz lay the back of his hand on the boy's damp forehead; his skin burned with fever.

"Koloran, you're sick. Have you felt this way long?"

"For a while. It gets worse at night."

"Look, I know you don't know me, but would you walk with me a while? At least let me help you get something to make you feel better. Would that be all right?"

Koloran nodded. Morvedraz stood and offered his hand to the boy, lifting him from his crouch, and the two walked slowly from the dark, damp alley and into the city sunlight.

Morvedraz led the boy to an apothecary who had a year ago elicited the Arbiter's help in settling a long and bitter property dispute with a neighbor. The apothecary had little wealth but offered Morvedraz life long medical care in return for his services. Morvedraz agreed, and the man remained satisfied in the Arbiter's debt. Now as he ushered the feverish boy into the medicine shop, he knew that the man's services would be worth any amount of gold he could have paid for Morvedraz' intercession.

"Morvedraz!" The apothecary beamed as the Arbiter entered the low-ceiling shop. "I haven't seen you down this way for months. What brings you this far from Long Street?"

"Rolim, this is Koloran." Morvedraz urged the boy forward toward the apothecary. "He is quite ill."

"Yes, I can see that." Rolim placed a hand on the boy's forehead. "Gods, boy, you're aflame with fever!"

"Rolim," Morvedraz began earnestly, glancing at the boy, "I'm finally in need of your services."

"Of course, Morvedraz. Come, boy, lie here." Rolim motioned Koloran to a padded cot in the corner. "Let me bring you a poultice for your head, and some herbal tea that will calm the fever."

Morvedraz watched the boy lying on the cot, sweat soaking his pale skin, his breaths quick and shallow, and felt the cold floor of the Dark Forest again on his own bare back, and the fever that had nearly claimed his own life again coursing through his body. His parents murdered—unbelievably by Dwarvani *waryers*—himself left for dead in the dense thicket of forest, he'd closed his eyes at what he thought would be his last glimpse of the setting Daystar over the tall trees. But when he awoke his fever had subsided, and a blanket covered his near naked body. He saw that he lay in a small field near where his parents' thatched hut now smoldered from just beyond the trees. A small fire burned next to him, and beyond it an ancient-looking Humani, clothed in purple robes, sat with his eyes closed, uttering incomprehensible whispers.

"You are awake, boy. Good. I thought that perhaps I'd found you too late. I worried you would not last the night. Come closer to the fire."

Morvedraz did as the old Humani had beckoned, felt as if helped forward by an invisible force. The fire was small yet burned with an intensity many times its size; the stones that ringed it glowed a strange, radiant hue the same shade as the Humani's robes.

"*What are you called, young Dwarv?*"

"*Morvedraz.*"

"*Ah, a very ancient name. What brings you ill and sleeping under the stars, Morvedraz? Wait, don't tell me... I see it clearly. Terrible... I am very sorry for your loss, my boy. I'm afraid that I can do nothing to quell your pain. But I can offer you the safety of my care. And perhaps...well... majik is not in your blood. Look, I am an old wizard. I have been alive since long before your parents were born. My majik is strong, but my body weakens day by day. Stay with me. Help me administer to my final years.*"

"*I... I don't know you, sir.*"

"*Of course not. I apologize. This is too much to ask of you at such a time of sorrow in your life. I am a fool to have allowed the thought into my head. Let me instead help you back to the Dwarvani kingdom. Surely your people will understand your plight and provide for you.*"

Though he knew not the consequences, Morvedraz understood that some bitter trouble had driven his parents, the last surviving bloodline of their family, to a damp, deep place in the Dark Forest, far from the kingdom in which they were no longer welcome. And the sight of the familiar-looking *waryers*—the glint of their axes, the flame of their torches—still haunted him both asleep and awake.

"*Sir... I'll go with you.*"

"*What's this? Are you sure, boy?*"

"*Yes.*"

"*Very well, then. Let us have some breakfast, and we will be off. Have you ever seen the great city of Antra, Morvedraz?*"

"*Only the gates, sir.*"

"*Well, then... You have much to see, my young friend.*"

When the memory faded from Morvedraz' eyes, he again saw the boy, Koloran, lying quietly asleep beneath a soft blanket, his breathing deeper, calmer now.

"Rolim, you know my quarters. They are well suited for a Dwarvani bachelor, but hardly appropriate for a sick child—"

Rolim only raised his open hand. "Morvedraz, think not another thought. The boy shall remain with my family until he is well and strong."

"Thank you, Rolim. I will not forget your kindness."

"Of this I have no doubt." Rolim smiled, then embraced Morvedraz. "You must excuse me. There are potions I must prepare for Koloran for when he awakes. Leave with only the thought of his recovery."

Morvedraz placed a hand on Rolim's shoulder and nodded, then returned to the noisy, teeming streets of the city.

Koloran did heal, though arduously and not without relapse. Yet Morvedraz remained confident in the apothecary's skill, and as winter turned to spring so did the season of Koloran's health bloom with new life. Though Morvedraz worried throughout the boy's lengthy recuperation, he nonetheless busied himself with preparing a proper residence for Koloran in the quarters above the wine shop. With the proceeds from his latest arbitration—a land dispute between two pompous yet fantastically wealthy citizens—Morvedraz purchased the large, upper unit of an adjoining building next to his own.

He called in a favor from a well-known Antran architect to join the third floor of the wine shop and the neighboring space into one large suite of living quarters: three bedrooms, an office, a common sitting room with fireplace, even a study complete with library, and a verdant roof-top garden. A team of designers outfitted each room, paying special attention that one bedroom would be appointed to especially suit a young Humani male. The office, Morvedraz would himself use, finally moving his modest desk from the cramped, dank basement, creating more space for goods.

He purchased finely-bound volumes to fill the library: books of history and poetry, drama and criticism, atlases with maps of every corner of the known world, great references and encyclopedias, and primers in each of the most prominent languages and sub-dialects. He had the garden filled with plants and potted trees and comfortable benches on which to sit and read or simply take in the view of the pale Antran sky beyond the rooftops. He closed the public area of the shop for an entire week and refinished all the cabinetry, the hardwood floors, the long counter that had lain for decades in a layer of grime and the sticky remnants of spilled wine. He even had the exterior wood repainted, double-paned windows installed on all floors, and a new sign hung to replace the tiny shingle that had sufficed for so many years, one that read only "Wine Shop." As the time grew near to introduce Koloran to his new home, Morvedraz had completed the remodel.

It was unusual enough for a Dwarv to live on Long Street, far from the section of the city that his own kind made their home. But to see such a drastic makeover in such little time was a sight to behold and drew attention away from the incongruity of where a Dwarv might live; the look of such prominent scenery rarely changed so dramatically in the city of Antra.

Morvedraz visited Koloran at the apothecary's every day during his season-long recovery. On a bright, wind-still spring afternoon, as Koloran sat in the window of the medicine shop gazing at a group of boys playing a game in the street beyond, Morvedraz watched from the front office and whispered to the apothecary.

"He looks well, Rolim. I can't thank you enough."

"He's fine now, old friend. A bit small for his age, but strong and healthy as he should be."

"Why is it that he only sits in the windowsill and watches the other boys play? Have you not encouraged him to join them?"

"I have, yes. In fact, the two of us sometimes go out together and begin a small game ourselves. Other boys arrive and join in. They're always friendly to him. I've never seen any teasing or fighting. But, after a little while, Koloran returns to the window and simply watches, or reads—he *loves* to read—and that's that."

"Well, then perhaps we simply have a natural young scholar on our hands, eh? He'll certainly have plenty to read at his new home."

"Still, encourage him to get outside. Play with other boys. He seems to have a propensity toward solitude, which is certainly not all bad and quite understandable considering his past. But he needs the practice of interaction just as much as he needs to read books and ponder great thoughts."

"Yes, you're right, Rolim. I will encourage him. Listen, please." Morvedraz placed both hands on Rolim's shoulders. "There is nothing that I possess that is worthy enough of the thanks I owe you. Consider your debt to me paid in full."

"Don't be ridiculous!" Rolim laughed. "I will always be in your debt."

"And I in yours."

"Then let us both remain so. Now, take your son home."

"One more thing, Rolim." Morvedraz lifted from beneath his robes a crimson sack. He laid it atop the apothecary's desk; gold zeks spilled from the brimming open top.

"Morvedraz! I can't possibly... I won't—"

"*Shh!* Not another word. You have spent your own money and time to heal this boy with little for your own needs. Now take something for yourself, make things a bit easier for your family. And I'm *still* in your debt."

Embarrassed at the amount of coin he'd just received, Rolim bowed his head, then reached for Morvedraz hand, held it in both his own, then slowly guided the hand toward his pursed lips. "Arbiter," he said after planting a kiss on the calloused knuckles. Morvedraz shook his head and placed his hand on the crown of the apothecary's head before pulling him upright. Morvedraz then walked to Koloran's spot in the window.

"Koloran, are you ready?"

"Yes." The boy smiled, then packed a small knapsack with a few books that Rolim had given him, and hugged the apothecary: "I'll see you soon, Uncle Rolim."

"Yes, you will, my boy."

"He means that," Morvedraz chided, wagging a finger at the apothecary. "Don't be a stranger on Long Street"

"Well, what do you think?"

Morvedraz smiled when he and Koloran walked into the solarium. A gentle breeze blew through the windows high on the wall and light poured through the glass skylight; a small bird wandered in and perched whistling on the branch of a potted tree.

"It's...amazing." Koloran spoke slowly and smiled.

"Yes, it is, isn't it? I hardly believed it myself when it was finished. This used to be a storeroom. Nothing but crates and old junk."

They toured the rest of the apartment; Koloran marveled at the library, and Morvedraz had to convince him that it would not disappear if he left it for a moment.

"Don't you want to see your room?"

The bedroom was painted a soft eggshell blue with chalk-white wainscoting and cove base of carved beech; the bed, dresser and closet—also a light beech—were built into the wooden walls. A small desk sat free in the center of the room, atop it a lamp, a quill and inkwell, and a thick manuscript. Koloran thumbed through the pages, found them completely blank.

"What's this for?"

"It's for you. To write."

"Write what?"

"Your thoughts, a story...anything. Koloran, listen..."

Morvedraz approached the boy and kneeled, placing a hand on his shoulder.

"I have welcomed you as my son, and I cannot tell you how pleased and proud I am to have the means to do that. But you are not so young that you can forget your past, your memories. Who you are, where you came from. It will always be a part of you, whether the recollections are pleasant or not. Write them down. Never forget them. You'll be glad you did in years to come."

The boy looked longingly toward the book, it's empty, unruled pages.

"I had them leave the desk free-standing so that you could move it to wherever you like in your room. I always believe that we do our best work that way. I'll leave you to get settled. Come down when you're ready and we'll get some supper."

Morvedraz turned before he disappeared down the hallway, watched while Koloran examined everything in the room, running his hand over the smoothly varnished surfaces of the bed frame, closet, and dresser. Then he took hold of the desk, careful not to topple the lamp and quill, and pushed it so that he could sit at the wide window and gaze down the busy expanse of Long Street.

As years passed, Koloran grew into a strong, lithe young man. He did make a few friends who'd come to visit him from time to time in the grand quarters above the wine shop. But, though Morvedraz encouraged him as much as possible, Koloran preferred a book and the quiet sunlight of the garden to the raucous play of other boys in the streets of the City. Morvedraz did not mind that Koloran's demeanor proved softer, more introspective than other boy's his age. His nature lent itself well to study, and study he did, proving he possessed abilities beyond his years. Morvedraz' plans for the boy to one day inherit not only the wine business, but the role of Arbiter, would require the skills of language, mathematics, history, knowledge of other cultures and races in order to successfully deal with the myriad of problems presented between quarreling parties.

But as he grew into his teenage years and beyond, the balance between Koloran's retiring, bookish nature and his social abilities tipped more and more. When engaging a foreign merchant who arrived at the tasting counter, Koloran would stumble through the conversation even though he knew the language fluently. While he could recite poetry and comprehend entire volumes written in strange tongues, something about social interaction threw him off, and the more he struggled with conversation, the more withdrawn he became. Visitors thought him strangely awkward, and familiar merchants and citizens of the City came to know Koloran as the efficient, polite, yet painfully shy assistant to the Arbiter.

Morvedraz came to understand that Koloran would make a decent, if somewhat acquiescent, merchant. The business was established and held in highest regard by both Antran and foreign clientele, and Koloran would need merely to maintain the level of quality and service that Morvedraz had forged. The role of Arbiter, however, Koloran would never master. He was too pliant, too unsure of his own stance on many occasions. Morvedraz could teach him to overcome this hesitancy so that Koloran might succeed in the wine business. But the Arbiter needed an innate resolve, a calm amid any circumstance, the likes of which could often be surprising, if not dangerous. Also, Morvedraz would not entrust the power of the amulet in someone who could neither fully engage its strength nor manage its consequences. He had learned throughout years of use that the amulet did not merely *act* upon empowerment; rather, it somehow commingled with the nature of the user. Its power would render a subject malleable, open to suggestion, but only if the one who invoked it possessed a means to work the situation and overcome his own fear of the uncertainty around him. He considered his own early attempts to use the amulet lucky at best. The first encounter over the Kwamadan wine had succeeded only because his will to mediate had proven great. One feeling that wavered his resolve could have easily resulted in a bloody fight, even his own death.

Though the idea left him uneasy, Morvedraz believed that Koloran needed a partner, an ally, someone of a different nature yet close enough so that the very thought of betrayal would be impossible. Koloran needed a sibling.

And so during each of his journeys south to Kwamada and Leth, Morvedraz sought to discover another less fortunate boy who would become his second son and equal apprentice to Koloran, yet who possessed the power of determination and fortitude required of Antra's next Arbiter.

2

Leaving her brother to clean up after a busy day at the shop, Nore ambled down Long Street, holding her head high and appearing taller than her diminutive stature to the smiling street merchants who paused to wave, hoping for a moment in her presence. But when they hailed and beckoned to her she merely smiled and stayed resolutely to her course.

Nore loved to stroll the crowded streets of the city at twilight, her favorite time of day, the bright Antran moon rising over the warm night sky. Unlike her brother, who rose early, often before the first rays of the Daystar lit upon the still shadowed streets, Nore thrived on the dark. Despite her stepfather's misgivings, she often spent entire nights walking the city, stopping to visit friends or to share a pint in a favorite tavern. She loved meeting people of different races, for, being now fluent in most of the wider-known dialects, she could converse freely and with the same charm she exuded in the common Antran tongue.

The one language she longed to hear, listened intently for in all her wanderings about the great City at night and amid the bustling wine shop by day, she never heard. Only Morvedraz spoke a few words of her native tongue, though mechanically at best. As a young teenager, she taught one of her girlfriends a few phrases, but when her stepfather discovered the girls speaking the language, he immediately sent the other girl away and bid Nore indoors. There he instructed, calmly yet firmly, that she was to speak this language only to him and seek it out in no other.

"But why?!" She'd demanded an answer, stomping her foot against the hardwood floor.

"Because it is my wish! Please, Nore. I ask little of you but that you do your lessons and learn the business of the wine shop."

"*Little* of me?! Between study and work, what time do I have? Barely enough to see any of my friends. What trouble can sharing my language cause?"

"Please, daughter. I have good reason—"

"What reason? Tell me why—"

"Enough. You will learn in good time. Until then, you have me to speak to. Now, go upstairs and finish your lessons for the day."

"You can't even speak it well. You sound like a child."

Nore whipped around and started up the stairs, muttering "*stupid old Dwarv*" under her breath in her own language, a phrase she thought unwittingly that Morvedraz would not understand.

He watched as she disappeared upstairs, smiling slightly and shaking his head. *You may think me foolish now, but you will understand one day.*

Morvedraz had learned only a smattering of Nore's language, and with difficulty, that which the old wizard had taken time to impart before his death. He'd found the structure of the grammar maddening, the intonations harsh and nearly impossible to pronounce. The wizard soon gave up any formal lessons and instead taught Morvedraz by rote only what would invoke the base powers of the amulet, only the most elementary of the secrets spelled out on the set of roughly hewn tablets that held the amulet's lexicon. The text told a story of an amulet of great power—the ability to influence the will of any subject—and how it had fallen into the hands of an evil wizard. The wizard used it to amass great wealth at the expense of all those with whom he had come into contact. But the power of the amulet turned against him as he attempted to seduce a young girl. The girl, barely a woman and still a virgin, had succumbed to the advance. But the girl's brothers discovered the wizard's deceitful seduction in mid act. Though he rose from the girl and attempted to invoke the amulet, the wizard remained lost in the haze of lascivious pleasure, could neither recoup his concentration nor abate his fear. The amulet's power inverted itself and instead magnified the wizard's emotions until he lay paralyzed, his powers rendered impotent; the brothers killed him easily.

But the tablets themselves were barely comprehensible to Morvedraz, and thus the story remained incomplete. Morvedraz assumed the tale to be myth until the benevolent wizard's dying day. With his last remnant of strength the old man took from his neck a smooth, elliptical stone, one side hewn flat and inscribed with words that Morvedraz recognized as the language of the tablets; he could barely pronounce them phonetically and had no idea of their meaning. But the dying wizard taught Morvedraz the correct pronunciation, and then explained that this incantation would indeed invoke the power of the amulet. The same amulet told of in the tablet's tale. Fearful of majik and skeptical that the feverish, dying *Humani* had not succumbed to his own delusions, Morvedraz declared to use the amulet only for the benefit of those for whom he invoked its powers. This he promised the wizard, who, upon hearing his adopted son's vow, released his last breath and closed his eyes for the final time. Morvedraz took the amulet from the wizard's neck and placed it around his own, determined only to hold it as a memory of his adopted father.

Later, he examined the tablets themselves and discovered that they appeared wrought of the same stone as the amulet. This drove his fear deeper, and he resolved to keep both the tablets and the amulet a secret and never attempt to invoke the power of the stone. Years passed, and the amulet became no more to Morvedraz than an item of deep personal sentiment, a hopeful good luck charm, until his fated meeting with the rival families over the Kwamadan wine. Only then, fearing for his very life, did he attempt to use the stone's power. Knowing the story of the corrupted wizard, how his own fear had caused the power to turn against him, Morvedraz held little hope that the amulet would assist him in regaining control of the struggle. As time passed and he reflected on the outcome, he determined that, indeed, the purity of his own purpose must have allowed him to successfully invoke the amulet's power. He feared more than anything else that the stone would fall into ignorant hands, and thus kept it hidden from even his most trusted apprentice, his own adopted son.

When he heard the strange, beautiful young girl speak for the first time the words he knew only as the language of the amulet, around the campfire in the Za-Zhirazani desert, a dual feeling of delight and dread filled him. There in front of him sat a child who doubtlessly came from the same land as the old wizard, a place he knew nothing of, only that it lay far beyond the Dwarvani Kingdom, beyond the unknown lands. The wizard had only spoken of his native land in vague, passing terms, as if protecting Morvedraz from some unknown danger. Morvedraz longed to hear of Leonora's past, of the land in which she'd been born, hoped to unravel more of the amulet's history. But the girl's memory proved frayed at best, driven deep within the cold, unreachable recesses of her mind. She only recalled a great conflict filled with terror and death, the images of her childhood mere shadows of thought from which she could not discern true memory from fantasy. Her earliest recollection began not long before the barbarian raiders captured her. She'd found herself naked but for some ragged men's clothes, her body bloodied and bruised, abandoned on the fringe of the Dark Forest. She'd followed the river south, but had missed the city of Kwamada and found herself lost in the desert. Wandering amid the small lowland trees near the northeastern border of Leth, the barbarians found her trying to warm herself with a few weakly burning sticks. She'd been in their bondage two moon cycles when the raiders encountered the strange, old Dwarv towing a train of pack animals and a large wheeled cart laden with goods, just north of Kwamada.

Nore often sat awake on the rooftop of a friend's home, long after her companions had succumbed to ale and wine, staring into the northeastern sky toward where she felt her homeland must be. Something about the alignment of the constellations looked familiar to her, though inverted, as if plucked from and placed in the wrong part of the sky. Tonight while she strolled the darkening streets of the City of Antra she looked up at the oddly familiar stars and listened keenly to the noise of the departing street merchants, the citizens headed home for the evening, visitors in search of a night's lodging or simply a comfortable place to take a meal and a potent mug. But she heard only the languages of the city and the known lands beyond.

"Nore!" Her name rang out suddenly from a darkened street corner. She turned toward the familiar hail and smiled. A city guard approached, armor dangling easily from his muscled shoulders, his hand poised upon the hilt of the wide sword on his belt. "Out wandering at night again, eh? Haven't I told you that these streets aren't safe for someone so young and pretty?"

"Don't you mean, young and *fragile*, Tolek?" But before he could reply, Nore struck a swift though muted blow just beneath the guard's breastplate, then circled skillfully away when he regained himself and grabbed for her arm.

"A little slow tonight. Perhaps one too many pints with your supper?"

"Come here, you little wench." The guard sneered and rushed forward, too quickly for Nore to avoid the advance. He took her wrists and bent her arms behind her back, forcing her tightly against his body. "Let's see you escape now."

"Who says I want to." Nore hissed and pressed her lips onto Tolek's mouth. He let his own lips part, then released his hold of the girl's arms, and she brought them quickly around his neck, raising herself onto him and pressing into his swelling groin.

"Your mouth is far too skilled for someone so young."

"Wouldn't *you* like to find out just how skilled my mouth is?"

"Indeed I would. Meet me after my watch is over, at Flannah's, just past the Hour of the Rogue. We'll share a pint. And then..."

"And then what?"

"And then you may demonstrate for me what skills you possess."

With one twist, Nore spun free of the guard's relaxed arms. "Maybe," she said over her shoulder, smiling and trotting away. "Maybe not."

"Tolek!" suddenly resounded from beyond the corner.

"Here, sir!"

"You're needed. Come at once."

"Uh-oh, better run before the sergeant has you thrown in the stockade. *Again*." Nore laughed and ran.

Teasing Tolek was one of Nore's favorite pastimes, as was similarly taunting any number of young men in the city. Indeed, she was known for her provocative public behavior, a reputation that would have normally been frowned upon in Antran society. But Nore's coquettish manner only served to enamor Morvedraz' wealthy clientele; where other girls would have been branded slatternly, Nore seemed held in an altogether separate regard. As far as anyone knew, she'd lain with no man. Once a handsome young son of a wealthy family, whom Nore had taunted over a game of *kare* at one of her favorite pubs, bragged openly to his friends that he'd met up with her later that night and that she had pleasured him repeatedly and in as many ways as he'd desired. When news of the false encounter reached Nore, she strode to the pub where the boy relaxed with friends. Upon seeing her enter, the young man smiled and rose to greet her. Nore met him with several swift, disabling blows and continued the beating until he lay bloodied and nearly unconscious on the ale-sodden floor. The boy, humiliated and banned from the pub, demanded that his father intervene in some manner.

"What is this girl's name? Who is her family?"

"Nore. Daughter of Morvedraz, the wine merchant."

Upon hearing this, the father landed a swift backhand across the boy's cheek. "Fool! Be more careful next time about whom you spread lies."

The father knew full well the value of the Arbiter's good graces, and the price to pay for betraying them.

Nore turned the corner on Long Street and headed west onto Little Market. She shouldered past the crowd gathering at Flannah's Tavern and made her way to her favorite table in a back corner. There she saw seated a young Zhirazani woman with long, ebony hair and skin the color of brown silk. The woman sat with one foot propped on the adjoining chair, her hand cradling a tall pint of ale.

"Andara," Nore purred when she sat, sliding her chair very close to the woman.

"Well, hello, darling. I thought you'd *never* show up."

"I had to pay a visit to our favorite guard. It's so funny when he thinks he's finally in control." She spoke through a devilish smile.

"Oh, you little tease. When will those foolish men ever learn?"

"Never." Nore laughed, then let out a small gasp as she felt the soft hand grasp her bare thigh and slide forward underneath her leather skirt until it rested against her undergarment.

"*Not here,*" Nore whispered, but with pointed breath.

"Oh, why not here? Do you know how much I'd love to see you writhing, sitting in a crowded tavern while the men of Antra looked on in envy?"

Nore's face flushed, then her mischievous smile widened. "Okay."

"Okay, what?"

"You can do whatever you want to me, right here, in front of the whole room."

The black pools of Andara's eyes widened.

"That is," Nore continued," if you can tell me what you're going to do to me—explicitly—in *my* language."

"That's not fair!" Andara pouted.

"Oh, come on! I lay next to you whispering it into your ear just night before last. Did you forget already?"

"You're language is barely pronounceable. Besides... you were purposely distracting me."

"Let's practice."

"Nore," Andara began wearily, "it's the Hour of the Rune. The workday is over. Can't we just sit and drink and speak in Antran?"

"*No. I want you to learn my language because then we'll be able to speak freely no matter who's around. You're the only one I wholly trust, my love, and this can be a way of ensuring that we'll be able to communicate with each other in any circumstance.*"

"I lost you after 'No'."

"You're not trying!"

"Nore, have a pint and relax. Please?"

"All right." Nore pouted.

"Hungry? I'll buy you dinner."

Nore shrugged and folded her arms and leaned against the wooden paneling of the back wall. "There's no one interesting here tonight. Let's go."

"It's way too early for *interesting* people. Give it an hour or so."

"I don't feel like sitting here for an hour."

"Then what *do* you feel like doing?"

"I don't know. I want to go somewhere where no one knows me."

"In The City?" Andara smiled and shook her head.

"Let's at least go over to The Black Chalice."

"If we're going to The Black Chalice I'll need more to drink first."

"Fine." Nore rose and spoke resolutely. "A pitcher of ale, and we go to the Chalice."

The Black Chalice tavern stood lighted by a single torch on an otherwise deserted street in the Rough Zirkot, an area noticeably absent of the wealthy, fashionable crowds who lingered on Long Street. The Chalice attracted a clientele from a dark yet prosperous fringe of society, the kind of people who legitimized their illicit dealings with an air of acquired gentility. Their brutish origins remained; inside the Chalice an innocent bump or spilled drink could easily result in bloodshed. But the regulars unofficially yet diligently policed the crowd so that when trouble began they could direct its swift and silent end. No sign marked the tavern's door, and potential patrons would need either glean the location through discreet inquiry, or pay for it outright. Neither method proved sure.

An enormous dark-skinned Kuzhani stood just inside the large yet unadorned entrance to the tavern. Those who knocked on the massive door watched rapt as a view port in the shape of a small chalice appeared near the very top of the door's lashed beams, and a huge set of yellow, virulent eyes peered downward, scrutinizing the hopeful patrons. The Kuzhani would inquire in a low, stern tone the nature of the visit. If the response proved acceptable, he allowed the patrons inside, casting a glare upon them that told in silent detail the fate should their motives prove trouble-some.

Morvedraz, of course, had forbidden Nore to go near the Black Chalice, which only drove her curiosity and desire to discover the hushed dealings that took place beyond the blank doorway. He knew that the Chalice housed the most wealthy of the notorious, and the most dangerous; indeed, he had rendered his services to many of them so that the streets of Antra would flow in commerce, not blood. Morvedraz asked for no payment for such arbitrations; the grateful parties would, without prejudice and in unspoken cooperation, agree jointly to ensure that no harm would ever befall the Arbiter. Nore only understood a fraction of the influence that her stepfather had over the clientele of the Black Chalice, but considered his demand that she stay away from the place grossly contradictory. If he himself could have dealings with the "businessmen" who frequented the place, why could she not on occasion share their generous company? The Chalice's loftier echelon agreed, and welcomed the renown young woman into their circles.

Nore and Andara walked through streets that thinned of crowds the closer they drew near the infamous tavern. Approaching the blank door they saw a richly dressed Lethani flanked by two muscled, armed attendants and a young woman in silken robes. The Lethani stood in heated debate with the small portal opened near the top of the door.

"It appears that the stranger has no idea with whom he's bargaining for entrance," Andara observed and smiled.

"I see a large headache in his future," Nore quipped, and the two girls laughed and stopped just behind the Lethani and his party. The Lethani's men leered at Nore and Andara as the man they served continued to debate with the set of eyes in the chalice-shaped port. Suddenly the eyes widened and a huge voice boomed out from behind the door in the Kuzhani dialect, "*Leonora, daughter of Morvedraz! Warm welcome to you and your companion!*"

The Lethani could not understand the salutation and jumped back as the door swung open and the Kuzhani stepped forward, blocking the entire Lethani party with one massive arm while motioning with the other for the two young women to enter.

It was barely the Hour of the Sword, early in the Antran night, especially early for the amount of activity that the girls hovered over, picking their way through the rumbling crowd toward their favorite spot. But when they approached the small table that stood raised with several others on a low platform ringed by a wooden banister, they noticed that a richly dressed man sat there. He leaned forward and spoke intently to two female Humani—one middle-aged, who nodded earnestly at the man's entreaties, the other very young, looking sullen and still.

Nore scrutinized the unusually thick crowd, then the interlopers. The two pints of ale she'd downed at the previous pub charged her demeanor. "Who are those strangers? Those are *our* seats."

"Gently, darling," Andara soothed. "We're lucky to receive the grand treatment we do since most of our drink charges go uncollected. Those three look like they're talking business. Come on. Let's go elbow our way to the bar and—"

"I'm not going to be crammed between sweaty criminals at the bar so some rich slaver can use our table to <u>buy a teenage whore</u>."

"*Shhhhh!* Nore, leave it alone." Andara wrapped her hand around Nore's upper arm and drew her close. "You know the trouble you can get into for that kind of talk. Look, he's not just some rich slaver. He's one of the most dangerous slavers in the city. I've only seen him at the market a few times, so he must be a newcomer. At first he'd simply hover in the back like he wasn't much interested. You know, just there to watch the bidding or something. Then one day a certain girl goes up on the block. Very young, but absolutely incredible. Skin like fresh cream, periwinkle eyes the size of gold *zeki*, long black hair the color of midnight. And when they, um, 'displayed her attributes'... I felt my arousal quite warmly._Anyway, the bidding was furious, and rich. The richest I'd seen in years. But just before the auctioneer struck the final gavel, *he* strolls up through the crowd, cool as a sea breeze, and lays twelve hundred gold *zeki* on the podium, *twice* the last bid. He turns then and smiles to the crowd, confident that no one would dare challenge, then takes the girl gently by the arm and leads her past me. I offered the usual security escort, but he just smiled and shook his head. I figured he must be packing something under that robe beside his manhood because he didn't have anyone with him and he didn't look like much himself."

"So, he has money, and he likes young girls like half the barbarians in here. So what?"

"I'm not done yet. He disappears with her, and after all the chatter about him just whisking her up with that unreal bid, the story dies. No one sees him around. Two weeks later I'm working. It was a slow day. All we had was a miserable looking lot—toothless, dirty, just poor, petty beggars. But at the very back of the wagon was a girl all curled up in the corner. She wouldn't move when I told her to hurry, so I walked over to her and pulled her up by her arm. Nore, I'd have never recognized her if it weren't for her eyes. Her hair had been shorn with some kind of dull blade, her face and what I could see of her body was covered in bruises and burns. She barely had the strength to stand. When I helped her to the wash room so she could at least clean up a little I saw a trail of dried blood down the back of her legs. She just collapsed into this horrible sobbing heap when I set her down on the bench in the shower. I asked her what happened, but she just looked at me with these terrified eyes. I calmed her down long enough to get her up on the block and out the door with a new sponsor, but I'll never forget those eyes."

Andara looked intently into Nore's own eyes, but her ale-fueled attention remained riveted to the man occupying what she considered *her* seat. She watched him talking and smiling, making gentle hand motions to punctuate his phrases. He was not handsome; his nose was too big for his face, hairline too high to cover his head, and he displayed a visible paunch. Yet he exuded a cool confidence that even Nore silently admitted could be alluring. He was also immaculately clad and groomed; his skin shone a golden hue even through the smoky haze of the Chalice. The older woman whom he spoke to directly looked most charmed. She was, for certain, no beggar. The girl—the woman's daughter, perhaps granddaughter—appeared quiet, but broke into a shy grin whenever the man glanced toward her. She had a slight body. Her flaxen hair shined and her perfect smile glinted in the candlelight.

"She looks like a little porcelain doll." Nore's tone gave up the sadness she felt at the sight of the girl, juxtaposed to the slaver.

"She looks like she's going to be *his* doll before too long." Andara echoed knowingly.

"How can they allow that? The Regent abhors sexual slavery." She paused, shaking her head. "The girl is barely old enough to bleed."

"If you're keeping enough of your gold in circulation, even the Regency can be a little near-sighted."

"This isn't going to happen. Not tonight." Nore took one hard stride toward the table before Andara caught her arm.

"Nore, are you crazy? There are probably a dozen blades aimed at anyone who goes *near* him! You'd be dead before you even got his attention."

Nore, seething, wrenched her arm from Andara's grasp. "Let's go to Zhakhar."

"Zhakhar won't to do anything, Nore. The man's buying drinks and keeping to himself: Zhakhar's only requirements. Now let's you and me just find a seat on the other side of the room and—"

But Nore had already turned and shouldered her way through the crowd toward the very back of the tavern. In a circular alcove, raised to give ample view of the wide interior, sat Zhakhar, proprietor of the Black Chalice. He rested his great bulk on the mountain of pillows lining the padded floor of the alcove while four young servants—two women, two men—attended to him. Zhakhar's appearance defied ethnicity, and he enjoyed spinning fantastic tales about his mixed ancestry—wealthy sea traders from Leth and ancient royalty from the Kuzhani jungles. Likely, his Lethani father had impregnated a Kuzhani slave girl, which would explain Zhakhar's light hair and dark skin. Nore approached and watched the master of the Chalice peer up from over the gold rim of his goblet.

"Ha, ha! The Arbiter's daughter. Papa out of town again?" He smiled and motioned Nore to approach. When she did she leaned forward and planted a warm kiss on his ample cheek. Nore rose and held her hand out toward Andara.

"Zhakhar, you remember my friend, Andara?"

"Indeed, I do. Warm greetings to you, lovely one. Come sit with me for a while, both of you, before you're off to more exciting encounters."

Zhakhar clapped his huge hands together once, and within a moment servants produced new pillows for the girls to lean against, and placed near each a silver tray with flutes of chilled, sparkling wine. "Now, you must have some special purpose for coming to sit with old Zhakhar other than to be friendly." He winked at the two who smiled appropriately.

"Zhakhar," Nore began carefully, "it's known that you run a very respectable establishment, and that all the interaction that takes place here, if not for mere diversion, is solely for the purpose of 'acceptable' business."

Zhakhar's eyes narrowed and his smile faded slightly. "What are you getting at?"

"What would you think if, say, sex-slave trading of an underage girl was taking place under your roof?"

Andara's eyes widened and she shot a frantic glance at her friend. Zhakhar's smile disappeared completely. He spoke darkly.

"No such business goes on under this roof, darling girl. The Regent of the Maj allows me to operate with no interference, and I don't let anything happen here that would cause him to need pay attention. And that would *certainly* cause him to pay attention. What you even bringing it up for?"

"We have reason to believe otherwise."

Every trace of humor washed from Zhakhar's face and he glared ominously at Nore. "Those are heavy words you speak, daughter. You best have some proof to back them up."

"Zhakhar," Andara interrupted, attempting to steer the tone of the conversation to a lighter subject, "I think perhaps that my dear girl has had one too many pints a bit too early in the evening."

"Stop it, Andara." Nore spoke, stern and lucid, then, in her own language: "*You know very well what that lunatic sitting at our table will do.*"

Andara understood the gist of the phrase and attempted to answer in kind, but faltered. Zhakhar then raised his open palm. "Enough! I don't understand the strange words you speak, daughter of Morvedraz, but I am inclined to investigate your charge, if only because I respect your father more than you know. Who is it here that you accuse of illegal slave trading?"

"There, sitting at my usual table. The one with the nose like a potato and the expensive robes. He's trying to buy the young girl seated beside her mother. I'm sure of it. Andara works security at the slave market. She's seen him purchase other such girls, abuse them, and then turn them back out onto the streets."

Zhakhar scowled maliciously and gazed at Andara. "Is this true?"

Andara nodded slowly.

"Behlar!" Zhakhar shouted, and one of the male servants scampered forward and knelt. "Tell Kor to secure the entrance—no more guests until further notice. And then escort the party seated there, to me."

He pointed to the table where the man sat now with his arm around the young girl, still conversing pleasantly with the older woman. "Tell them that Zhakhar would like to make their acquaintance and thank them for their generous patronage."

Nore and Andara watched the attendant step quickly through the crowd and approached Kor, the Kuzhani doorman. He leaned forward to hear Behlar's whispered message, then immediately lifted a heavy beam and placed it securely in its stanchions to bar the entrance before striding toward the table where the three sat. The *Humani* feigned a smile and held his head high as Kor leaned over and whispered to him. The man stood and motioned the woman and girl to follow. Nore's heart beat harder as she watched the group approach. Andara grasped Nore's arm, and she felt the cold grip course through her body.

"Master Zhakhar," Kor announced, "Valthan of Leth, and his companions."

"Thank you, Kor. You may take your post back at the entrance. Please, dear friends, sit with me for a bit. I haven't seen you here before and wish to welcome you to the Black Chalice."

Valthan smiled and motioned the woman and girl to sit. He knelt beside them and bowed his head toward Zhakhar.

"Master Zhakhar, how fortunate we are to have lingered. We were just about to leave for the evening and would have missed your invitation. It's an honor." The Lethani spoke in a warm, gracious voice.

"The honor is mine to welcome a new patron, especially such a generous one. I see that you are partial to Kwamadan wine. Only my most notable patrons have the means to savor it in such quantity."

"I've been most fortunate in business lately."

"Indeed." Zhakhar motioned briefly with his hand and glanced in a direction outside the alcove. Within moments several servants had placed trays laden with platters overflowing in rare foods and decanters of Kwamadan wine, along with brandy and aged *kororah* sticks. Nore noticed that, as the servants produced the delicacies in a flourish that captured the attention of Zhakhar's visitors, other emissaries of the Chalice stealthily and silently positioned themselves nearby, their faces stern, eyes sharp as the hidden blades they readied.

"This is very generous of you, Zhakhar. I can't tell you what a pleasure it is to sit in your company."

"Yes, yes... But, please, you haven't introduced your companions."

The woman smiled attentively at Zhakhar's reference while the girl, obviously frightened, avoided the eyes of everyone in the booth.

"Well," Valthan began with only the slightest pause, "this is Lenah, my sister. And Samare, her daughter...who would be my niece."

"Who *would* be your niece?" Zhakhar asked, sensing the Lethani's hesitancy.

"I mean, Lenah is my sister by marriage. My brother's—rest his soul—wife. Samare is their adopted daughter, and so my niece only through the fortune of my brother's good heart." He smiled at the girl.

"I see. So your brother is dead."

"He's been missing for several months. We believe that he must have fallen prey to raiders in the desert."

"A terrible end." Zhakhar looked at the woman, whose face remained impassive, then at the girl, down whose cheek a single, silent tear rolled until it splashed on the silken pillows.

Valthan thanked Zhakhar for his concern and helped himself to great quantities of food and wine. The woman nibbled perfunctorily from her plate, and the girl ate nothing. After the better part of an hour Valthan lit a *kororah* stick and puffed mightily, reclining against the pillows, his face now red and sated. The woman and girl still sat stiffly upright.

"This is really a pleasure." Valthan began to wax, the wine and smoke warming him. He sighed. "You know," he said to Zhakhar in a fraternal tone, "they warned me about this place when I arrived in the city."

"*Really?*"

"Oh, yes. I was making discreet inquiries as to where I might encounter those interested in more rare and lucrative merchandise than might be found in the street markets, and of course The Black Chalice was on everyone's lips. But they told me that it was a closed club, you know? Very discriminating. If the doorman didn't like my looks, I could well end up thrown off of the cliffs into the great river!"

Valthan laughed loudly, a bit too loudly even against the swelling background noise of the crowd. He seemed to sway in his seat, his demeanor giddy and relaxed, but lacking the keen sense he'd possessed only a while ago.

Nore had grown weary of what looked like Zhakhar's coddling of the likely criminal. The wine warming her stomach warmed her temper as well. "You seem really broken up about your lost brother, Valthan," she sneered. "Was he as fond of Kwamadan wine as you?"

She'd intended on catching him off guard, lulled by the wine, but only succeeded in alerting him to her suspicion. Valthan recouped his persona of a patrician merchant, smiling at Nore.

"Perhaps it's *you* who are too fond of Kwamadan wine." He laughed, glancing toward Zhakhar who shared in his mirth with a broad smile. Andara caught Nore by the forearm just before she sprang forward to strike Valthan. She leaned toward her friend and whispered in Nore's own language, "*Don't be fool!*" Nore reclined against the pillowed wall of the alcove and crossed her arms, allowing her right hand to sneak beneath her tunic and wrap a ready grasp around her dagger.

A young female servant slipped into the rear of the alcove nearly un-noticed by all but Zhakhar, who leaned back away from the group to hear the servant's whispered message. He smiled up at her and nodded when she bowed, then fled.

"Valthan, share a brandy with me, would you?" Zhakhar said. "You do well to mask your emotion, as a good businessman should. But, indulge my sentimental side; tell me of your brother."

Valthan heaved a great sigh as if to quell his sadness and collect his thoughts. Both Nore and Andara listened intently, sensing a purpose behind Zhakhar's accommodating charm. They looked toward the woman, Lenah, whose face appeared drawn with lines, her body tense. Samare sat with her knees drawn up tightly to her chest, back very straight, and, for the first time since she'd approached the alcove with her mother and Valthan, she focused the great pools of her azure eyes intently on Valthan and Zhakhar.

"My brother," Valthan began, his voice dark and hoarse, "was a fool. I'm sorry, Lenah, I mean him no disrespect. But, traveling far from a civilized population, with no escort and few arms, and with such valuable cargo! It's a wonder he hadn't fallen prey to raiders years ago."

Zhakhar watched Lenah's face; her glance darted about the alcove and her face grew pale. "Perhaps Lenah has heard enough, Valthan. She looks quite ill."

"I'm fine, really," she said, forcing a smile.

"Indeed..." Zhakhar intoned deeply, then to Valthan, "you know, it's strange that an experienced traveler, as I'm sure your brother was, would embark on a journey through the desert unescorted."

"Armed escorts cost money. My brother chose to risk danger rather than diminish profits."

"Tell me, what was his cargo that would have profited him so greatly? I find it odd that anyone, no matter his avarice, would risk losing not only his entire stock of goods, but his very life."

"I wish I could tell you. I only know what Lenah shared with me—that he left under cloak of darkness with a great train of carts and animals, bound for Leth, and was due back in one month. But two months passed and he never surfaced. It was then that Lenah contacted me that I might attempt to learn what had happened to him. Did he have trouble selling the goods, whatever they were? Did he sell the cargo and remain in Leth, a wealthy man with a new identity? This we never discovered."

"And, how was it that you assumed him killed by raiders?" Zhakhar continued to Valthan. "Did you not seek him in Leth?"

"I traveled there myself and made many inquiries. Fortunately, I possess the means to gain the information I sought. A local merchant told me of a band of barbarians who'd come through town not a week before my arrival. They were overheard in a tavern, bragging of how they found a lone fool in the desert. They didn't admit anything directly, but implied that the cargo they now possessed would not have been theirs had this traveler not fallen ill to the wasteland's 'harsh elements,' so far off the main trade route."

"And they wouldn't disclose what the cargo was?"

"Not in certain terms. Only that they intended on presenting it to their chief, and that he would be most pleased."

Zhakhar nodded and relaxed his bulk against the silken pillows. He took a large swallow from his snifter of brandy and drew deeply from the rich *kororah* stick, exhaling billows of smoke that clouded the space of the alcove. When he did so, four cloaked emissaries who had hidden themselves in the nearby crowd silently drew near and stood circling Valthan's back. When the wary Lethani, slowed by food and drink, attempted to rise, the cloaked men each drew back their robes. Seeing the gleaming blades of razor-honed steel ready in the men's hands, Valthan eased himself back down to the floor of the alcove.

"Master Zhakhar, these men are surely friends of yours?"

"They're among my closest."

"Why don't they sit and have a drink with us?"

"They don't have time. They've come here at my request for a very specific purpose."

Zhakhar nodded to one of the men who slowly removed the veil that covered his face. Valthan, perspiring clearly now, sat motionless.

"What's the matter, Valthan?" The unmasked emissary spoke with a tone of pointed sarcasm. "Has the wine upset your stomach? Suddenly you look unwell."

Valthan gazed up at the man's face, his scowl deep, as if engraved. "Do I know you?" Valthan offered weakly. The emissary answered by driving the metal tip of his boot into Valthan's ribs. The Lethani groaned and doubled over, clutching his side.

"Master Zhakhar," Lenah began pitifully, "I suspected him from the beginning! I thought he knew too much about—" Zhakhar swung the back of his great hand toward Lenah, catching her squarely across the face. The imprint of Zhakhar's knuckles swelled clearly on her cheek.

"No one's addressed you," Zhakhar growled, then motioned to two of his female servants. His face softened and he turned to Samare who had remained clutching her knees to her chest, eyes wide. She looked surprised, indeed, though not afraid or even apprehensive about what seemed to be happening to her mother and uncle. Rather, her face shone with a hopeful expression; she'd not fully understood her uncle's motives in adopting her, nor her mother's for agreeing, but wanted no part of either side.

"Samare," Zhakhar began softly, "why don't you go with my girls for a little while. They'll get you something more suitable to eat." The servants smiled toward Samare and helped her from the pillows. She scampered away with them, looking back only once at her mother's reddened face.

Valthan had recovered from the kick and sat upright again. "I demand an explanation for this barbaric treatment! What have I done to you to deserve—"

"Your voice sickens me." Zhakhar growled and motioned to the four emissaries. One drew the curtain of the alcove swiftly shut while the second unfurled a large throw rug onto the plush pillowed floor, then joined the other three who deftly pounced upon the struggling Valthan, forcing him onto his stomach and tightly binding his wrists behind his back and his ankles and knees together. When he lay struggling against the cords and spitting obscenities at all around him, the emissaries rolled him into the rug. One kneeled on his chest while two others held his head still, pinching his nose shut to force his mouth open for breath. The fourth emissary, the one who had questioned the now helpless Valthan, slipped on a pair of studded leather gloves and began prying at Valthan's clenched mouth. The Lethani resisted, and the emissary tired of the protest. He drew the dagger and smashed the butt end of the handle against Valthan's mouth, breaking his front teeth. The Lethani groaned, allowing the emissary a firm hold, stretching Valthan's tongue to the point of tearing.

"Let me show you, Valthan, how we treat the rapists of children in the City of Antra."

The emissary drew a long dagger, both edges thin as razors, and glided the blade across the meaty base of Valthan's tongue. The blade appeared at first to only scratch the surface, drawing no blood. But then Valthan jerked his head, and as he did so the entire length of his tongue separated, remaining clutched in the emissaries hand. They stuffed dirty rags into his mouth to staunch the blood and muffle his screams, then rolled him into the rug.

Nore and Andara still sat to Zhakhar's left, gazing at the scene they'd witnessed, the events that they had initiated through their suspicions. They watched the emissaries raise the struggling bundle over their arms and await direction from Zhakhar. The master of the Black Chalice then took the woman, Lenah, whom he held by the arm, and with one flick of his hand tossed her into the middle of the alcove.

"Confess your crime and you may live."

"But, Master Zhakhar! I am still her mother! She needs me! How can she survive—"

"Tell me your plan!" Zhakhar bellowed.

Lenah sobbed and looked toward Nore, who glanced away.

"I wanted her to grow up like you," Lenah said, "strong and beautiful. The only way I could ensure she'd grow up at all was to see that she was taken care of by someone prosperous, someone with the means. It was my husband's idea, to assist Valthan in his business by transporting the goods at night. Valthan agreed to pay us a huge profit if we only succeeded in transporting the cargo from Leth to the City of Antra. This saved Valthan the enormous price of security for his merchandise and still assured us money beyond our wildest hope. We'd be able to provide for Lenah. But, then my husband never returned, and suddenly I owed Valthan the price of his shipment. Five thousand gold *zeki*! Where was I going to get five thousand?!"

"So you were willing to sell your daughter as a whore."

"What? No! The arrangement was that he would adopt her, she'd become *his* daughter and be educated in business, indentured to him, yes, but because of her intelligence and abilities—"

"Ridiculous. Haven't you realized what Valthan's *business* is? Don't you know what that 'cargo' was that was lost? Little girls like your daughter. What else do you think is worth five thousand gold pieces? There were ten of them, all about your daughter's age, some even younger. And Valthan paid a raiding party of Barbarians a small but ample sum to find your husband's route and kill him before he got a mile outside of Leth. He knew that bringing in that many girls to be sold would raise suspicion. So, your husband losing his shipment put the liability on you. He knew you couldn't pay the debt. But he knew what would bring him as much if not more than ten ragged girls from who knows where, barefoot and scarred, without any social graces, some not even virgins. Your daughter—ever take a look at her from across a room? Her skin looks like fresh cream, her hair like spun silk. There are men who'd pay greatly for the thrill of torturing one so perfect."

Lenah's mouth gaped open in abject horror, then she bowed her head and sobbed. Zhakhar hefted himself to his feet and strode toward the woman. He leaned toward her and took her chin in his hand, raising her face toward him. Their eyes met.

"I'm still not sure you didn't know the whole plan, but I can't prove it. And, unfortunately, stupidity is not a crime. So you're going to get your daughter and go home. And if you ever have any wild schemes about getting mixed up with some pimp like Valthan, you'd better do it in another city."

Zhakhar motioned to the now-still roll of rug that the emissaries held. "But first, I want you to witness what happens to people like him, just so you have no doubt about my sincerity and its consequences."

Zhakhar pulled Lenah to her feet and motioned her toward one of the emissaries, who held her firmly by the arm.

"Throw him off the cliffs into the great river. But make sure he's conscious so he can watch where he's going."

With these words the rolled rug came to life again, struggling against the emissaries hold. They beat it viciously with their feet and fists until it stilled once more, then exited the alcove through a hidden passageway in the back wall, Lenah in tow.

Zhakhar turned to Nore and Andara. "Way too much excitement for one night." He shook his head and sighed, opening the curtain of the alcove again and smiling upon the familiar crowd. "Why don't you two have another drink with me. There's plenty of brandy left." He said this and sat, motioning for the girls to do the same.

"You knew all along." Nore spoke, her tone deep with admiration. "You knew he was after the girl."

"Of course I knew. But I couldn't let on about it. I don't have anything to do with what the Regent of the Maj disapproves of, remember? He doesn't ask, I don't tell. I knew Valthan's scheme as soon as he arrived. I have eyes everywhere, especially the slave market. Do a lot of side business there. But not slaves. And surely not children. I just got lucky this time. Old Valthan approached the wrong bunch of raiders with his little plan. They're all on my payroll. Soon as they saw what the 'cargo' was, they alerted me. I've had men around Valthan for weeks, just waiting for him to make a wrong move."

"And the girl's father?"

"We hid him in Leth with other friends. He'll join his family, his debt erased with Valthan's dip in the river. But he'll still owe me."

"Zhakhar, did you hear anything about another girl?" Andara asked. "She was beautiful. Long, black hair—"

"Eyes like the color of the midday sky? Oh, yes. Wish I could have stepped in before he got his hands on her. He specialized in brokering the most beautiful young girls he could find for his clients. I won't even describe what they did to her." He sighed and gave up a slight shudder.

"Afterward—when they brought her back to the market—I found her in a cart." Andara's tone grew even more hopeful. "She was purchased again by a man I didn't recognize—"

"At my request. I can always use good help around here."

Zhakhar glanced across the room and nodded, and from within the crowd a young woman picked her way toward the alcove, serving tray balanced in one hand. When she approached, Andara saw that her hair had grown in to shoulder length, that her wounds had healed well, and that the weight she'd gained had rounded her hips and breasts.

"How may I be of service to you, Master Zhakhar?" She spoke and bowed her head.

"I want you to meet two friends of mine. This is Nore, daughter of Morvedraz, Arbiter of Antra. And this is Andara, Nore's dear friend. Ladies, meet Melora."

The girl walked toward Nore and Andara who remained seated and bowed to them. Then her eyes met Andara's, and Melora smiled widely.

"It's you! From the slave market!" Melora exclaimed, a single tear coursing her left cheek, then continued, quieter. "You were kind to me, after...what they did."

"I'm sorry I couldn't have done more."

"But, you didn't *have* to do anything. You could have just ignored me." She said this and leaned slowly toward

Andara. She placed her small hand on Andara's shoulder and slowly kissed her cheek. "Thank you."

"My pleasure," Andara said smiling.

"I work for Master Zhakhar now. Full time. He treats me very well." Melora turned to beam a wide smile at Zhakhar. "It's so nice to meet you, Andara. And your friend. I hope you'll come and visit me."

"We sure will." Andara smiled.

"Thank you, again." Melora spoke, then glanced at Zhakhar who smiled and nodded. The girl skipped back into the Chalice crowd.

Nore nudged Andara. "'*We sure will?*' Sounds rather enthusiastic, my love."

"Oh, that was a euphemism." Andara shook her head. "You're really something, Zhakhar. Quite the hero."

Zhakhar huffed. "The man was jeopardizing my business. No one in this City's going to do that, I don't care how rich he thinks he is. Besides," he added, "she's far too small a wench for a *real* man." He winked and smiled.

The girls rolled their eyes and rose. "Well, we're going to reclaim our table. I think we've had enough excitement for one night, too."

"Stranding me so early? All right, lovelies. Take care, and don't you be strangers."

They smiled and stepped from the alcove into the hot, sweaty crowd.

3

"Well, was all that interesting enough for you?" Andara chided when she and Nore picked through the crowd toward their usual table.

"Oh, it was okay. You know: we saved a girl from being enslaved, helped seal the fate of the man who'd have sold her, and got our table back. I guess that's pretty good for any given evening."

"And you said you were bored."

"Well, now that we've vanquished the Chalice of evil, I'm bored again."

Nore smiled, and Andara laughed and shook her head. They sat scanning the room from their raised table. The crowd had thinned since Valthan's expulsion; likely those who'd heard the nature of his business and wished to transact with him realized what his sudden disappearance meant and had wisely taken their leave. Melora brought the girls another carafe of wine and chatted with them for a while, and a few of the tavern's regulars stopped by their table to visit. More and more patrons exited the Chalice's door, and within an hour only a small familiar circle remained.

"Okay, now this looks more like a family reunion than the most infamous tavern in Antra," Nore said. "Let's grab a bottle of brandy and—"

But just as Nore spoke she saw Kor pull open the huge entrance door and step aside to allow in a *Humani*. He stood alone in the middle of the entryway, eyes wide, scanning the room as if searching for someone. Kor urged the man forward so that the doorman could secure the entrance, and the man strode slowly between the tables.

Nore and Andara had never seen him before. They had never seen anyone who looked *like* him before. He appeared neither young nor old; sometimes the light, wispy hair on his head shined yellow in the lamp light, other times silver; his amber eyes drooped tiredly with dark circles against their underside. He was about average height for a *Humani* and looked lithe yet muscled like an athlete. They watched him walk to the middle of the tavern and turn a slow complete circle, as if still searching, and, not finding whom or what he sought, dropped into the first empty chair nearby. He slouched, one boot thrust outward against the floor, the other drawn in to maintain balance.

"Well, things just got interesting again," Nore said and smiled.

"No doubt. Who do you think he's looking for?"

"Or trying to avoid. But now he just looks like he's going to fall out of his chair. Maybe we should get him a refreshment." Nore waved Melora over. "Melora, would you please bring a boot of ale over to that man, courtesy of us?"

Melora nodded and brought the tall, foam-capped tankard to the stranger, nodding her head toward the table where Nore and Andara sat. The girls prepared to smile when the man acknowledged the courtesy by a wave, or a nod, perhaps a smile of his own. But he never did, never looked up from the boot sitting on the table in front of him, only nodded slightly to dismiss the serving girl. He neither picked up the boot to drink nor pushed it away, just sat still and watched it, almost guarding against it, as if it would animate at any moment. The girls looked at each other, bemused.

"Maybe he's even more tired than he looks."

"I guess..."

Then suddenly, with no preparation, no warning, the man lifted his head, like an animal responding to an unfamiliar sound, and cast his stare directly at Nore. She gasped slightly from the surprise and found that she could not look away, though she tried.

"Gods," Andara said. "His eyes look like yours."

Just as Nore opened her mouth to respond an enormous pounding erupted against the entrance door, startling everyone in the tavern. Zhakhar even stood and strode out of the alcove to see if there were a problem. The pounding sounded more like a battering ram instead of a knock. Kor hesitated to open the view portal for fear the tiny opening would be enough to weaken the door and splinter it. Zhakhar made several hand gestures toward various emissaries in the tavern, and suddenly a dozen or more of them scrambled to different directions, some exiting through side doors and secret passages, others up tall, dark stairwells to the upper floors. After the commotion of deployment subsided, Nore noticed that the stranger, too, no longer sat at the table; the boot of ale still trembled, nearly knocked to the floor.

As suddenly as it had begun, the pounding ceased, and almost immediately one of Zhakhar's faithful returned with the okay, and Kor pushed open the great door. Six Dwarvani sprawled in front of the entrance, their faces bruised and bleeding; they lay about a long, wooden battering ram. Zhakhar motioned that they be brought inside. Kor strode forward and grasped two Dwarvani in each hand by the back of their shirts and dragged them from the entranceway. The other two stood on their own efforts at knifepoint and hobbled inside the Chalice. Emissaries threw a bucket of water onto the four whom Kor had dragged in, and the Dwarvani struggled to their feet. Zhakhar strode toward them.

"Just what do you mean trying to break down my door?"

"Forgive us, please! We thought the building empty, except for the fugitive. There are no markings on the door, no sign—"

"What are you talking, 'fugitive'?"

"We saw him enter through the doorway. We were sure he was hiding inside! If we didn't hurry—"

"Shhh..." Zhakhar whispered, holding his hand up toward the silenced Dwarv. "I'll give you one last time to say something that I understand, and if not I'm going to tell these men around you to cut your throats. So, you think for a moment, and come up with what makes sense."

The Dwarvani who appeared to be the leader glanced quickly at his cohorts, then strode forward slowly. Heaving breath, he raised his sweating face toward Zhakhar.

"Good sir, I apologize for our intrusion and will gladly pay for any destruction we may have caused to your door," the Dwarvani began, but was interrupted by Kor's mighty laugh. "Ha-ha-ha! Kor's door like wall!" he bellowed in broken Antran, and patted the thick, massive wood which appeared, indeed, undamaged.

"Continue," Zhakhar directed.

"We're sent from the majesty of the Dwarvani Kingdom to track down the murderer of one of our oldest and most respected citizens. The fugitive is desperate for any information concerning a majik amulet that may have passed through Dwarvani hands nearly one hundred years ago. Only a few were alive who remember that time, and the fugitive found all of them. The last one swore that the amulet had found its way to Antra and was held somewhere in the City—he told us so, before he died of the wounds inflicted upon him by the fugitive to coerce the information. It was this tragedy that brought us to your great city. The fugitive wasn't hard to track down, and a few inquiries and gold pieces later, we found him wandering the Hilo district, making inquiries of his own. But he saw us and we chased him toward your door. We watched him enter, and hurried to follow, but the entrance was sealed tight by the time we reached it."

"Why didn't you just knock?"

The Dwarvani cast his gaze toward the floor and just shrugged. Zhakhar sighed and shook his head.

"Do you have proof, of your mission?"

"Yes. A letter of appointment from the Dwarvani Royal Council." He produced a scroll from within his robes. "If the fugitive procures the amulet, he'll become next to invincible. There'll be no way of apprehending him. We *must* find him and stop him. Or," the Dwarvani added hesitantly, "find the amulet ourselves and destroy it."

Zhakhar read the scroll, saw that the seal appeared authentic. "All right, Dwarv. Your mission appears legitimate, but if you ever come to my door again, it better be with a pleasant knock and a sack full of gold. Now get out of here."

"Thank you, master, thank you. We'll take up no more of your time." And with this the six shouldered their belongings and quickly stumbled toward the Chalice door. The leader turned toward Zhakhar just before exiting.

"Kind sir, would you happen to know where we could find a Dwarvani wine merchant named Morvedraz? He may have information to assist us in our task. At least, according to our slain brother."

"Never heard of him." Zhakhar scowled.

The Dwarvani nodded once, then disappeared behind the closing door.

Nore and Andara had listened intently to the entire exchange between Zhakhar and the Dwarv and now sat staring at one another.

"I need to go and warn Koloran. My father's not there, and six Dwarvani against my anemic brother isn't exactly a fair fight."

"What about the stranger? He's got to be this fugitive they were talking about. He has to be hiding here somewhere. I'll see if I can find him."

"Patience, daughters." Zhakhar spoke in a wary tone. "Take three of mine with each of you. Let not a pair separate."

Andara nodded, and Nore stood calmly and waved toward Zhakhar who in turn motioned to three of his most skilled emissaries; they would accompany Nore back to her home and assist in quelling any trouble that arose. Andara slipped into the dark corridors of the Chalice with another three emissaries and began exploring the maze of hallways and rooms that laced through the building off of the main tavern. Some of these served as private conference areas, guest rooms for the especially wealthy, or mere storage. Andara felt certain that she'd find an unexpected visitor behind one of these doors. But after searching for nearly an hour she and Zhakhar's most skilled men found only a stray rat or two amid the narrow hallways and dark rooms.

Nore directed her escorts to remain near but under the cloak of the long shadows opposite the dozens of torches that gave light to the city streets. If they encountered the Dwarvani party—or the fugitive of whom they'd spoken— neither would likely be scared off by a lone girl. When she approached the wine shop, all appeared normal. A dim light shone in the uppermost quarters, and the front door remained locked. The emissaries did a thorough patrol in and around the vicinity of the shop but found nothing out of the ordinary. Nore checked on Koloran; he'd long ago fallen asleep in the library with a book in his lap. She then blew out the flame of the single lantern and crept silently downstairs. To the men who'd accompanied her, she gave each a bottle of very good wine, for which they thanked her and bowed respectfully before leaving her alone in the dark security of the wine shop.

Finding the Chalice's chambers empty, Andara emerged again in the tavern room, Zhakhar's men in tow, just as Melora rang the brass bell to sound "last call." She strode to the alcove as Zhakhar stood directing his servants to close the Chalice for the evening.

"That's far too much commotion for one night." Zhakhar's intoned. "Word will likely reach the Regent's ear by first light. His emissaries will cover this place like black on basalt. And what about the other who came in just before his majesty's Dwarvs?"

"We searched the whole place, every corner of every room. It's as if he disappeared."

Zhakhar scanned the room intently. "Behlar! Kor! Search every crack! We may have a hidden guest."

The two bid several of Zhakhar's emissaries to follow as they began a second search of the entire premises.

"One more before bedtime, lovely? You should remain and spend the night in your usual suite, for safety." Zhakhar said to Andara, directing her to follow him to the bar.

"Thank you, Zhakhar. I need it after tonight."

The two sat at the long bar side by side, staring at the tavern's reflection in the back-bar mirror behind the rows of ornate bottles. Melora brought them a flagon of brandy before retiring to her quarters for the night. Zhakhar poured them each a tall glass of the warm amber liquid and they sat sipping silently for a long while, each ruminating over the night's events.

"Isn't it odd," Andara began, "that Dwarvani would be in search of a *majikal* object?"

"Odd? It's unheard of. They're scared to death of *majik*. Some won't even use an apothecary's herbs. So all of a sudden these show up swearing there's Dwarvani dying for their knowledge of an amulet. Makes no sense."

"And what could they want from Morvedraz?"

"He's the most renowned Dwarv in the city. He'd be the first place they'd start."

A rush of voices and footsteps echoed from one of the corridors beyond the tavern floor, and three emissaries emerged, their hands wrapped firmly around the arms of the stranger who'd appeared just before the Dwarvani. Zhakhar and Andara turned toward the commotion and watched the servants lead the stranger forward. His clothes appeared soaked from the shoulders down and an acrid odor emanated from his body.

"We found him crouched inside a barrel of sour wine, Master Zhakhar."

Zhakhar eyed the stranger sternly. "You must be wanting to hide very badly if you're willing to spend the night submerged in vinegar. What's your story, boy? You the one the Dwarvani lookin' for?"

Zhakhar spoke in a common street dialect, a rapid, abbreviated version of the standard Antran. The stranger only stared at Zhakhar with a bewildered expression.

"Speak up, boy! You're trying my patience, and I really don't want to throw anyone else off the bluff tonight—"

"Pardon, please, great master," the boy began, his voice grave and rough. He spoke haltingly, pausing at inappropriate places that broke the rhythm of his sentences, like a child reading from a primer. "I am but a...stranger in thy land and have...learnt little of thy tongue."

"Where ya from, boy?"

The stranger shook his head.

"Where do you come from?" Zhakhar annunciated the proper sentence with unusual care.

"I am born in the land south of the City where grow the fine grapes."

"You mean Kwamada?"

The stranger nodded hopefully.

"You don't look like anyone I've ever seen from Kwamada." Zhakhar spoke low, almost to himself, looking skeptically at the young stranger. "In fact, you don't look like *anyone* I've ever seen—"

"Anyone except," Andara whispered into Zhakhar's ear, and his eyes grew wide with realization.

"Gods, girl, you're right."

The stranger looked quizzically back and forth from Andara to Zhakhar.

"I have an idea." Andara looked intently at the young man. "Stranger," she began in formal Antran, then, straining, constructed an awkward phrase in the language spoken only by Nore: "*What be that you are called?*"

The stranger gasped and drew backward, his eyes wide and mouth agape. "*You know my language! How's that even possible? I was told that there was no one, no one left from our bloodline but me. I'm the last one. And if I don't—*"

"Whoa!" Andara interrupted, shaking her head and raising both hands. "You're going to have speak way slower than that. Now, come on, work with me. *What you are called?*"

The stranger nodded and said deliberately, "*My name is Khaleo. And yours?*"

"Andara," she said, pronouncing each syllable distinctly. "And this is Zhakhar," she began, wanting to explain Zhakhar's status—"*he...father of...house,*" she managed, holding her arms wide and looking about to indicate the entirety of the Black Chalice.

"Ah!" the stranger said, immediately dropping to one knee and bowing before Zhakhar. "*Forgive me, sir! I am both displaced and ignorant. I meant no disrespect to you or any of those in your charge.*"

The stranger looked hopefully between Andara and Zhakhar.

"Uh, he said," Andara began, "that he's...really sorry. I think." She shrugged.

Zhakhar waved his thick hand, dismissing the apology and indicating the stranger to stand. Zhakhar turned to Andara. "We need to find out what exactly our friend here is saying."

"I'll go get Nore."

"Take a team with you, just in case you run into any stray Dwarvani."

Andara nodded and headed toward one of the secret exits, four of Zhakhar's black-cloaked assassins following close behind.

Nore poured herself a glass of wine and gazed out the window at the leaden clouds shrouding the Antran moon. She thought to light a candle but decided to remain in the darkness and allow only the moonlight to illuminate her surroundings. The clouds had gathered and thickened, and the weak, ghostly glow cast only a gray pallor into the dark interior of the tasting room. Still, she enjoyed the cool air full of the scent of wine, the dark paneling and roughly hewn timbers. These were her first memories of the wine shop—the scene she'd taken in when she'd arrived, just five short years before—and despite the opulence of the luxurious floors above, the simple environment of the ground floor gave her the most comfort.

She'd thought of waking her brother and warning him about the Dwarvani, but decided against it. What would he do? Wing a book at them? Hide in the cellar? Her father would be home by the Hour of the Drug the next day. She'd stay close to the shop tomorrow, help Koloran for the day, then talk to her father when he arrived.

After checking every window and door, Nore finished her glass of wine and had lifted her foot onto the first step toward the upstairs quarters when three sharp knocks at the wine shop door made her pause in mid stride. She did not start from the surprise, only turned with movement even and silent, and padded toward the door, her soft leather boots not so much as creaking the wooden floor. When she stood facing the entry she said in a normal voice, "Who's there?"

"*Your best friend.*"

Nore had taught Andara the phrase—your best friend—in Nore's language, and told Andara to use it only when matters of great urgency were at stake. Hearing Andara utter the warning, Nore drew in a quick breath, then unbolted the door. Andara and two of the emissaries entered, the other two remaining invisible but close enough to the entrance to strike a killing blow if one proved needed.

"What's wrong?"

"It's way too complicated to explain. You have to come back to the Black Chalice."

"Now?"

"Yes, now. Please, Nore. Believe me. You won't be sorry."

Nore sighed heavily, but strapped her dagger to her thigh, grabbed a leather cloak from the stand next to the entryway, then followed Andara into the night. The clouds continued to obliterate the moon that would have normally cast a false daylight, rendering anyone who wandered the street plainly visible even at the late hour. Nore and Andara walked briskly and silently, two emissaries completely out of site but only seconds away at any moment; Nore had beckoned the other pair to remain at the wine shop, in case Koloran awoke to the noise of Dwarvani.

When they arrived at the Black Chalice, Kor had already opened the viewport; his enormous eyes shined through it like beacons, scanning for Nore's arrival. The door swung wide when the girls approached, and the Kuzhani quickly ushered them inside and replaced the heavy stanchion.

"Welcome back, daughter." Zhakhar sat at a table in the center of the room, empty now but for him, Kor, and the stranger, who sat stiffly next to master of the Black Chalice. "Sorry to roust you so late, and after everything that happened tonight, but we need your help. Come on over."

Nore walked forward, her head high, and stood in front of Zhakhar and the stranger. She gazed toward the white-haired young man. Zhakhar placed a hand on his shoulder and nodded. The stranger then looked up directly into Nore's eyes.

She tried to mask her astonishment; no one in the city had ever seen another being with eyes like Nore's: large, and with the slightest elliptical shape, the color of warm amber. In some areas of the city, Nore was known as "the girl with the golden eyes." But the stranger's eyes matched hers to almost every extent, though his were smaller. She noticed then that his silver-white hair looked the very color and texture of her own, perhaps a bit lighter. Nore's heart beat hard and she breathed in deeply.

Acting on instinct, she spoke in her own language. *"Who are you?"*

"I am Khaleo of the Zhoryan royal family."

Nore gasped and brought her hand to her opened mouth to quell a prelude to a sob. Her short life seemed to play itself out in her mind; so much of it, so many of her thoughts and dreams were based on the fantasy that someone somewhere else could speak to her and know her origin. She recalled the endless hours when, as a younger girl, she would speak to herself in her language and answer herself in kind. She remembered the pained attempts that Morvedraz had made to engage her in conversation, attempting to satisfy her desire to discover her roots, to give her a sense of self. She thought of lying next to Andara's warm, bare skin under a silken sheet as they gazed out the window on a midsummer's night; where her lover saw the Antran stars all in place, Nore saw a strange reversal of order in the sky. Those were her only remnants, her unknown language and the belief that somewhere far away from the City of Antra lay a place where others like her lived, where the constellations coursed the sky naturally in their proper juxtaposition.

"Where do you come from?"

"My family was the last bloodline of the royals who were wiped out by Dwarvani raiders, almost two hundred years ago. We'd been in hiding since I can remember. They're all gone now. I'm the last. Or, I thought I was. Until I saw you."

"Listen," Zhakhar interrupted, "I am going to speak very clearly for you. Do you understand?"

"Yes."

"Tell me as well as you can, why are you in Antra?"

"I must to find...uh...I know not the word. Majikstone. It belong to my family, stolen by... man...many, many years past. Never found. Then Dwarvani tell story...magikman... who travel with young Dwarv...he carries stone. Dies. Dwarv disappears—"

"You're talking about an amulet."

"Yes! Powerful..."

"What kind of power does it give the bearer?"

The stranger shook his head, not understanding the question. Zhakhar grimaced impatiently, but checked his frustration and spoke more slowly, simply. "What can you do with it?"

"Ah!" The stranger exclaimed, his face lit with apprehension, then took a deep breath and looked into Zhakhar's eyes, his smile now completely faded.

"Anything," the stranger whispered.

"That's not possible."

"Yes. Possible."

4

Armed with only the amulet, Morvedraz had grown accustomed to traveling alone, which had not only grown his reputation as a Dwarv of power, but allowed him to expand his wealth far greater than any other merchant of The City. While the price of armed passage through the wilderness often depleted whatever modest profits a merchant could hope for, venturing into the vast deserts and dark forests alone could cost the traveler not only his gains, but his life. Yet time after time, season after season, year after year, the old Dwarv left the gates of The City, his face replete with an air of confidence and success that he bestowed with a smile to each shopkeeper and street vendor he passed. And they in turn felt a like confidence as they watched The Arbiter disappear beyond the gates, their sense keen that prosperity would continue so long as he returned.

Though steadfast and stubborn as any Dwarv, Morvedraz' aplomb shone with more polish and grace than even some of the most noble members of the City's society. Much of this was, of course, gained as a side benefit of using the amulet. The stone would not only latch on to the untrue user's fear and amplify it, it would conversely enhance the subtle confidence of the bearer whose heart sought only to benefit those around him through the amulet's *majik*. This is not to say that Morvedraz was not a special Dwarv to begin with; his mentor the old wizard knew as much long before finding him on the forest floor.

Any Dwarv of above average intelligence and wit could have learned from the wizard's lessons, but any Dwarv's latent fear of *majik* would have rendered him incapable of even accepting the wizard's tutelage, let alone refining his personality along with such skills. This incongruity was well known not only throughout the City, but the world of Antra as a whole.

But for every inhabitant of Antra whom Morvedraz had helped, no matter their excess or lack of wealth, no matter their race, nor standing within the City's society, every one who thankfully owed the Arbiter, there lived one who mistrusted the Dwarv's very existence. Morvedraz had known this for years; to make such enemies was a natural part of doing the business in which he engaged. But he had never worried as much about them as he had of late.

You are getting too old for this, he intoned to himself as he sat around the small campfire listening to the blustering of his team of sleepy horses. *What am I to do? Koloran is an efficient assistant, but has neither the head nor the stomach to carry on as Arbiter. Nore's ambition is great, as is her courage and skill with both hand and blade. But I fear she is too vain to resist the temptations the amulet could bring her, and too proud to choose her mind over her dagger to solve conflict.*

Morvedraz knew he must make a choice, and make it soon. As a younger Dwarv, his journeys proved far more than mere ventures to acquire goods. But he tired of the wilderness, saw the quelling of a barbarian's rage or the slaying of a lurking beast no longer adventurous but merely troublesome, almost tedious distractions. He longed to retire to his land in Kwamada, tend to his vineyards in the cool of morning and sip chilled wine in the evening shade, perhaps even in the company of comely companion.

His stout Dwarvani legs ached from the journey, so much so that he'd stopped for the night with the basalt cliffs below the city in view on the horizon. Never before had he spent an extra night in the wilderness when the soft down of his bed beckoned only a half days journey ahead. But the half-day walks had of late turned to full days or longer. He did not want to drag himself through the gates at midnight looking like an exhausted common traveler; he'd hear the Gardzi's ridicule if he did, and would have none of it. No, *I'll wait until first light. Let the chilled waters of the Great River and a cup of blakwine heighten my senses, then stride into the city gates at noon, tall and smiling—well, tall for a Dwarv. Shout to the Gardzi that they should have seen the young wench I'd had to finally chase from my bed this morning in Leth...*

It was, of course, equally as dangerous sleeping in the desert with the city in plain view as it was days from the nearest small village. In fact, with the sheer volume of traffic in and out of the gates, it was more likely to meet up with undesirables very near the center of civilization than it was in the middle of nowhere.

Morvedraz knew of a sheltered place just a few hundred yards from the road. Several high boulders stood exposed in a circular pattern near the river. From a distance they looked to border the chill of the water, but the old Dwarv knew that they actually formed a small rock-enclosed area where the soft sand of the riverbank made a restful bed, and the thick stone of the boulders kept the river at bay. His horses could drink as they liked from the calm pools at the water's edge.

Morvedraz sighed at the thought of a warm fire and the pliant sand beneath his aching body. He tugged gently on the horse's lead and the team angled off the road and into the more formidable terrain of the desert. The light had dimmed as the sun sank below the high horizon of the mountains, and the entire landscape grayed into dusk. When night drew near and Morvedraz found himself in unfamiliar regions, he often placed his hand beneath his robe and held the amulet, allowing its warmth to emanate around wherever he walked. This cast a protective aura of great distance in every direction, but also drained the amulet's power that could be used for a singular incantation, lessening its effect, and Morvedraz relied upon this method only when he was certain that an unknown foe lurked nearby. He had no thought to use the amulet now, in an area he considered familiar and safe.

When he neared the rock circle he thought he heard a knock and shuffling, but dismissed it as the rushing water dislodging yet another stone from the muddy bank. In another instant, however, the small spot of worry that had momentarily traveled across his mind transformed into a large blot of fear. When he'd rounded a corner of the cliff, Morvedraz found himself flanked by a small group of beings whose race he could not discern from the darkness. He felt a presence behind him and knew at once that the group had surrounded him. He thought to reach for the amulet, but quickly decided against it, unprepared as he was and not willing to chance its capture.

He stood silently for a moment, then, growing wary of the standoff, risked first contact in hopes of gaining the upper hand.

"Who are you creatures lurking in the dark? You like to scare the life from an old Dwarv!"

A general sigh emanated from all around, and suddenly the sparks of a flint flew about, like a tiny fireworks display. A torch flamed to life, and the entire group of lurking unknowns shone clearly in the firelight. They were Dwarvani, looking quite ragged and road-weary, but otherwise more peevish than dangerous. They had not drawn their weapons, but merely placed their hands on the hilt of their short swords, an odd lack of preparation on the part of their usually tenacious race. But when Morvedraz gazed at each their faces, lit by the glow of torchlight, he saw that the measure of their weariness hung heavier than he had ever seen on a Dwarv. They looked more than tired; they looked beaten.

The torch-bearing Dwarv stepped forward and faced Morvedraz directly.

"Good Dwarv, be greeted warmly. I apologize for the less than amiable approach, but we have encountered all manner of beasts in this wilderness, the likes we've never seen."

"No apology is necessary. But, tell me, what has happened to you and your companions? You look as if you've fought a mighty battle."

"This I will share with you presently. First, let us be properly introduced. I am Glavan, second adjunct and emissary of the Dwarvani King."

Glavan spoke slowly with his chin raised. Morvedraz saw that the Dwarv's tone meant to ply humility and reek impression. Never had he heard such a lofty title bestowed upon someone who looked like a slave market reject. However, Morvedraz felt lucky that Glavan's own ego had betrayed his identity; if the beleaguered emissary knew the true Dwarv who stood laden with goods, Glavan's greeting would have been less than welcoming.

"Master Glavan, it is an honor and a pleasure to encounter not only my race, but those of the royal court," Morvedraz intoned with proper humility, and abbreviating his proper name in an attempt at concealing his true identity. "I am Morved, a merchant based in the City."

"It looks as if your business is quite successful, Morved. Those are among the finest mounts I have seen."

"Thank you. Indeed, I have been most fortunate."

"You must spend much time traveling in the wilderness to have found this location without the aid of torchlight. We were lucky to have stumbled upon it after slaying several wretched gnar worms that attacked us from the deep pools upstream."

"The gnar worms are troublesome, indeed."

"Tell me, good Dwarv, how is it that you travel alone, with only a dagger that looks more accustomed to slicing cheese than the throat of an enemy?"

Morvedraz smiled at the gibe. "I use a good deal of prudence, and not a few tricks that I've learnt these many years. You must remember that these flatlands are as familiar to me as the Dark Forest is to you."

The Dwarvani cadre mumbled in wonder at Morvedraz small challenge to Glavan's smugness, and for a moment Morvedraz thought himself in danger. But the murmurs became light laughter, and another somewhat less weary looking Dwarv approached the light of the torch.

"Glavan, quit badgering our cousin, for goodness sake! Let's get a fire going and start supper before we all collapse." He spoke and patted Glavan on the back, then turned toward Morvedraz. "Good Morved, I am Kaljero, *primary* adjunct to the Dwarvani King. It is an honor to meet a Dwarv who has gained such high success in the Great City. In my village—during normal times—I am, too, a merchant, but none of your standing. Perhaps we may discuss your methods of trade after supper. I would likely learn something of value from your counsel."

"I would enjoy discussing business with you. But first, please, let's make that fire. My old stomach growls!"

All six Dwarvani, despite their obvious weariness, sprang about, lighting torches, gathering wood, unpacking the supplies that remained from their trek. Unfortunately for them, two of their pack mules had been lead away by a trio of Kuzhani thieves—the identity of whom the Dwarvani never saw, and thus attributed the disappearance to *majik*. These particular mules carried most of the food and ale, and the Dwarvs had subsisted for several days on water and dried roots usually reserved for the animals.

However, to celebrate their encounter with the good Dwarvani merchant, 'Morved,' Kaljero instructed his team to bring out a small portion of actual dried, spiced meat and a dozen fresh apples from his own pack. Morvedraz took notice of the leader's generosity, knowing full well that the withered Dwarvs would need all the sustenance they could find simply to make sight of Kwamada, where he assumed they were headed, it being the closest town of significance at around three days trek.

The Dwarvs took their captain's lead and served the fair swiftly and gladly to their honored visitor. Kaljero sat down next to 'Morved' and placed a flagon of water before him.

"I must apologize for such anemic libations, but our ale vanished along with our pack mules some three nights ago. It was a mysterious disappearance, indeed. I posted two guards with the animals, allowing each to alternate their sleep four hours apiece. As the one turned to wake his counterpart, he thought he heard a small sound like laughter, but muffled, as if from a distance. When he shook the other awake, he leapt to his feet and pointed wide-eyed over his friend's shoulder. The other turned and gazed at the place where the mules were tied, only to see two empty ropes and a pile of steaming turd."

Morvedraz could not contain a smile, and his cheeks flushed. "It appears that your guards met up with Kuzhani."

"Kuzhani? What sort of *majik* is this that it causes one's animals to vanish, leaving only a pile of their excrement behind?"

Morvedraz could only smile more broadly at Kaljero's urgent tone and attempt to keep his laughter to himself. "Dear Kaljero, 'Kuzhani' are not *majik*. They are people of the desert. They know it like we know the feel of our favorite hammer as we pound a new sword at the anvil. And they move upon you as stealthy as sleep."

"Ah! And they frightened our poor animals such that they lost their bowels?"

"No, indeed! They are quite gentle people. But they are prone to, shall we say, a very *basic* brand of humor...and they enjoy leaving a calling card." Morvedraz smiled wider still, and could no longer contain his laughter. He erupted in deep belly laughs, and tears sprang from his reddened eyes. Kaljero at first felt aghast at the prank, and his mouth fell and eyes bugged. Then he, too, shook his head and his smile widened as his own laughter grew and match that of his guest's.

"Good Morved, we must speak at length after supper, for there is definitely much that I may learn from you," he managed before laughter overtook him.

As the Dwarvs finished laying out the modest fair, Morvedraz excused himself from Kaljero's company and walked unnoticed to his own team of horses. He leaned against Elihra, his favorite, and lead silver mare, patting her soft nose as she nibbled his finger, searching for an apple. *Ah, they are dear, these simple Dwarvs,* he thought and watched the group bustle about the firelight. *I forget how much I've changed, living among all sorts of peoples, and engaging in the interests that I do. I feel almost out of place among my own.* He then unsheathed his dagger and quickly razored through a heavy twining that secured a portion of his cargo. From within—and against his better judgement—he pulled several bottles of wine, a wheel of hard cheese, and sealed box of *kororah*. He hoped that he'd forged enough good will with Kaljero that this offering would be accepted without suspicion; they were rare enough for common people of the City, and unheard of luxuries for Dwarvani emissaries on march in the wilderness.

Morvedraz returned to the fireside and found the gathering of Dwarvs huddled together staring at their small meal, Kaljero keeping sternly vigilant nearby to prevent one of the poor wretches digging in before 'Morved' returned from wherever he'd gone off to.

"Begin the meal, please!" Morvedraz beckoned heartily as he approached the Dwarvani leader, who in turn nodded to the lesser Dwarvs. They took the direction without hesitation and grabbed for the meager rations. "But, if it please your leader, accept these offerings in accompaniment," he added. Even Kaljero's face, accustomed as it was to the strong stoicism of leadership, widened and brightened as he saw the cheese and bottles of a deep colored spirit.

"Good Morved, what are these bottles? Looks like the darkest ale I've ever seen!"

"It's not ale. It's wine."

"Wine! We have not seen anything like it in months."

"What about this?" Morvedraz said and held up the cedar box for Kaljero to examine.

"What does it contain?"

"*Kororah*. It is a *tabak*, rolled thickly and long in sticks and smoked. Try one after your meal. These are of a medium strength and should suit our cheese and fruit and accompany the wine well."

Morvedraz sat next to Kaljero and showed him the proper method of opening wine, which the leader did so deftly with each bottle, then pouring to the brim of the cup each outstretched hand until every Dwarv sat with his own. Morvedraz insisted that he serve the Dwarvs—emissaries of the King as they were—and Kaljero yielded to his guest's resolve. Morvedraz unsheathed his dagger and sliced the wheel of cheese as thinly as possible to extend its flavor to all present. He enjoyed this modest gesture, supplicant as it were. It reminded him of the easy days of only presiding over his wine shop, presenting a plate of cheese and fruit to happy tasters across the counter. He smiled and even gave a chiding look at Glavan who smiled in return, feigning comfort with a crimson face.

Kaljero implored his guest to relate tales of his travels and of his business ventures. "Master," Morvedraz answered, "my travels are hardly adventures at all. I've been taking relatively the same path back and forth from Leth for thirty-odd years. In the beginning, the going was dangerous, I'll admit. But, as I said before, I've learned quite a few tricks since, and even more important have secured friendships strategic to my safe passage. The creatures must be avoided, to be sure. But far more dangerous are the thieves and raiders who from time to time scavenge this land. For, after all, they can steal not only your life, but your profits as well." Morvedraz smiled, and the group laughed in kind.

"Morved," Glavan began inquisitively, "you said that you stay to the same path in all your trips, but still have problems with neither beast nor thief. You must have made friends with the very sand that supports your steps!"

All the Dwarvs, even the cautiously diplomatic Kaljero, thought the small challenge of this comment both humorous and relevant, and their laughter soon faded to rapt silence.

"You are wise to consider this, good Dwarv," Morvedraz began, "but, though the desert may be a place of vastness and large danger, it is often the small details that pass notice which lead to one's demise." Morvedraz paused for dramatic effect and saw that the tactic had worked; each face around the fire held its still and wide-eyed expression. "You may recall that I said my path was 'relatively' the same. The vastness of this wilderness is both bane and advantage. This is true for several reasons, the most obvious being that, trudging the slow trek in any direction seems to leave one visible for miles, and likewise vulnerable."

"Are you saying," Glavan interrupted, "in that it *seems* to render you visible, that you know a way to disguise yourself?" The Dwarvs nodded toward each other, muttering many an 'Ah!' at their cohort's supposed discovery.

"In a manner of speaking, yes. But not as you would know a disguise," Morvedraz said soothingly, and pretended to adjust his tunic and relax into the explanation. As he did so the Dwarvs debated eagerly amongst one another the secret of their guests "disguise," and as they did, Morvedraz crossed his arms and reached imperceptibly beneath his tunic until his hand lay softly atop the amulet. He mouthed the words silently—all that was necessary for him for such subtle work—and felt the warmth emanate.

He did not wish to deceive the Dwarvs, simply to quell their curiosity.

Never having ventured this far from the Dwarvani Kingdom, the emissaries of the King had only heard tales of the creatures that wandered the vast wilderness of the Zhirazani Desert and Dark Forests beyond the populated areas of the greater known world. They had thus considered many such tales myth—who would have believed that fifty-foot worms could routinely rise with menace from quiet pools of water? They had encountered a variety of beasts during their journey, so many that their typical Dwarvani resolve had shrunk, and they'd often found themselves in swift and perilous retreat.

Morvedraz, his hand wrapped firmly around the amulet, imparted to the company several 'secrets' for avoiding this beast or that—facts that were common knowledge in The City, yet unknown to the Dwarvs. They sat with mouths agape, nodding their silent gratitude for the revealed knowledge. In the end, Morvedraz succeeded in relating to the Dwarvs information that would be valuable to them in their trek through the desert and beyond, yet not divulging anything that could not be gleaned from overhearing a tale in a pub.

The amulet's effects receding, Morvedraz opened another two bottles of wine and passed them to his left and right. The Dwarvs took the bottles, drew from them, and passed them to their respective neighbors, who did the same. Soon the entire group of Dwarvs, save their leader, lay snoring softly around the campfire's dancing flames. Kaljero kindly and softly crept to each of his charge and pulled a blanket from their packs over their shoulders, then placed two thick logs of dried hardwood onto the fire. He picked up a half-full bottle from where a sleepy Dwarv had let it fall and strode next to Morvedraz. Sitting cross-legged next to him, Kaljero sighed heavily.

"They're good Dwarvs, all of them." Kaljero whispered, leaning close to Morvedraz. "They're just single-minded, and loyal to a fault."

"As are most."

"Even Glavan has the best intentions."

Morvedraz stopped himself from voicing the obvious question: *Intention toward ...what?* Instead he offered, "I'm sure that's the case," trying to sound as if he took the comment in stride.

"He will not be satisfied with your simple beast-avoidance tactics, as will the others. He knows better."

"How's that?"

"Come now, friend. For we are friends, aren't we? Though we've treated each other far more leniently than we'd have wanted, if out of necessity, we've grown some trust. You may ply the others with wine and food and a few tales common to more sophisticated travelers. But Glavan has been beyond the forest a few times, so to speak. And his curiosity borders suspicion."

"What are you saying?"

"What I am saying, *Morvedraz,* is that you may be well served to take both a cup of *blakwine* and your leave of our campfire long before the Daystar begins to pale the desert sky. I will be up long before them and will attest that you wished to reach the City before the markets opened."

Morvedraz sat stunned, less from the bold suggestion that the Dwarvani leader had just given than from hearing his true name aloud on Kaljero's lips.

"Kaljero, I don't understand—"

"We don't have time, Arbiter. And 'Morved' will not fool Glavan much longer." Kaljero spoke naturally, as if offering wine, even passing the bottle to Morvedraz.

Morvedraz sat perplexed at both *how* he'd been discovered despite the amulet's power, and *why* Kaljero seemed to be allying himself. He took a long draw from the bottle and turned toward the Dwarvani leader.

"Why are you doing this?"

"Because, I'm on your side."

"But, what side is that? And for what reason should I be on one rather than the other?"

"You put the group to sleep too early. It would have behooved you to keep them up a while and learn from Glavan himself of our charge, for now there is no time for me to go into detail. Suffice it to say that we're looking for the amulet."

Morvedraz felt cold pierce his stomach and course through his body. He sat so still for several long moments that he forgot to breath, and at last took a deep gulp of air.

"I don't know what you mean."

"I didn't think you would, until I saw my company, Glavan included, list into pliancy as if they were drugged."

"The wine is potent. It's from—"

"Enough." Kaljero cast a dour glance at Morvedraz. "Your only advantage is that *they* don't think you have the amulet either, not even Glavan. And even if you did, he would not think you would dare use it. They do, however, believe that you know of its existence and may even have information that could lead to its whereabouts. Glavan is certain of it, and will press you further. This is why you must leave at once."

"But, what are Dwarvs interested in an amulet for? And by charge of the King? That is extraordinary—"

"There is no time," Kaljero said and rose. "Let's get you on your way."

Morvedraz struggled to his feet, looked about at the snoring Dwarvs, then walked a few paces away, still reeling from being discovered. Kaljero followed.

"I took the liberty earlier of leading your team several hundred yards down river. You'll find them tied to a tree branch next two large boulders and a small pool."

Morvedraz heard the description and immediately thought of Nore, of the place where she'd first bathed and taken his offer of clothing. He could use her now. Her mercenary training would allow her to easily subdue a half-dozen tired Dwarvs should anything go wrong. But, why did he think anything would go wrong? Their leader was on his side, whatever that meant.

"Wait." Morvedraz stopped, turning to face Kaljero squarely. "Why is it that I should trust you? Perhaps you're leading me into a trap. Your Dwarvs could sneak downstream and be waiting to ambush me before I reached the horses."

"Why in the name of Purim would I do that?"

"Yes," suddenly rang crisp and clear from ahead of where Kaljero and Morvedraz stood facing one another. The voice startled them, who'd been conversing in stealthy whisper, and they jumped away from the approaching figure of Glavan, sword drawn.

"...why, indeed, would my leader wish to cause you any harm, good *Morvedraz?*"

Morvedraz feigned a casual manner and began, "Dear Glavan! Do put aside your blade and—"

"Quiet." Glavan stepped forward in three quick strides. The point of his short-sword hovered inches from Morvedraz heart, inches from the amulet itself. Glavan then turned toward Kaljero.

"Leader, why are you ushering our friend away at such an unsafe hour? And for what purpose?"

"Lower your sword at once, Glavan! This is a direct threat to our fellow Dwarv, and at least an insult to me."

"At *least*." Glavan's sword followed the path that his eyes had taken toward Kaljero. "You help this Dwarv escape who has information we seek. Tell me why!"

"I have questioned him. He knows nothing! He has been kind and shared with us part of his very cargo that we may not starve in the desert. His goods are perishable and must get to market before the heat of the sun turns wine to vinegar!"

"And what questions have you put to him to determine his ignorance? Why did he conceal himself from us?"

Morvedraz cleared his throat and lowered his arms, open palms out, then took a slow step toward Glavan.

"Glavan, you asked me this night how I've not been killed in the wilderness. One way is to never, never admit to anyone who I am, be they Barbarian, Humani, or Dwarvani. In the case of Dwarvs—particularly those of the Court—I thought it safe enough to simply change my name yet retain the rest of my identity. I want you to know me, but my reaction is to protect myself. Who knows what level of ill *majik* could have possessed you? And my caution is not merely for the protection of my own profits and skin. There are literally hundreds in the City who would suffer if I fell to peril!"

Morvedraz spoke these words clearly and convincingly, for they were all true.

"You are the Arbiter?"

"I am."

"You've been witness to many strange and dangerous artifacts in the course of your...business."

"I have."

Glavan dug into his back pocket and produced what looked like a folded piece of parchment. He neither lowered his eyes nor the point of his sword, but held the parchment out toward Morvedraz.

"What is this?"

Morvedraz took the parchment haltingly from Glavan's hand, unfolding its sharp creases. The parchment was faerie-wing thin and opened to a much larger piece than Morvedraz first suspected. He held the outstretched sheet against the light of the moon and gazed upon it.

"It appears to be a rubbing." Morvedraz strained to see the characters embossed thereon.

"Yes, I know. What does it say?"

"I don't know."

"Really? Do you often carry around stone tablets of a strange mineral carved with runes of an unknown language? Or were these part of your 'perishable cargo'?"

"What are you saying, Glavan?" Kaljero demanded.

"I did the rubbing! From tablets I found among his goods! Look at it!"

Glavan then drove his sword into the ground and held the rubbing with both hands toward Kaljero's widening eyes.

"Gods...it's the language of the amulet." Kaljero spoke with a bewildered tone, more to himself than anyone else.

"Very good, leader! You recognize these from the tiny scraps that we were shown us by the King before we departed. It was thought to be the last remnant of this cursed tongue. But our friend Dwarv here has an entire alphabet full of it!"

Morvedraz raised a hand to clasp the amulet, but the moment he moved three Dwarvani daggers appeared from the darkness and pressed against his neck and chest.

"Glavan, this is madness!" Kaljero boomed. "Release him at once!"

"I hate to think that you are this naïve. In fact, I know better. So, my only conclusion is that you are somehow involved in this deception, good leader."

Glavan gave a quick nod of his head. The remaining hidden Dwarvani stepped from the shadows and placed a hand on Kaljero's shoulder. With the reflexes of a seasoned *waryer*, Kaljero stepped to one side and, using the Dwarv's own momentum, threw him easily to the ground, then drew his sword. For a moment the company froze, not willing to attack the captain to whom they had sworn allegiance. Kaljero used this instance to strike a flat blow toward Glavan's blade and knock the sword from his hand. The Dwarvs who had surrounded Morvedraz now stood stunned in fear, unsure of what their next move should be

or whose lead to follow. They paid little mind to Morvedraz, who stepped back out of dagger range.

"Put your weapons down, all of you," Kaljero ordered.
"Our friend has decided to leave us, and he is free to go."

"Free to sell his secrets to the Zhor and attempt to destroy the Dwarvani Empire!"

"Silence, Glavan! I shall deal with you later."

"You shall deal with me now." Glavan dove for his
sword, catching the hilt deftly and barrel-rolling, then
springing to his feet.

"Congratulations, Glavan. You have just earned yourself a long stint in the dungeons."

"For what? Keeping you from committing treason?"
Glavan countered, and the two struck at one another simultaneously. Their steel clashed, and sparks flew into the
black backdrop of the night.

The other Dwarvs stood agape at what was happening
around them. Noting their inattention, Morvedraz quickly
ducked a hand underneath his tunic and grasped the amulet, murmured the ancient words and watched as the rapt
Dwarvs dropped cross-legged to the ground, still gazing
at their dueling superiors, but letting their daggers fall
thoughtlessly to the sand. Morvedraz repeated the incantation and now focused on Glavan. In a moment he slowed
and stepped back, gazing at Kaljero confusedly and stag-
gering somewhat. He took a deep breath and lowered his
sword, then looked at the blade in his hand as if neither the
appendage nor the weapon belonged to him. His eyes then
bulged, and he drew a deep breath.

"No!" he screamed. "I will not let this cursed *majik* ruin
me!"

Glavan took two labored strides forward and, with
an upward slash, struck at Kaljero. Morvedraz, surprised
at Glavan's resilience, clutched the amulet tighter and repeated the incantation with more force. This dropped Glavan to his knees as if struck from behind with a mighty

blow. Morvedraz repeated the words again, and Glavan collapsed to one side, the sword slipping from his hand, and lay staring blankly at the sand in front of his face.

Morvedraz then turned toward Kaljero, intent on application of the same majik on the Dwarvani leader in an attempt to mask his collusion, but when Morvedraz turned he saw Kaljero leaning against a great boulder, a deep gash from his shoulder to his abdomen pulsing out in rhythm a stream, red and thick, to the steady beat of his heart. Morvedraz rushed to his side.

"Come with me, quickly, while the others are still subdued!"

Kaljero looked to move in slow motion, swaying his head toward Morvedraz. "It does not appear that I shall be doing anything quickly, Arbiter."

"Sit then, so you don't fall. I'll be back as soon as I can."

He helped Kaljero ease himself down the face of the boulder and come to a weak crouch at its base. Morvedraz ran as quickly as his stiff legs would permit, toward the point in the darkness where his team should be waiting. His lungs burned from deep erratic breaths, and pain shot through his joints as if bare bone scraped against itself with no cushion of cartilage. When he thought he would collapse before ever finding his way he heard a low neighing and shuffling of hooves in sand. He slowed to a gasping walk, trying to quicken his pace but felt as if a force pulled him back the harder he strode forward. At last he saw the large white outlines moving against the dark of the river in their background, trudged to Elihra and placed both arms around her wide muscled neck.

"We must hurry!" he whispered to her, for a whisper was all his strength would allow. "Kaljero needs us..."

And as if she had been at his side the entire strange evening, even as if she understood his words, Elihra neighed and shook her head, freeing herself from the rope tied loosely around the tree limb, bidding her team to move.

Morvedraz thought for a moment to unbridle her and lead her alone, which would be faster. Then he realized that not only would raising Kaljero's wounded body onto the tall mare be impossible, that raising his own spent Dwarvani self that high would be nearly so. He took several deep breaths and calmed himself, then lead the team up river toward the Dwarvani company.

When he approached he saw that the lesser Dwarvs huddled around the still somnolent Glavan who now sat with his head between his knees. Morvedraz saw no sign of Kaljero. Then from out of the darkness to his right he heard a wheezing call, seeming to emanate from the boulder itself. He walked carefully toward the sound, his eyes still on the Dwarvs, and found Kaljero lying in the cold sand, his head propped against a rock.

"You are wise to have hidden yourself, my friend. Glavan is coming to. Come on! Let's get you out of here."

Kaljero forced a smile at Morvedraz, then squelched his moans of pain as best he could. The only vehicle Morvedraz had able to transport the wounded Dwarv was a low wheeled cart towed by the last horse. It contained only Morvedraz essential travel items—blankets, extra clothing, some food—and proved at least as comfortable as the course sand of the riverbank. He leaned Kaljero against the pile of blankets and helped him climb onto it as best he could. Not looking back toward the Dwarvs, Morvedraz pulled Elihra's rein and started the team north into the dark desert toward the City. He would stay away from the main highway in case the Dwarvs decided to follow, thinking not even Glavan foolhardy enough to attempt the blind desert.

But when he turned the team away from the Dwarvs he heard a smattering of disquiet voices, the loudest of which he recognized as Glavan's. Morvedraz continued forward, not haltingly. Then the voices grew nearer and more clear. Morvedraz quickened his pace until a single shout stopped him.

"Dwarv!" Glavan called, still groggy, but more charged than before. "Your evil *majik* may stop us for the moment, but it will not hinder our purpose."

Morvedraz turned and strode forward, hand clutched safely around the amulet, and faced Glavan.

"If you only knew, Glavan, the true nature of my *majik*, you would question *your* purpose. I have saved hundreds, perhaps thousands, and created the prosperity of tens of thousands with a simple—"

"Enough! Go. We have no power to stop you. But next time, when there is an entire regiment of Dwarvani *waryers* pressing you instead of a tired few, see how your *majik* will falter. Now, give us our leader so that we may judge him."

"He meant no harm to you, and he is near death. You have no means to revive him. I will take him to the City where skilled apothecaries may still—"

"No! Despite his crimes he would doubtless rather die an honorable Dwarv than be subject to more of your de-basing *majik*!"

With this declaration Glavan had regained more of his strength, enough to push Morvedraz swiftly and firmly to the ground, then raised his sword unsteadily yet high and took aim at Morvedraz' neck. The other Dwarvs un-sheathed their daggers and swords and rushed toward the two.

Morvedraz used his stout Dwarvan strength to re-pel Kaljero away, then struggled to his knees. He shout-ed once, but still the Dwarvs charged and Glavan looked to muster enough strength for a deciding blow. Gripped with more anger and fear than he had ever experienced, Morvedraz did two things he had never done, things he had sworn to the dying wizard so many years ago he *would* not do. First, he tore the amulet from its chain and held it openly toward his adversary. This alone stopped the

Dwarvs in their tracks and even caused Glavan to falter and pause. Then, Morvedraz pointed the amulet toward the group and thought with definite purpose enraged images of each who sought to harm him, and shouted in full and violent voice the words to wake the amulet.

Instead of a pervasive warmth that usually emanated around Morvedraz, the amulet instantly heated until its glowing sapphire blue radiated nearly white, and the ancient runes on its surface beamed blood red. The heat erupted with such intensity that Morvedraz had to drop the stone. It landed flat against the desert floor, but appeared to grow in size and brightness and to even emit a sound like a gale rushing through a forest. The terrified Dwarvs simply froze. Glavan forgot his aim at Morvedraz and instead tried to strike the amulet where it lay. But as soon as he turned to face it the radiant heat appeared to concentrate into a single beam that shot straight into the air, disappeared into the darkness above, then with imperceptible swiftness directed itself downward at Glavan. The beam struck him in the chest, and he immediately withered to the ground, his face instantly losing all its rage and resolve until he took on the expression of a simpleton. But the beam did not stop once Glavan appeared subdued; rather, its heat and luminosity intensified, so much that Morvedraz squinted and then had to look away.

He shielded his eyes for what seemed a long time while the rushing thunder continued around him. He could perceive from the light dancing on the sand and surrounding boulders that the beam had moved several times, not randomly, but with rhythm and purpose. Then, just as suddenly as it had begun, the light vanished, and the only sound present was the bubbling of water over the smooth stones at the bottom the nearby river shallows. Morvedraz took a deep breath and turned toward where the Dwarvani company had stood. He squinted into the darkness, waiting for his eyes to adjust to the sudden change. He saw forms, five of them, lying still on the ground, not even showing the rising of breath. He quickly ran to his packs and found a flint and struck flame to a torch. When he approached the body that had been Glavan, he gasped and grew physically ill.

In removing the amulet and using it not as an indirect influence but as a direct extension of his own hand, and further crystallizing the distinct image of his enemy in mind as he voiced the incantation, Morvedraz had transformed the amulet from an effective deterrent into a ferocious weapon. Used as a shield, as it always had been, the amulet protected him by bending the will of any subject around within a given distance. Used as a direct force, the intensity of the amulet's power had magnified exponentially; what would in a lesser degree weaken one's resolve and dull one's mind now burned through the brain like a fire erupting from within. Once the mind was gone the power turned itself to the body, withering it with the same intense heat. What Morvedraz found left of Glavan was a singed torso, its head and limbs burned completely away, reduced to smoldering stumps; the body was no longer even recognizable as a Dwarv. The metal of his scabbard and armor had melted completely and pooled into the cool sand like molten metal poured into crude molds. Morvedraz looked to where the other Dwarvs had stood and saw four similar forms, smoke rising from each withered corpse. The sweetly sickening stench of roasted flesh filled his nose, and he turned and ran to the river.

He vomited steadily for several pained minutes, finally clearing his throat long enough to take a long, acrid breath. He remained there for some time, well into the Hour of the Basilisk. Indeed, he felt the influence of the Basilisk on him, for the entire scene wreaked of madness. Finally he regained his composure and washed himself in the frigid water, then stood and proceeded back toward the scene. His team still stood ready to venture out. Kaljero still lay on the open cart, unmoving but breathing shallowly. Morvedraz walked to Elihra and pulled her lead away from the river. Suddenly a rush of wind rose from the open desert and seemed to push Morvedraz backward. He felt the loose chain cold around his neck.

"The amulet!" he whispered, though there was no one near to hear him, then walked toward where he thought it had dropped. He had let the torch fall into the river when he'd retreated from the burnt corpses and thought not to strike another flame. But when he approached the place where he had stood he saw a faint glow in the sand. The amulet had illuminated itself, with no incantation, like a homing beacon. Morvedraz hovered over it, so familiar to him yet now so strange and frightening. Still, he knew it could not remain there in the desert and be discovered by anyone, especially the party that would eventually strike forth from the Dwarvani Kingdom in search of their lost comrades.

He reached toward the glowing amulet, his hand trembling. When he touched its still-warm surface he jerked his hand away, as if the stone would again radiate its white heat. But it only glowed a soothing blue, emitting its usual warmth. He picked up the stone and looped it back onto its chain, crimping the bent-open loop into shape so that the amulet dangled securely again from his neck. He then hurried to the horses and immediately lead them toward the main road to the City, hoping he would reach the gates before the Daystar uncovered what had happened in the wilderness while the Basilisk still ruled in its madness.

5

Zhakhar stood with his arms crossed, looking skepti-cally at the hopeful stranger. "So, Khaleo, is it?"

"Yes."

"All right, Khaleo. I'm not sure if what you're saying is the truth, a lie, or something in between, but either way you don't speak Antran well enough for me to tell." Zhakhar turned to Nore.

"Daughter, I don't want to put you into any dangerous position just because you happen to understand this *Hu-mani*, but if you wouldn't mind a favor—"

"No, it's fine." Nore answered immediately, unable to wait any longer to hear her language other than in her own mind. "I want to."

"Good. Thank you. Now, I'm going to bed. Kor, escort Andara to guest quarters. I think it's a good idea if you stay here tonight, lovely. Just for safety."

Andara nodded, then turned to follow Kor, touching Nore on the shoulder as she passed.

"Nore, I'd like you and Khaleo to speak alone for a while, without us all staring at you. See if what he's saying sounds real to you. After you're done, just ring the bell and Kor will show you both to quarters. I want to keep every-thing inside tonight, and sort it all out in the morning."

Zhakhar, weary of the night's troubles, turned then and strode resolutely to the stairs and up toward his suite. Kor disappeared down the dark hallway out of the sight of both Nore and Khaleo, but took a quiet seat in a deep shadow from which he could spring should any trouble arise.

Nore motioned for Khaleo to sit at the round wooden table, and he did so thankfully. She then poured them both a brandy that Zhakhar had provided, sliding the tall, narrow glass in front of the stranger. She watched him sip gingerly, contained a laugh when he emitted a small cough; he drank like a child given his first thimble of watered-down wine at a family dinner table.

"You don't drink much, do you?" Nore spoke absently in Antran, then, checking herself, repeated the phrase in her own language.

"I drink wine. In Kwamada. This is much stronger. What is it called?"

"It's brandy. And don't tell me you're from Kwamada and have never had brandy."

Khaleo nodded and stared shamefacedly at the table. "I've been staying in Kwamada, but I wasn't born there."

"No shit."

"What?"

"I said, that's obvious."

"Ah."

"So, let's have it, then. Where are you from? What is the language called that we're speaking? And why is it that you and I look like first cousins?"

"Because we are."

"What?"

"We are of the same bloodline of the Royal Family of Zhor."

"Zhor? You've got to be kidding. That sounds like something a child would make up."

"Perhaps to your ears, that are used to the Antran language. In our language—"

"Just what is our language."

"Zhoryhan."

"Okay."

"Zhorhai is to the far north, beyond the Dwarvani Kingdom, so far that none of the peoples in the known lands of Antra would have known of its existence. The Dwarvani rarely speak of it, though it were they who discovered it, and they who destroyed it."

Nore glowered. "But, Dwarvani care only about the metal they mine, the ale they brew and the meat they raise to sear over an *open flame. They have no ambitions toward war unless provoked, certainly no interest in wiping out an entire race. What would possibly have brought their wrath upon your people?"*

"Our people."

"Whatever. What's the reason?"

"Unfortunately, it was we who would have encroached upon them."

"What do you mean?"

Khaleo sighed, his shoulders hanging slack and his face drawn as if in shame.

"There was a time, over a hundred years ago, when a faction among the Zhorhai royal family rose against the traditions of prosperity-through-peace and charity toward the lesser beings who dwelt around our kingdom—

"What's this 'lesser beings' crap? You think you're above other races? You think because of your alleged majik and complicated language that Kor couldn't crush your head like a Kwamadan grape if you slighted him like that?"

"No, please, that's not what I meant. It's that...there were peoples, hundreds of thousands of them, living in and around the Zhorhai kingdom, who had not the means of resource and commerce from which we were most fortunate to reap our riches. The practice of the royal family had always been to share—give to others in need, because we could. And for no other reason that they were beings under the realm of the same gods as were we. We sought them out, we protected them, we fed and healed them. And they prospered and lived in the gentle light of the shining tower of the Zhorhai palace. They bestowed upon us their knowledge of agriculture, their skill at hunting and fishing. We could create vast armories of forged steel blades, but they possessed a keener skill at wielding the sword, and shared their skill with us without prejudice. Our races intermingled in the markets, in the forests. Some even intermingled their blood..."

"You mean, they married?"

"And had children, strong in the tradition of the Zhorhai and its wealth, and more strong in the heritage of those whose very sinew hummed with a strength we did not possess, a precision that grew

stronger in the hybrid offspring than any pure Zhorhai union could have ever produced. They were revered by the royal family, brought in and treated as blood in kind. There was talk that their entry into the royal bloodline would strengthen it and help do battle against those who would strike down the values that our race had held for millennia."

"So, what happened to them?"

"They were attacked as were the thousands who'd bred with Zhorhai to produce them. Few escaped."

"How many?"

"I can only confirm one, for certain."

"Where is he?"

"She." Khaleo paused, and Nore watched as the stranger took a deep breath as if to prepare for Nore's reaction. *"I'm speaking to her."*

Nore gasped and stood, taking several steps backward and staring at Khaleo with dagger eyes; from deep within the dark corridor she heard Kor's breathing quicken.

"But, you're talking about something that you say happened a hundred years ago! How could I possibly—"

"Leonora." Khaleo spoke Nore's proper name, paused, then continued. *"Do you have any idea how old you are?"*

Nore remained standing, glaring at the one who was at once so strange and so familiar. Though she'd known the language within her mind she'd never had the ability to engage in an audible conversation with another being in this *Zhoryan,* as Khaleo called it, since being discovered and saved by Morvedraz; she had no memory of her prior life. But the lilt and rhythm of the phrases came to Nore effortlessly. Her skills with a blade of any length—from the dagger strapped to her thigh, to the swords of Morvedraz' armory—had always felt like the very extension of her own arms, her movement with their weight balanced and fluid; there were few in the *Kolej of Waryers* who could best her in competition. And then there was the undeniable longing, the pulling force she felt when sitting in the uppermost terrace of her home at night, when the constellations in the sky looked reversed, and she felt a strange, strong yearning each time she gazed toward the north.

And the mystery behind Khaleo's question made Nore question herself: *How old could I be?*

"*So, back up for a minute and tell me what did this 'faction' of Zhorhai did.*"

"*They rose against the Royal Family by infiltrating the highest councils and most influential committees, where decisions of state were made. They made secret contact with the other peoples who'd benefitted from the Zhorhai's beneficence and promised them more than they'd ever been given: equal footing for all their people with the Zhorhai, intermingling of all races to form a complete union. Of course, they were deceived. The rogue faction only needed them for their skills with the blade. Once they solidified power, their intention was to enrich just enough of the other people's leaders so that they could remain in control.*"

"*But, why? Why upset such a balance between races when it was benefitting everyone?*"

"*Quite simply, greed. They had no wish to share the Zhorhai wealth with others for the mere reason that it was beneficial to them. They wanted to amass wealth and power unto themselves. And when they'd succeeded and driven our side of the Royal Family into exile in the forests that ringed the Kingdom, they thought to extend their power. That's when they began plans to invade the Dwarvani Kingdom.*"

Nore took a deep breath and exhaled audibly, then sat back down at the table.

"*Khaleo, if this is all true—and I'm not saying it's not—I have a deep sympathy for you and your people—*"

"*You are my people.*"

"*I may look like you. I may be able to do the things you say I should be able to. But that doesn't mean I belong in Zhorhai. I have no connection, no memory—*"

"*Please, Leonora, hear me out. You're the reason I've travelled these thousands of miles. You're the last hope to lead our people back from obscurity and establish the Zhorhai kingdom once more.*"

"What?! Listen, Khaleo, I just wanted to learn about my background, my origins, where I'm from. And hopefully find someone who shares my language. But, I'm not traveling those same thousands of miles back to some place I don't even remember. And I'm certainly not going to lead any uprising—"

"It wouldn't be an uprising. There isn't anyone to rise against, anyway. The Dwarvani took no prisoners; they slaughtered all they found, then retreated back to their own lands. Fortunately, some were hidden and enabled to escape—yourself included. The others just need training and support until they can band together and perform on their own. You have the innate skills with weaponry that they lack, and though they don't possess your dexterity, you can teach them maneuvers that they could use to protect themselves, to return to the kingdom and rebuild it."

"Khaleo, listen: My father is a very important person in the City, and I'm treated with a respect and attention like almost no one else. I'm learning my father's business. And, he's not getting any younger. He needs my help. My brother, Koloran, is a good bookkeeper, but he doesn't have the personality to grow a business, let alone learn the skills of an arbiter. And, I love Andara very much. What I'm saying is, I have a life in Antra, one I'm lucky to have, because if Morvedraz hadn't stumbled upon that particular band of barbarians on that particular route through the desert, I'd be a slave, or dead, by now."

"Morvedraz is your father?"

"Yes! Who do you think the Arbiter is?"

"I had no idea. I mean, I hadn't made the connection. I must speak to him. I must find out what knowledge he may have of the amulet."

"He doesn't have any amulet." Nore spoke with immediacy, not considering the charge. "But, he spoke my name when he found me, in Zhoryhan, if that's what you call it. And he knew a few words. Speaking to him is like talking to a three-year-old, but he still learned the words somewhere. So, I don't know, maybe he could help you. But, I'm not traveling thousands of miles to someplace I've never been just to—"

"You don't have to travel there."

"What do you mean?"

"I mean, you don't have to walk, or ride a horse, to get there."

"Then, how..."

"The amulet. With a particular incantation, it can be used as a teleportation device."

"You're kidding." Nore lapsed back into Antran out of surprise at the thought of *majik* teleportation.

"What?"

"Are you serious?"

"Yes. As I implied to Master Zhakhar, the amulet can be used for almost any purpose, as long as one knows the proper incantation. I know only a few. And the tablets that contain the entire lexicon of the amulet's powers were lost in the great struggle, when the Dwarvani overran the Zhorhai city and drove our people into the wilderness."

"All right. Listen. First of all, you don't have the amulet. Second, it's really, really late. I'm exhausted. Let's get some sleep. In the morning we'll fill in Zhakhar about all of this. He's definitely someone you want on your side if you spend any time in Antra. After, we'll go to the wine shop and talk to my father."

Nore watched as Khaleo nodded, then stood. Kor appeared in the entryway to the hall and with a wave of his huge hand beckoned the *Humani* forward and toward a room for the night. Nore followed the two toward the guest quarters, taking a corridor on the left and moving quietly toward the room she and Andara shared when they stayed late at the Chalice. She eased the door open and closed it silently, stepped toward the layered down of the comforter and removed her tunic and sandals, draping her clothing over the back of a side chair and slipping naked underneath the heavy covers. When she did she felt Andara stir and press against her, Nore's breasts seeming to meld into the radiating heat of Andara's back. Nore reached her arms around and cupped her lover's own small, pert breasts, but soon let her grasp relax and fall onto Andara's hip as sleep overtook them both.

The hopeful light of the Daystar had finally crested the peaks of the great mountains, lifting the wasteland of the desert from it's cold obscurity and casting warmth onto Morvedraz' weary shoulders, but the gentle heat brought him no comfort. For though he hurried toward the gates of the City to seek aid for Kaljero, vowing silently never to use the amulet as he had and allow its powers to twist into destruction, the single thought he could not wrest from his mind continued to plague his every sore step: *You killed Dwarvani.*

He had possessed not the slightest inkling that the amulet held such devastating power, yet this fact failed to assuage his shame and only drove the feeling of failure further into his consciousness. *If I'd have only been more curious, more ambitious to learn the entirety of the amulet's powers, I might have discovered its ability to kill and made certain I'd never have put myself in a position to rely on such terrible capacity. But it was not within my Dwarvani nature. And I can't read the damned tablets! The wizard died before teaching me. I only know the single incantation to ply my will onto others gently, gracefully. I could have asked Nore to translate the tablets. But, that would have meant revealing the amulet to her, and I could not take the chance on its existence being known to anyone but myself. This is what the wizard warned greater than anything else: never, never, under pain of death, tell anyone about the amulet.*

Morvedraz, now approaching the ascent that led to the gates of the City of Antra, bid Elihra to stop, and as she did the other horses followed her lead and obediently halted their steady march. He took a deep breath and gazed at the gates at the top of the rise, then walked toward the tarp-covered wagon that held his goods, patting his horses' flanks as he strode. He reached beneath the burlap tarp for a water sack and opened its spout, tipped his head back and poured a long stream into his open mouth. Then he knelt to where Kaljero lay and placed a hand on his shoulder. Morvedraz was glad to see the Dwarv's chest still rising and falling with breath, more so when he opened his eyes and even attempted the slightest hint of a smile.

"We're almost to the City gates. Take some water. Then I'll cover you for the last stretch of the journey."

Kaljero parted his dry lips, and Morvedraz squeezed the bag, careful to give the Dwarv just enough water to sooth his parched mouth. He patted Kaljero's shoulder, then spread an extra tarp over his entire body, hoping that the *Gardzi* would not scrutinize his load any more so than normal. Of course, he could use the amulet to influence the sentry, but the plight of the *Dwarvani* party still pressed heavily against his heart, and he decided to reject his usual methods and hope his stature held enough power to sway the *Gardzi's* eyes.

When Morvedraz and his team stood immediately outside the towering gates of the great city, he heard a guard hail him from the sentry tower on the left, raised his hand toward the sound of the hail and smiled, though the Daystar's rays obscured the guard's face, and Morvedraz could not discern if the sentry were familiar, or strange. Nonetheless, and after only a short pause, the gates rumbled, then slowly began to part, pivoting inward on their huge iron hinges until the entryway into the City stood wide open in front of Morvedraz' thankful eyes. He raised his head high and maintained the artificial smile, feigning a confident stride as he tugged at Elihra's reign and urged her and the team forward.

He glanced to his left, saw two *Gardzi* lazing against the parapet wall of the watch tower that protected the Customs House, where ordinary merchants would be required to pay the necessary tariffs before entering the City to sell their wares. Luckily, Morvedraz had long ago negotiated special arrangements with the Customs officials to pay a yearly sum on his projected revenues, and it was understood that these projections would be far, far lower than their actual worth—the price required to keep the skills of the Arbiter on retainer. Though the *Gardzi* were aware of Morvedraz' stature, they nonetheless enjoyed chiding him with mostly good nature, still deeply envious that a Dwarv had risen to such a level of power within the merchant ranks of the City.

Morvedraz smiled and waved toward the two, who smirked and jerked their heads backward in greeting, the mugs of hot Blakwine they held steaming the steel of their breastplates.

"Quite a sunrise, wasn't it, men?" Morvedraz always found that engaging the *Gardzi* with casual pleasantries tended to disarm their surly nature.

"Ha, Morvedraz! You must have packed that load before the Daystar's rise. How lumpy and disordered it looks! What did you do, kill a gnar worm and stuff it under your tarps?"

"Unfortunately, I nearly encountered a roving band of Kuzhani thieves when I stopped to water the horses at the Great River. So yes, you're right; I had to pack quickly and in the dark to avoid being noticed."

"You don't look so well yourself. Far more harried than you usually appear. Are you fretting about something in that load you should disclose to us?"

Curse you, bloated Humani sloth, Morvedraz thought, but maintained his wide smile. He recognized Tolek, the guard who always flirted with Nore, and the thought burned in Morvedraz' chest that this oaf might paw at his daughter, even though he knew she'd cut him quickly and gravely if he ever crossed the line.

"No, no, Tolek. I'm simply an old Dwarv, and running from thieves on these short, bowed legs is not the best way to prepare to enter the great City. I do apologize for my appearance."

"No matter. Get yourself home, then, and we'll be happy to help your poor horses by relieving the weight of their load."

Yes, of course you would, you fat drunken toad. You'll have fin-ished the wine long before the Daystar reaches its apex!

"Oh, certainly! Please, lower down a gunny sack and let me fill it. It's my pleasure."

The *Gardzi* must have anticipated Morvedraz' return, for they'd already staged the line and sack at their feet, and now hurriedly and anxiously lowered it before any of their superiors might take notice.

Morvedraz placed the four bottles—two red, two white—of Kwamada's most recent vintage in the sack, tied it tightly, and watched it disappear up into the Day-star's glare and toward the *Gardzi's* eager mouths.

"Good day to you, Morvedraz!"

"And to you as well, Tolek!" *Would that you choke on your first swallow.*

And with another hearty smile and grateful wave, Morvedraz bid Elihra forward, and the team pulled easily toward the entrance to Long Street. Though Tolek would surely now be concentrating on opening his newly ac-quired delicacies, Morvedraz nonetheless waited until the team were clearly out of the tower's view before urging Elihra forward into a trot, looking backward with concern to ensure that the small cart carrying Kaljero did not jostle. Morvedraz himself had to match his horses' pace, a feat he would not usually attempt, though he knew now that ev-ery moment counted, if the injured Dwarv were still alive.

Hold on, friend. Only a few blocks more and we'll be in front of the apothecary's door.

Rolim had lain awake well into the hour of the Basi-lisk, a damp strain of worry painted across his brow. As the saying went, word travelled at the speed of the Daystar's rays in Antra, especially when it involved strangers from faraway lands, and the prospect of violence. He'd thought to spend a gentle evening at the pub, his wife away visiting relatives in Leth, his children, now almost at *Kolej* age, off

involved in their own preoccupations and not even feigning interest in spending time with their old father. But, no
matter, he thought; they were happy, as far as he could tell.
And, when was the last time he'd hunched over a friendly
bar, a frothy ale poised for his lips, and the hope of engaging company awaiting his eager ears, perhaps with tales of
the greater world than he'd ever have access to, holed up in
his apothecary's shop.

Tonight, the tales would be numerous, indeed.

When the doors to Flannah's Tavern nearly splintered
with the great weight thrust against them, all went silent
inside the pub, and every head pivoted, eyes wide with an-
ticipation, toward the open door. And from the darkness
beyond the portal emerged a line of Dwarvani the likes no
one in Antra had seen in long memory: heavily armed, clad
as if for battle, faces creased and stern.

The company took a table and hailed for drink, looking stiff and out of place amid the common working people
of Antra seated with no other thought but to relax for a
few meager hours before returning to the next day's toil.
But before this night was finished—and it would be long
hours till then—the pub's patrons would hear tales the
likes they'd never heard, bringing excited fascination to
them.

Except for Rolim.

Gradually, the Dwarvs relaxed amid the amiable
crowd around them, shed their swords to the arms check,
let their beards down and did what Dwarvs do best: eat,
drink, and tell tales. And these Dwarvs were not shy, relating the entirety of their journey, all the way from the
Dwarvani Kingdom, in pursuit of a marked fugitive.

"And, what was his crime, that you come so far a distance?"

"Murder! And conspiracy to overthrow the Dwarvani
Kingdom!"

"Murder I can see, but to overthrow an entire kingdom? It would take tens of thousands of *Waryers*! No one possesses such an army. How could one Humani possibly challenge an entire race?"

The lead Dwarv, colonel of the Royal Guard, stood to engage the question, as all other voices faded to silence.

"How else would such a possibility occur? Through *majik*! A *majik* most potent, most destructive, and most evil."

Rolim had listened quietly yet intently from his station at the bar, smiling some, nodding, sipping his pint, yet the inkling of concern that began to foster itself in the background of his consciousness now throbbed with pain inside his forehead, and made his face flush with fear.

Dwarvani. *Majik*. A fugitive, who looked like no race anyone had ever encountered. Rolim's thoughts sped immediately to images of Morvedraz: his immense wealth; his uncanny abilities; his strange-looking, if beautiful, adopted daughter. Yes, the Dwarv's stature was unchallenged, and would remain so, he having ensured the continued wealth of almost every powerful family in the City. But you wondered, as did Rolim, how in the gods' names did a Dwarv ever attain such abilities, such—if we could use the term, so unlikely applied to a Dwarv—powers? And, Nore was, indeed, a most charming and engaging girl. But, one could not deny noticing her appearance: who among any known races had hair that transformed from flaxen to silver and back again by no means of dyes or other unnatural shading, but by a simple alteration in the angle of the Daystar's light? Who had eyes the shape of almonds and larger than any Humani woman ever seen, and colored the hue of brushed gold?

All these thoughts coursed through his mind that night at Flannah's, even after he'd decided he'd drunk his fill, heading out into the chill of the Antran night and toward his quarters above the apothecary's shop, as he lay in bed, straining to sleep. He hoped, desperately so, that his intuition would prove wrong. But when strange Dwarv's arrived speaking of conspiracy, *majik*, and a fugitive with silver hair and golden eyes, Rolim could imagine nothing else but that Morvedraz would somehow be involved, and that, no matter in what regard this involvement might be, it would require calling in the great debt Rolim owed to the Arbiter of Antra.

And he would be right to worry, for as the hour of the Basilisk faded toward the Jewel and the light of the Day-star pierced the loose blinds of his sleeping chamber, Ro-lim jolted to full consciousness with the resounding crash of a fist pounding the wooden surface of his front door.

The three sharp raps stung Morvedraz' hand, but he repeated them in succession, hearing not the slightest stirring from inside the apothecary's shop. He found this more than odd; Rolim rarely ventured out, and surely nev-er overnight. But after what seemed a painfully long time, Morvedraz finally heard the rumble of footsteps negotiat-ing the narrow wooden stairwell, then shuffling across the cold tile floor, the clatter of keys and the creak of widening hinges.

"Morvedraz." Rolim spoke the name with no inflec-tion of surprise, and this startled the Dwarv more than the harried moments of waiting he'd spent in front of the apothecary's locked door; it sounded as if Rolim had al-most anticipated the arrival.

"Rolim, I need your help. Open the gates to your yard so that my team might lead the cart inside.

Rolim nodded—gravely, Morvedraz thought—and moved toward the rear of the shop and to the courtyard out back. Morvedraz lead Elihra toward the left side of Rolim's building where the two whitewashed swing gates opened onto a small courtyard covered in grass, a clothes-line strung to one side, a simple wooden bench the only other adornment. Elihra plodded forward and stopped when her nose almost touched the wall opposite the gates; the horses and cart nearly filled the tiny yard. Morvedraz moved quickly to the rear of the cart, bidding Rolim to follow.

"What is it you want me to do?" Rolim spoke flatly, almost warily, Morvedraz thought.

"Old friend, what's the matter? You sound as if you're addressing a stranger from the Rough Zirkot."

Rolim's eyes widened somewhat and he shook his head. "Forgive me, Morvedraz. Sleep escaped me last night, and I was only beginning to doze when your knocks jolted me awake."

"I apologize for the hasty entrance, but I assure you the situation is most serious."

Morvedraz flipped back the burlap tarp, revealing Kaljero's bloodied torso, the rough blanket on which he lay soaked through with red.

"Gods, Morvedraz! Quickly, help me get him inside."

Morvedraz unhitched the small cart and the two picked up one end and rolled Kaljero into the apothecary, then hefted the entire cart onto a table in the back. Rolim's instincts as a medical provider overrode his skepticism at least for the moment, and he sprang to treat Kaljero's wound, cutting the bloodied leather tunic away from his skin, cleaning the wide gash and applying a poultice and clean bandages.

"You're lucky, friend Dwarv. The blade appears to have entered you at a fairly acute angle, so the wound is not as deep as I'd feared. If you'd been struck head on..."

"...I would not be lying in your presence." Kaljero spoke in a graveled whisper. "Thank you, friend."

"He should be fine in a couple of weeks. But, Morvedraz, I need to speak to you."

Rolim angled his head toward his office, then strode in that direction. Morvedraz nodded, then followed the apothecary inside, who closed the door behind them.

"Rolim, thank you for your kindness and skill. I feared he would be lost. He was wounded a half-day's journey from the City."

"What in the gods' names happened?"

"I encountered a party of Dwarvani in the desert. They quarreled amongst themselves, and the fighting became grave, as you can see."

"And the Arbiter had no power to persuade them away from the sword?"

Morvedraz furrowed his brow in displeasure at the question's obvious implication. "Unfortunately, it was about *me* that they disagreed. I attempted to engage them without revealing my identity. They took it as an attempt at trickery."

"I should think they would. Why didn't you just tell them who you are?"

"Friend, I have my reasons."

"Yes, I suppose you do." Kaljero's tone turned skeptical yet again, and he scowled at Morvedraz.

"What's wrong? Why do you use such a tone with me? Have I offended you somehow?"

Kaljero sighed. "No. I'm sorry. But I worry, Morvedraz. Your wounded friend out there and those others you encountered are not the only strange Dwarvs to grace us with their presence."

"What do you mean?"

"I was at Flannah's last night, and a party of Dwarvani clad for battle showed up, regaling all who'd listen with tales of a fugitive Humani who is wanted for murder and conspiracy in the Dwarvani Kingdom. Perhaps this is the same group who took offense to you."

"No. They fled south." Morvedraz spoke with his eyes lowered, away from Kaljero's.

"You're certain? But, no matter. Morvedraz, the Humani they described is said to have hair that changes shade, from flaxen to silver, and eyes the color of gold." Rolim paused. "You must realize who has those same features—"

"Of course I do." Morvedraz spat out the phrase, cutting off Rolim's sentence, now maddened at his old friend's demeanor. "Nore has nothing to do with any unknown fugitive. If they share features, it's just some strange coincidence."

"But, Morvedraz, no one has ever seen anyone who looks like Nore. If suddenly another Humani appeared looking similar, wouldn't you be curious?"

"I'd be more curious as to what possible motive you have for worrying yourself about a situation that has absolutely nothing to do with you. Now, let me pay you for your services today and I shall be on my way."

Rolim's eyes widened and he held up his open hands, understanding now that he'd bested Morvedraz' patience and had no intention of falling from the Arbiter's good graces.

"Morvedraz, please! You hurt me. You know that you owe me nothing."

"Very well. Look after Kaljero. I need to get my goods to the wine shop. I'll return this evening to check in."

Morvedraz opened the office door and started toward the back entry of the shop, then paused and turned back toward Rolim. "Old friend, please know that I'd never put you in danger. That I swear to you."

"I believe you, Morvedraz. My worry is only that danger may put itself to me with no intention of yours."

Morvedraz frowned, nodded, then hurried to his team of horses to usher them toward home.

6

Ah, another day, another book... The thought coursed absently through Koloran's mind when he opened his eyes to the Daystar's rays streaming through the un-curtained window of his small bedroom, having woken earlier in his chair centered between the library's tall bookcases, the volume of Antran poetry he'd been reading heavy on his chest. He'd tossed the book onto a wooden table and sloughed off to his quarters adjacent to the library's stacks. Morvedraz had at first challenged the boy's desire for a bedroom located next to the library—wouldn't he rather be in a more spacious suite on the middle floors, as were his father and sister? No, he'd replied with a calm certainty; he only wanted to be near the books.

And it would be wise for Morvedraz not to dismiss his son's bookish proclivities as passive or in some regard lacking masculine force, for though a book remained Koloran's first desire—more than sport, business, even the pretty young women who accompanied their well-to-do fathers to the wine shop—he practiced his favorite undertaking with no less assiduousness than would a *waryer* practicing the stroke of his sword. Koloran knew that he'd never possess Nore's athleticism, and thus shunned swordplay or other activities that might involve physical contact, let alone armed combat; his only weapon would be the consciousness that resided in his eager mind, and, unknown to his father, this would prove a weapon most effective, and most potent.

Indeed, the boy studied far darker and more heady subjects than Antran poetry. Koloran had begun, long before he'd have the actual means to acquire such text, to venture into the far streets of the City to the bookshops whose inventory greatly transcended the standard classic literature and popular tales, but branched into areas of interest that many might consider arcane, perhaps taboo, some that the *Maj* would even deem illegal. Yet if one possessed the will to inquire of their availability—as well as the means with which to acquire them—a world of secret knowledge lay open for the taking.

Though Morvedraz supplied him with an ample allowance, the books Koloran sought required a far higher sum than the collected *zeks* of a teenaged boy. Still, he had been blessed with a penchant for patience—unlike his sister—and after two full years of saving that culminated in his nineteenth birthday, had finally accumulated enough for the price of his first tome: *Ancient Spells for Success & Profit*. Koloran knew that he'd need another way to acquire the money necessary to fuel his curiosity other than to wait for his meager allowance to build, and this volume, tucked between dusty tomes high on a shelf in a shop called Centhum at the outskirts of the Rough Zirkot, loomed over Koloran's head as well as his curiosity. Surely this aged doctrine would allow him to increase the funds he'd need to nourish his desire for knowledge.

The volume was thick and ancient, but the green dragon-skin covered boards and troll-tendon stitching of the wide spine showed little wear. After Koloran handed the hundred zeks to the bookseller, the old Humani slid the tome across the dusty counter and into the young one's eager hands.

"That's quite a valuable book for such a young man to possess. Where did you come by the means for such a purchase?"

"I saved my allowance for two years."

"Two years! I'm impressed. That's quite the show of restraint. You must have a tremendous love of rare books. Are you starting a collection?"

"Yes."

"Well, this is a fine edition for your first volume. It's in near perfect condition. There's hardly a crack in the spine. It's as if it'd never been opened."

"Have you ever tried any of the spells yourself?"

"Spells? Oh, no. I'm sure they're merely flowery verse, no more potent than the swords and shield hanging there on my wall. Just decorations. And, truthfully, most of the writing in it is far too small for my old eyes to make out."

"I guess I'll be finding out myself, then."

"Well, enjoy the book. And if you *do* manage to turn rocks into gold, please let me know!"

Koloran watched the old shopkeeper's mouth stretch into a humoring smile, then tucked the book carefully into his knapsack and hurried back toward Long Street and his sanctuary above the wine shop, where he would, indeed, begin a most successful study.

The ancient Antran characters were at first difficult for Koloran to interpret; U looked like V, V like B; and many letters of the script appeared nearly alike when printed in succession, so that M, N, U, V and W looked together in one long jagged line of indiscernible characters, the peaks and valleys of a tiny mountain range. The first word of each paragraph began with an enormous initial red letter replete with a filigree of flourishes and calligraphy the likes Koloran had never seen. But after a while he grew familiar with the unusual lettering, and began to unlock the tome's secrets. Fortunately, he did not skip the Forward, as a less scrupulous student might have, since the print was so tiny that it looked nearly incomprehensible. But with persistence, and the help of his father's magnifying glass, he learned within the confines of these tiny words an important lesson, one that would prove crucial to his future success:

"Seeker of knowledge in the abundance of nature and of the gods, read this Forward carefully and numerous times! For only it con-

"Well, alright then," Koloran said aloud, acknowledging the book's warning, and indeed began to read—slowly, carefully—the directions of the Forward. He skimmed the entirety of the book's prelude first; the text was long and tedious, giving lengthy and exceedingly specific instructions, incantation by incantation, as to how to invoke each spell: precise days of the week and hours of the day and night must be headed; the manner in which the caster must hold his arms up, palms wide open and head high toward the Daystar or the depthless night sky—representing his acknowledgement of the abundance and beneficence of nature and the gods—must be performed with exactitude; even the volume with which to voice the incantations—louder than in common conversation, but not shouted—must be heeded. And the most daunting direction of all: "*You must learn the spells in succession! Skipping any to invoke a later incantation will render all useless!*" upon which Koloran heaved a sigh, and began to read the instructions of the first spell.

It took him the better part of a month to fully absorb the requirements for only the very first, simplest and seemingly least potent of the spells: "*Gathering the Forces of Induction.*" Yet the forward explained clearly that this *pre*-spell must be learned and practiced with expertise were any of the other spells to function. Koloran studied the procedure scrupulously, waited for the precise day and time, the proper declination of the Daystar's rays, and after intoning the ancient words, waited. For what, he was not certain. The Forward, while being precise in its explanation of process, described no indication of expectations of the spell—no clue of the results. He did sense a feeling of warmth, as if acknowledging that the abundance that awaited him had been validated by the very forces of nature. But it was a very subtle result, indeed.

Still, he continued, spell by spell, poring over the details of the Forward, making certain that he performed every step with the utmost precision. The results remained less than concrete, though he had no indication of what concrete results he should expect. And though the titles of the incantations grew in successive prominence—*Expansion of Personal Power; Attraction of Enriching Avenues; Maintaining Prosperity*—all their respective results seemed to render Koloran with nothing more than a positive feeling. Yet he persevered, and, having completed the instructions for all preceding spells throughout the better part of a year, finally allowed himself to gaze upon the title of the tome's final incantation. He'd not even peeked beyond the steps of the spell he'd been studying, fearful that this might somehow render his efforts invalid. And when he finally came to the pages that outlined the last set of incantations, the frankness and clarity of the spell's title struck him with more than surprise. It was no amorphous rendering, hinting at power or abundance or determination in some abstract manner. Rather, the book's final chapter heading stated clearly: *Spell to Multiply Physical Wealth.*

"If you, the reader of this most ancient volume, have persevered as the Forward has directed and never wavered from the instructions therein, and if you have faithfully and successively performed the incantations exactly as prescribed, building a solid foundation in the esoteric attainment of Prosperity, then you have arrived at a most fortuitous and concrete conclusion. For many have sought to reap the riches implied that the spells of this book hold, yet few have ever practiced the required steps properly and meticulously enough to allow the final spell to invoke its power. Most would ignore the Forward; many attempt short-cuts and negate their abilities to work with the spells at

all, discounting their power. If you have chosen wisely, you shall now embark on an experience the likes many in the physical world would give their entire fortunes to discover, for the rewards will be many times that which they would ever relinquish."

Koloran thought this instructional preamble to the last spell odd; none of the other spells had commanded such a flourishing prequel. But he plunged into absorbing the final steps quickly though carefully, which, as he read in the dim candlelight of the library, proved far simpler than for any of the previous sets of instructions:

"Repeat in succession the incantations of all the other spells, focusing your attention on an object of value, such as a jewel or gold piece. After having done so, and then after acknowledging with upstretched arms and open palms a final thanks to nature and the gods for sharing their abundance, lower your arms, hold your still-open palms over the valuable object and repeat: multiply yourself in the name of all that is good. Do this until the desired result is attained."

Koloran felt relieved that the final incantation should be so simple, yet realized that to perform all the previous spells' ritualized steps, one after the other, to build up to the final spell, would take the better part of a day, and must be conducted in a solitary place to avoid disruption, and at a very specific interval and with precise timing so that the angle of the Daystar would be at the proper declination.

I must make an excuse to take an entire day away from the wine shop and venture into a remote area in order to enact the final spell. I'll tell Father that I need a break, that toiling every day is a burden while Nore ambles about the City, flirting with the Gardzi and getting drunk at the Black Chalice, where Father would forbid her to even enter.

And the next morning—the Day of the Dream, which Koloran thought fittingly symbolic—he did engage Morvedraz in such a conversation.

"Father?"

"What is it, Koloran?"

Koloran faltered only slightly, seeing the creases of strain on Morvedraz forehead as he balanced the logistics of orders and inventory.

"I need to speak with you."

"I seems you are." Morvedraz spoke without raising his eyes from the ledger on his desk.

"Um, yes. Well... I need a day off."

Koloran watched as Morvedraz, scowling, slowly shifted his gaze from the accounts at which he stared to his son's face.

"I do not understand. What is this you speak of, this '*day off*'?"

"I mean, I need a day to myself. A day in which I may do as I please, as does Nore. More often than you know."

"I'm very aware of your sister's indelicacies and shirking. I may be an old Dwarv, but I'm not a stupid one. But, you are the male of the house after me. You must focus on conducting the business of this shop, for it will be yours one day, and I will not have it fall into disrepair."

"Father, I understand, and have toiled here since the day you brought me to my new home. That is nearly twelve years."

"You know you always have my blessing to go and do as you need. So, go. But why does this take an entire day?"

"I wish to venture into the desert. Seek a quiet spot where I might meditate, absorb the beauty of nature, as opposed to the constant din of the City, from which I have rarely traveled all these years."

"Hah! Beauty of nature! Do you know that bands of thieves roam the desert? Do you know that foul beasts lurk behind rock cropping and beneath the surface of the Great River? That there is no food and little water, save the river's, where you might lose the very hand you dunk into the icy ripples for a drink—"

"Yes, Father, I know all of this. For you have taught me well. But, I am... I am now a man. And I would like to experience some of this strange land for myself."

Koloran watched Morvedraz sigh.

"Koloran, Koloran... Very well. You speak true words. And I admit that I have sheltered you here. But, do you blame me? After finding you in the condition you were when we met, that I would not want to shield you from any such malice that might come your way?"

Morvedraz face strained with a look of regret, but Koloran walked toward his father, opened his arms, and, though the reciprocal gesture proved at first less than willing, took Morvedraz in embrace, holding him close and tightly. Eventually, the old Dwarv relented into a hug, and Koloran allowed his grasp to slacken.

"I do love you, Father. For all you have done. Not just for me. But for Nore. For the Great City. I just want some time for... Myself."

"I know. And I understand. So, take your, 'day off.' Such an odd term. But, whatever you call it, choose a period between two of the Daystar's fallings and successive risings, and it shall be yours. I suppose that would actually equal two...*days off*."

"Thank you, Father."

Koloran smiled widely at Morvedraz, a physical sentiment he rarely bestowed upon anyone. He turned to start the three stories of steps toward his quarters, but halted when he heard his father's voice, prominent, yet subdued.

"Koloran."

"Yes, Father?"

"I want you to know that... Despite this very long time, and after so much struggle between us..."

"What, Father?"

He saw the old Dwarv double over, nearly crumpling into tears, though he held them back and composed himself, steadying his weight against the rail of the tasting room counter.

"I love you, too."

Koloran, to his amazement, watched tears spring from Morvedraz' eyes and stream down his leathered cheeks. The son made motion to run to his father, who caught the gesture before it formed into action and held up a stiff palm. Koloran relented and allowed Morvedraz this private time of emotion, but retreated with the joy that full rendering of the final spell would not only be possible, but would happen within one cycle of the Daystar.

Koloran woke early, far earlier than he normally would have, for he'd shunned reading for pleasure the night before his trek into the desert and focused his concentration, as if beginning anew, on the successive steps of instructions set out in the forward of *Ancient Spells for Success & Profit*. He skimmed the sections he'd memorized completely, but backtracked and reviewed them again, lest he lapse into a feeling of certainty that he'd done enough, that his efforts had proven sufficient to unlock the rewards of the final spell; he would not let himself do this, for he could not be certain until after performing the incantations of the last conjuring that any of his earlier efforts would have proven effective. Thus he labored until the Daystar's rays nearly crested the horizon outside his window, relenting because his weary eyes no longer possessed the power to remain open.

And sleep he did, far later than he'd planned, until the Hour of the Dagger on the Day of the Mage. Still, he persisted, though his first "day off" was nearly half gone, and he noticed the smirk on his father's face when Koloran plodded sheepishly toward the front door of the wine shop at well into the Hour of the Dragon, a rucksack slung over his shoulder, opened the door and stepped into the bustling commotion of Long Street at midday.

He felt almost delirious, unaccustomed to the crowds, the noise, the sights and smells and general goings on about the Great City, usually tucked away in his room, the library, or the small office downstairs, where he balanced Morvedraz' books. But he continued, shrugging off his hesitancy and trepidation, thrust his chest out and held his head high, pushing through the crowds around him that would have impeded his steps; he would make his own steps today, he'd decided. Even when passing the *Gardzi's* tower, leaving the main gates of The City, when Tolek hailed him with surprise and wonder—Koloran had rarely been seen this far from the wine shop—he did not lower his face to the ground, but held it high and smiling toward the guard.

"Koloran! And where are you about to? Venturing not only away from Morvedraz', but out of the City proper?"

"I'm taking a day off. Two, actually."

"Day off? Whatever that means, I hope you've packed well for a trip into the desert!"

"I believe I have. Take care."

"I shall. And I hope Morvedraz has prepared you for your journey."

Koloran smiled at the guard, one he knew fancied the attention of his sister and longed to attract the attention of her father; for influence and profit, Koloran thought, drove the Humani's desire far more so than Nore's ample breasts. And though Tolek smirked and discounted the young man, only known as the wine merchant's obedient servant, Koloran let his words remain within himself but guided his thoughts to project his destiny.

Just give me a little time, Tolek, and it will be me that you seek an audience with, over both my sister, and my father.

When Koloran had walked for the better part of an hour, long after listening to the scraping of the huge beam that barred the gates of the City of Antra slide into place and the laughter that punctuated the *Gardzi's* final farewell, he stopped, never before having turned to gaze upon that which receded behind him. He'd followed the path of the great river away from the City, choosing to avoid the more widely travelled road that skirted the western banks and the Dark Forest in the distance, and cross over the river's expanse, heading steadily toward the Garnet Desert. And then he did turn, and for the first time in his life saw the City of Antra not from within the depths of its own confines but from a distance that seemed to create within him such a feeling of exposure that he at first felt frightened. There beyond the barren landscape he'd crossed loomed the City, high above the great river, but it's towers and spires appeared dwarfed by the sites of the world around it, those Koloran had only read of in geographies and viewed in atlases. And he felt even tinier, a mere speck amid the endless expanse of wilderness surrounding him.

Still, he quelled his fear and turned toward the wide plain before him, having crossed the river at Lorzkar, continuing on, step by trudging step, until he'd reached the edge of the desert. He hiked around the sharp height of a steep diatreme thrust through the depths of the world from far beneath the surface of the known lands, thousands of years before the races would evolve and populate Antra and beyond, and found a curved outcropping of rock on the side that directly faced the Garnet Desert. Weary now after walking until the Hour of the Sword, Koloran decided that this semi-sheltered nook would make a fitting stopping point for the night. He'd decided to rest first, take some food and sleep until early the next morning, then begin to recite the incantations just as the Daystar's rays announced the cresting of the Hour of the Jewel. But after he'd built a fire and made a supper of hard cheese and dried spiced meat—washed down with a purloined half-bottle of his father's Kwamadan wine—and lain down on his bedroll to rest his eyes and fall into what he'd thought would be a deep and dreamless slumber, he found that, even after the relaxing warmth of the wine, he could not sleep at all.

In fact, he could not even keep his eyes closed, lying on his back and staring up at the constellations of the night sky, so much more dense and bright in view seen from this far away from the City's torches and lamps. He tried, though ultimately found the attempt futile, to cover his eyes with his blanket, tuck himself as snuggly as possible in the thick folds of his coat, and lapse into sleep. But sleep would not come.

Koloran experienced insomnia often but had never considered it a liability, for it allowed him time to complete his wine shop work early, leaving him with more time to read. And despite the dark circles that often ringed his eyes, he considered this ability far worth the price of a bit of grogginess that a mug of blakwine would likely wash away. So this night in the Garnet Desert Koloran decided to take advantage of the extra time bestowed upon him by lack of sleep and begin the recitation of the spells, to work until morning when they should be completed, and let the final spell perform whatever *majik* it would yield as the Daystar's rays crested the high hills in the distance.

Having studied *Ancient Spell for Success & Profit* like a literary scholar would a treasured work, Koloran had gleaned from its depths details and consistencies that a casual reader would have missed; he'd realized rather early on—after only his third poring over of the Forward—that a distinct pattern of timing followed each spell. The first spell was a nighttime spell, to be raised and voiced in the Hour of the Moon. Each thereafter followed the hours of the night into the rise of the Daystar, the final spell culminating in the Hour of the Jewel, which Koloran thought most befitting, given his surroundings. And so he decided, as he looked into the night sky at the constellations above whose alignment signified the Jewel, that this would prove the perfect time to begin the complete recitation of the successive incantations.

He built a fire, even though Morvedraz had warned against it, for light in the desert might attract as unsavory a visitor from a hungry creature to a greedy band of thieves. But Koloran ventured out of the rock formation after stoking the fire and into the open desert from which any intruder would approach, walked the entire perimeter of the diatreme, and saw that the curved outcropping of rock fortuitously held within its border all light from the low flames within. Feeling charged with confidence at this discovery, Koloran trotted back to his nook and began preparations for the final spell.

He began after a bracing mug of *blakwine*, and soon found that the concentration he applied to each successive incantation took him completely out of space and time; the hours crept by, but by the sheer expertise he'd gained in studying the Forward, Koloran met all the time requirements naturally, sensing the proper temporal alignment of each incantation and reciting it in perfect pitch and cadence. When the fire died he did not hesitate, but continued, not feeling the chill of the early desert morning, and as he competed the penultimate spell realized that the Daystar's beams warmed his face.

Finally, the moment had arrived. Sweat rolled down his forehead and his hands trembled slightly as he turned the page that revealed the final words. He reviewed the steps required—the simplest in the entire volume—took a deep, cleansing breath and began the ritual. But when he came to the spell's end, he realized the crucial element that he'd unwittingly left behind at the wine shop, so unused to carrying items of worth since Morvedraz supplied at will anything Koloran might want or need: he'd forgotten to bring an item of value on which to focus the force of the final spell.

But instead of panicking or interrupting his concentration, he simply allowed his calm, even breath to escape his lungs naturally, held open his hands high toward the rising Daystar, and thought. And in an instant he knew the answer: *Your in the Garnet Desert! Reach around you...* He did this with still-open palms and felt the raw garnets that lie about the perimeter of the diatreme literally jump into his hands. He piled them in the manner the Forward had instructed and, palms open above them, repeated: *Multiply yourself in the name of all that is good. Multiply yourself in the name of all that is good...*

Koloran opened his eyes and realized that he'd been asleep, but for how long he could not immediately tell. The Daystar appeared just past its apex: the Hour of the Dragon. While he knew where he was, and why he'd traveled there, he somehow could not remember completing the steps of the final spell. Still, he felt the same calm warmth inside his chest that all the other spells seemed to invoke, and wondered if the words he'd spent so much time and effort to master were simply, as the old bookseller had assumed, nothing more than flowery verse. He sighed and rubbed the sleep from his eyes, then pushed himself into a sitting position in front of the dead embers of his fire, and when he looked down in front of the cold, charred wood what he saw struck him with such surprise that he gasped audibly.

Garnets. Dozens of them, lying in a perfect concavity of sand. Not the few rough, dull stones he'd gathered with ease in his enchanted hands, exploded from the confines deep beneath the world's surface by volcanic eruption and scattered haphazardly about the perimeter of the diatreme, but perfect polished stones, their hue the color of Kwamadan wine, stacked in a completely symmetrical pyramid. He rubbed his eyes again, making sure the vision was no illusion, then reached for the stone at the peak of the pyramid. He held it up to his eyes; the gleam in the crimson surface shone perfectly, refracting the Daystar's rays.

Then he heard a sound, unlike anything he'd experienced in the past two days in the desert, and for a moment held himself completely still and listened with his eyes closed to the murmur of the wilderness around him: the hum of the breeze embracing the craggy formation of the diatreme, the rustle of wind through shrub and bush. He could discern nothing strange. But still he heard in his mind his father's constant warnings echoing the dangers of the wild, and quickly but quietly packed his knapsack, pouring the polished garnets into a leather pouch and tucking it into an inside pocket of his coat, and began the long march back toward the bustle of the City of Antra.

He would be a half day late, and he knew his father would not be pleased, likely fraught over Koloran's absence, so he hurried as best he could along the route he'd taken the day before, careful to be wary of both sight and sound. When the city of Lorzkar loomed on the horizon, Koloran saw a puff of dust rising from just in front of the city gates a quarter mile away. He thought to tuck himself behind a rock or tree, but realized that all the terrain around him was flat and without feature for as far as he could see. Instead, he began to walk ninety degrees to the right of the path he'd taken, hoping that whoever—or whatever—had made the desert sand rise in the distance would miss him. But after he changed direction he noticed that the rising dust did so as well. When it neared he realized the shape of a horse, but when the animal drew nearer Koloran saw that it had no rider, though it wore a saddle and harness. He stopped then, knowing he could neither hide nor outmaneuver the large beast, but when it came upon him, whinnying at the sight of him, Koloran smiled at the discovery that the white mare was Elihra, Morvedraz' own prized lead horse; he must have sent her along the path she'd known so well in search of his missing son.

Koloran patted Elihra's nose and reached for an apple in his knapsack, feeling the tickle of her lips on his fingers as she greedily crunched the ripe fruit. Then he placed his right foot into the stirrup and heaved himself onto the mare's sturdy back, and when he'd secured himself, rapping the reins around his hands twice, Elihra turned and began a steady trot back toward the City of Antra.

They made good time, and when Koloran had unsaddled the mare and brushed her, laying a blanket over her weary back, he turned and found himself in front of his father's petulant face.

"Back a bit late, aren't we?"

"Yes, father." Koloran answered and bowed his head toward the straw of the stable floor. "Forgive me. My experience in the desert was...most amazing. So much so that sleep did not come for me until well past the hour of the Daystar yesterday."

"You mean, you lay awake the entire time of your journey until just the day before?"

"Yes."

"That must have been some potent meditation you embarked upon. Did it satisfy your curiosity about the outside world?"

"Somewhat, father. I would like to return there."

"So, you'll be wanting more, *'days off'*?"

"Yes, but, not for a while. I hope you understand."

Koloran watched Morvedraz sigh and shake his head, then turn and begin a slow walk toward the residence entry to his compound.

"Just let me know when, which days, and the like. And you may do as you wish."

Koloran listened to the words his father spoke as he walked away and raised his left hand in a dismissive gesture that at first troubled the boy. But when he wrapped his mind fully around what Morvedraz had said—that all he would need do would be to provide the time he wished to himself—he smiled, realizing he'd achieved what he'd never expected: unbridled time away from the wine shop, whenever he needed to exact abundance by means of the spells.

The next day Koloran strode the length of the Rough Zirkot resolutely, head high and gaze direct into the eyes of anyone who looked to challenge his presence, and all eyes who did so faded upon seeing the radiance in his own. He felt more forceful, more bold, even taller than he'd ever felt, for when he walked he held his head high and chest out. He stepped resolutely through the doorway of Centhum, the bookseller where he'd first encountered and later procured the *majik* volume, and hailed for the proprietor.

"Oh, young man! I hope you've enjoyed the book you'd purchased. Perhaps you've come back to consider other worthy volumes?"

"Indeed. And, also to give you a token of thanks."

Koloran watched as the old Humani merchant wrinkled his forehead and pressed his eyes into a squint.

"Thanks? I provided you a book, you provided me pay. For what other service could I deserve thanks?"

"You told me to come and tell you if I'd turned rocks into gold. I have not done so."

"Ah, well. That was to be expected—"

"But I have turned sand into garnets."

The shopkeeper's yes widened, and he looked on Koloran with narrow, skeptical eyes.

"What in the name of the *Maj* do you mean?" The shopkeeper spoke in a furtive whisper, his eyes intent on any outside his windows who may have overheard.

"I don't think we should invoke the name of the *Maj*. He may not be terribly keen on my methods."

Koloran reached into his tunic and produced a leather draw-string pouch, opened the wide mouth and poured into his hands a dozen perfect polished garnets. He held them in his open palm high toward the shopkeeper's gaze, then gently poured them onto the surface of the counter.

"My boy! That's many hundred zeks worth of stones! How in the gods' names would I—"

"Fret not. They are yours, to keep and to fund whatever venture you wish." Koloran paused, then turned his ice-blue eyes toward the shopkeepers milky brown gaze.

"However, if I were you, I might wish to pursue other tomes of, shall we say, exceptional quality, as was my first purchase. For they may prove to be equally prosperous for us both."

The shopkeeper's smile widened. "I understand completely. Please return in four cycles of the Daystar, and I should likely have yet another volume that will provoke your interest."

Koloran held out his open hand, felt the strength of the shopkeeper's in his own grasp, then turned and left the book store, headed toward the gem broker on lower Long Street, where he would change the remainder of his gems into *zeks*.

7

When Nore opened her eyes she saw the Daystar's rays filtering through the lace curtains of the room, and the lean, lithe form of Andara, naked and leaning against the window frame, arms crossed and head tilted to one side. She appeared to gaze absently at the rising Daystar, but Nore saw from the lines on her brow that she strained with concern.

"Come here." Nore's still sleepy voice rasped. But she grinned at the brilliant white gleam of the Kuzhani girl's smile.

"Hey, sleepy." Andara jumped onto the bed and landed next to Nore, who held the covers open, and the two intertwined their arms and legs, pressing their bodies together.

"Please don't stop holding me," Andara whispered.

"What's wrong?"

"Everything that happened last night. The *Dwarvani*, this Khaleo person... It's just unsettling. And knowing that somehow you two are connected. I'm just not sure what's going on, or what's going to happen."

Nore looked into the dark pools of Andara's eyes. "You are the most important person in the world to me. You and I will be together regardless of what happens—"

"Nore, I know you're strong. And you're resolute. And stubborn. But you can't know that."

Nore's face slackened into sadness, but she quickly recovered and her expression turned to stern determination.

"Yes, I can. Because it's my will, and I will *make* it happen."

Andara shook her head, then tucked her face between Nore's cheek and shoulder.

"I hope you're right, my love."

"When have I ever been wrong?"

"Not yet."

Nore sighed and whispered into Andara's ear: "Trust me."

"I do. It's the rest of the world I don't trust."

Nore propped herself up on one elbow and looked again into the endless dark of Andara's eyes. She thought to speak, but decided instead to simply lose herself in the moment of gazing at the beauty beneath her, parted her lips slightly and pressed them into the plush pillows of Andara's own, their mouths melding, velvet tongues intertwining, and each young woman silently deciding to allow herself to be lost in the passionate moment, rather than worry about the day—and the future—ahead.

Zhakhar had risen earlier than any of the inhabitants of his establishment that morning, unable to sleep past the Hour of the Jewel, well before his usual rousing, after a night of intricate and discerning management of the Black Chalice. The situation with the Lethani whore monger had not thrown him; he'd prepared for it for weeks, yet the fact that such degrading commerce occurred at all— even under the watchful eyes of the Regent of the *Maj*— disturbed his very being. And this strange Humani who looked like Nore... He sounded supplicant, almost reverential; Zhakhar did not trust him. Whatever intricacies of tale he'd spun the previous night, the master of the Chalice knew that the story must possess far more detail than he'd heard so far. And to Zhakhar's seasoned intuition, Khaleo's sincerity seemed...somehow, *too* sincere, as if through his humble straightforwardness he really intended to deceive, to conceal his true purpose.

Zhakhar took a cup of *blakwine* and strode down the stairs to his office overlooking the vast expanse of bar, tables and private alcoves that made up the main room of the Black Chalice, intent on planning out a strategy of how to deal with this stranger, and the trouble Zhakhar felt certain would follow.

"Good morning, Zhakhar."

Nore's ample curves rounded out her tunic and almost smoothed the wrinkles it had gained the long night before.

"Good morning, daughter. Your clothes seem a bit worse for wear today. Let me get you a fresh set."

"No, Zhakhar, don't. You spoil me as it is. And a few wrinkles never bothered me anyway."

"As you wish. Where is your darling girl?"

"Dozing. She was up way too early, pondering all that happened last night. And not feeling good about it."

"As was I, daughter. As was I." Zhakhar spoke in a grave, low tone. "So, tell me about your conversation with Khaleo. Was it enlightening?"

"I'll say it was."

"How so?"

"According to him, we're cousins."

"*What*?"

"And not only that, but I'm some sort of hybrid race, a mix of his and another that possessed far more skill at the blade than his people."

"Well, if he's telling the truth, that would explain why I've never seen your skills bested."

"I'm from a place that was called *Zhor*."

"*Zhor*? You've got to be kidding."

"Evidently not. It was so far beyond the Dwarvani Kingdom that no one in Antra had ever discovered it. I'm the only known surviving member of a special class of 'Zhorhai' royalty. Oh, and I'm two-hundred fifty years old. I guess I was only about a hundred seventy-five or so when Morvedraz found me in the desert."

Upon hearing this Zhakhar's eyes widened and his mouth dropped open; not much exacted surprise from the wise, wary merchant, but this detail seemed too fantastic for him to hold back his usually checked emotions.

"How is that even possible?!"

"I guess we age well."

"Nore, this all sounds preposterous."

"I know. And I'd think so, too, if I didn't speak an unknown language fluently, feel that, though I love the City of Antra, that I'm pulled toward a place far, far from here every time I look in the direction where this *Zhor* is supposed to have been. And look like no one else anyone has ever seen. Except Khaleo."

Zhakhar took a deep breath and considered all that Nore had described. However fantastic the details seemed, neither she nor anyone in Antra would deny that Nore's origins, and all that was unusual about her, remained a mystery.

"Well, what's compelled Khaleo to venture this far in search of you?"

"He wants me to go back to where *Zhor* was, find the exiled inhabitants, or what's left of them, and help establish the kingdom again."

Zhakhar rolled his eyes. "That sounds like a fantasy novel."

"Oh, and we don't have to ride horses or anything. There's a *majik* amulet that will transport us. Khaleo says he knows the spell. And my father's supposed to know about it."

"Your father, the Dwarv, has a *majik* amulet? Oh, please..."

"Yeah. I know."

"Very well. I want to speak to Khaleo myself. My interrogation skills might prove useful, maybe poke a few holes in his story and uncover anything he's hiding from us."

Zhakhar turned toward the darkened corridor that led to the sleeping quarters. "Kor!"

The huge Kuzhani emerged within moments and paused to receive his leader's direction.

"Go and rouse our new acquaintance. See that he gets a fresh set of clothes and a hot mug of blakwine. Then bring him here. There's much I need to discuss with him."

Kor nodded and disappeared into the corridor and toward the guest quarters where Khaleo would be sleeping.

"Well, I believe this ought to be a very interesting discussion. I'll need your help, of course, to translate for me?"

"Sure."

"Thank you, daughter. And then we should get you back to the wine shop. I'm sure Koloran will be most upset that his little sister is shirking her tasting room duties yet again."

Zhakhar and Nore both started when Kor rushed from the corridor into the light of the office, his dark face awash in an even darker than normal hue.

"What's wrong, Kor? And where's Khaleo."

"Khaleo, not."

"Not what?"

"Not. Gone."

"That's not possible." Zhakhar clapped his hands twice, and within moments a dozen of his armed emissaries stood waiting for orders, ready to strike.

"Seal the doors and windows. Search the entire place, barrel by barrel. Recall that our guest takes to swimming in vinegar."

Khaleo felt more than surprised that Zhakhar had allowed the stranger to be quartered in an unlocked room, for the Kuzhani merchant's distrust of his guest was palpable to Khaleo's keen intuition, a heightened empathic sense that his race possessed, the knowledge of which he'd purposely not let slip to Nore. After slumber had caught up with the entire inhabitants of the Black Chalice, after even Kor, stationed in the hallway, uttered too small and delicate a snore that such a large being should possess, Khaleo set upon finding an escape route from the Chalice. He knew there must be several, one on each side of the building, leading to the street and alleyways outside; Zhakhar's emissaries moved too quickly in and out to be restricted to the front door.

So he hunted, taking silent steps in the dark, with only the sensation at his fingertips to guide him, wall by wall, keg by keg, for nearly three hours, and finally came upon a nook so small that he'd at first disregarded it as simply a chipped place in the stone. But he thought twice, and prodded inside the indentation, first forward, then side to side, then down, to no avail. It was when he applied a slight amount of upward pressure with his fingertip that he felt the switch give way, and when it did the seam in the wall in front of him parted, and he felt from outside the cold rush of the Antran night. The opening was barely wide enough to allow him to exit, but he managed to wriggle through after getting stuck for only a moment. When he stood panting from the effort in the dark alley behind the exterior wall of the Black Chalice, the wall sealed itself as if it sensed the exiting stranger, the stone blocks appearing seamless yet again.

Certainly not the hatch that Kor slips out of, Khaleo thought and smiled, even allowing himself an audible chuckle, then hurried from the alleyway and toward the silent street, intent on searching the City and finding the wine shop where he felt certain that he would also find the amulet.

After the better part of an hour Zhakhar's patience had worn thin. "Enough!" he bellowed, and upon hearing the command all emissaries searching the Chalice returned to the main floor where their master had positioned himself along with Nore, waiting in vain for Khaleo to be discovered and brought forth.

"Forgive us, master Zhakhar. We have searched everywhere. Unless the stranger has the ability to transform himself into the air we breath, or turn himself invisible, he is no longer inside our confines."

"Well, at this point I'm ready to believe that he might have the power to do both. Perhaps he's the very table upon which sits my mug!" And with a heave, Zhakhar pulled the heavy dagger he kept hidden within his robes, thrust the tip toward the table with such force that it penetrated clear through the thick wood, bouncing the legs completely off of the floor, but when it landed remained simply a roughly hewn piece of furniture, the buried dagger standing straight with its hilt toward the ceiling.

Zhakhar sighed. "Do not apologize. It is not your fault. It was unwise of me to think he'd simply spend the night so that I might interrogate him in the morning. His supplications lulled me from my usual resolve. Perhaps this is yet another power the stranger possesses. In any case, all of you are my trusted few, and I value and appreciate your efforts. But do this: go with stealth and speed to Morvedraz' wine shop. Nore, I have a feeling that Khaleo wants a private audience with the Arbiter, one in which the skill of your blade and the potency of my emissaries would be far absent. Go now. Seek out your father and secure his safety. I will organize an inquiry here and send forces to the far reaches of the City, until we find our crafty friend, Khaleo."

Upon hearing Zhakhar's words, Nore felt a cold sensation in the center of her chest and a heavy feeling of dread sink into the pit of her stomach.

"If he so much as touches a whisker of my father's beard I will slash his throat from ear to ear."

"Settle yourself, daughter. If you find him, bring him here. We need the information that resides in his living mind more than we need his blood flowing like so much spilled wine. Swear to me that you'll do as I ask."

Nore glanced at the ground, the scowl on her face drawing her cheeks toward the direction of her gaze, then back at Zhakhar's face.

"I swear it."

"Thank you. And if he has brought any harm to your father, after I'm through with him, you may dispatch him as you will."

Nore nodded, and with an animal alacrity only she possessed moved swiftly toward the door, the dozen emissaries in tow, sprinting toward Long Street and her father's unwary presence.

It was a fine morning, the Daystar beaming with what seemed an extra intensity, so much so that Morvedraz thought that a walk was in order. He'd spent the week worrying about Kaljero, though his every visit to Rolim's had proven that the wounded Dwarv's progress toward full health sped along, as the apothecary had predicted. He had no idea yet how or what he'd do with the convalescent Dwarv upon his full healing, but when he puzzled and considered the situation for so many hours, thought it would be a fitting time for a break.

"Koloran!"

"Yes, father?"

"I'm going to walk to the cheese stand at the other end of Long Street. I feel like some fresh air and a snack."

"Shall I accompany you, father?"

"No, no, it's fine. Stay and open the shop at the appointed hour. It's only about a half mile, and I could certainly use the exercise."

"Very well, father."

"I'll see you in a little while."

The streets were still nearly empty, with only the early delivery carts and their attending drivers stopped in front of storefronts to unload the day's goods. Morvedraz enjoyed this early time better than any other part of the day, when the air was still fresh and the streets barely inhabited, before the bustle of commerce and din of crowds choked off the very air he breathed. But he knew his friend

Erib would be unloading the wheels of cheese fresh from farms that abounded in the outer fields west of Kwamada, and he always held back a special few that had extra age on them because he knew that they suited Morvedraz' palate.

When Morvedraz rounded the corner where Long Street intersected with the bustling outdoor market, there was Erib, busily lugging huge wheels from a driver's cart to his small warehouse behind the stand.

"Good morning, Erib!"

"Hah! Morvedraz! What a delight to see you, my friend, on this fine morning. But surely you have not come for your usual allotment. You'd need your horses and cart for the size of wheels I've reserved for you!"

"No, dear Erib, I'm simply enjoying the early morning air and a stroll that I desperately needed, but thought that a fitting destination would be where I might procure a small snack." Morvedraz grinned and glanced lustily at the ripe quarter wheel of sharp cheese, its aroma wafting heavily about, that lay atop Erib's counter.

"My friend, of course! Here, let me slice you a plate. You'll marvel at the succulent nuttiness of this one."

Morvedraz heaved himself onto one of the wooden stools that stood in front of the counter.

"My friend, I know it's a tad early, but might I suggest a small glass of some of your finest that you gifted to me? It's the perfect accompaniment!"

Morvedraz usually kept a strict regimen about drinking: never before the Hour of the Sword, and never more than two glasses of wine, so this suggestion of Erib's felt oddly and guiltily out of place. Nonetheless, Morvedraz felt a certain ease about the morning, a full gratifying sensation of security that enveloped his very being this day; he was wealthy, of course, beyond anyone's dreams; he was respected, revered in fact, by most inhabitants of the City, and feared by the few from whom such sentiments counted; he loved his children, and they loved him in return; and, he was approaching that age when he'd relinquish much of running the business of the wine shop to Koloran. Of course he'd remain involved in his duties as Arbiter, for he felt a great sense of responsibility for the fabric of commerce and prosperity that his role in the life of the City had created, and he would maintain this wellbeing with his every ounce of strength, until the inevitable day that his strength would fail him. But, otherwise, he found himself relaxing more often—even allowing himself one of these odd "*days off*," as Koloran called them. It titillated him for the sheer guilty pleasure of taking a day unto himself for no other reason than that he could.

Perhaps that son of mine is a greater innovator than I'd given him credit for! He may not be the most competent business owner, but he certainly knows how to take care of himself...

And so it was with this relaxed sense of self and lapse of his usual Dwarvani wariness—he'd not even looked around at who might be approaching from behind him before putting the glass of Kwamadan wine to his lips—that Morvedraz would enjoy his morning snack, and as a result allow the events of his very demise to be swayed into action.

Khaleo shuddered in the early morning cold as he darted about alleyway and empty street, searching for signs of a prosperous neighborhood that would contain a wine shop. Though the darkness lent him stealth it also chilled him, and though the Daystar would reveal him and his unusual appearance to all who'd encounter him, he still felt relief at the warming rays when they crested the horizon.

He pulled a knit cap tight over his head, covering his flaxen hair and smallish ears to disguise himself as best he could. Still, the warm amber hue of his large elliptically-shaped eyes beamed forth to anyone who passed him, and though he tried to keep his shoulders hunched forward and head tucked toward his chest, he still met lengthy stares when any passerby looked him carefully in the face.

But the early morning streets still lacked the crowds he'd learned to avoid during the day by sleeping at cheap inns until well after the Daystar's falling, and the merchants and delivery people he encountered felt ultimately far more concerned with their commerce than the odd-looking stranger who'd passed by; perhaps he was some variant of Lethani, his features simply exaggerated by the combination of shadow and early morning glare.

On he walked, for hours, until just before the Hour of the Jewel, when he approached a large intersection of streets and looked up to see in the distance a most curious sight: a Dwarv, seated upon a stool in front of what looked like some sort of food stall. The creature's stoutness and girth betrayed his race quite clearly, and Khaleo felt his spirit brighten for the first time since he'd escaped the Black Chalice; surely a Dwarv, any Dwarv, would know of Morvedraz, perhaps even be acquainted with him. What he did not realize, had not even let himself believe might be possible, was that the discovery of this lone Dwarv snacking in the early morning hours would bring Khaleo closer to everything that his long, long journey had hoped to accomplish.

Morvedraz almost dropped his glass, not expecting the hearty hail from behind him, one that in earlier times of his life would not have surprised him, for his vigilance would have been sharper, his every mundane action carried out with far more precaution.

"Good morning, friend Dwarv! I see you've found a vendor who's opened early and is serving. I'm famished myself. Would you mind if I took a seat beside you and shared your company over a plate of cheese?"

Morvedraz expected a fellow merchant, perhaps even one he recognized, at least a well-to-do traveler unfamiliar with the customs of conduct within the City, but when he turned to gaze at the face of the one who'd just greeted him and placed a warm hand on his shoulder, he let forth a low yet audible gasp.

"Who are you?"

"Ah, wary as a Dwarv should be! I am a sojourner to the City and all its wonders. I come from Kwamada."

"You don't look like anyone I've ever seen from Kwamada."

Khaleo sensed something that he could not at first pinpoint in this Dwarv's demeanor. Surely he'd be suspicious. But there looked to be a faint glint of something in his eyes... Could it be—recognition? And his face grimaced with trepidation the likes that Khaleo had not expected. A Dwarv was exuberant. A Dwarv was gruff, perhaps course and a bit uncouth; but this Dwarv emanated an emotion that was to Khaleo as palpable as it was surprising: fear.

"I'm not *from* Kwamada, but have been staying there quite some years. A beautiful area. In fact, I'm thinking of retiring there."

"As am I."

"Really? Such the coincidence! And a fine choice of destinations, I might add."

Khaleo spoke in fluent, flawless Antran, the ruse he'd played on Nore, Zhakhar and all he'd encountered in the City far removed from his current interaction with the Dwarv, so much so that he felt that conducting himself like a fellow countryman rather than a distant foreigner would be an advantage.

"My, that glass of crimson nectar does look inviting, even at this early hour."

"Please. Help yourself." Morvedraz pushed the bottle toward Khaleo.

"Oh, no! Not for me, friend Dwarv. My constitution is quite delicate, I'm afraid. If I took even as small a dram as yours, I'd fall fast asleep."

"Perhaps a mug of blakwine, then. Erib always keeps an urn full and hot."

"No, I'm afraid that blakwine would send me into such frenetic fits I'd hardly be able to sit! But, kind vendor," he directed at Erib, "a plate of your finest would be most appreciated."

"Of course, sir. I am Erib, cheese merchant. And this is—"

Morvedraz' habits had not yet gone so slack and his senses were not yet dulled by the few sips of wine that he was unable to cut off Erib before his unwitting yet misplaced courtesy could disclose what might prove at least unwise, ultimately dangerous.

"—Bolim, son of Gretlag, of the Dwarvani Kingdom. My father brought me to the great City when I was a teenager, and I swore I'd return and make my fortune here." Morvedraz smiled, unaccustomed as he was to pretense, especially about his own persona, but he thought he'd done a good enough job, perhaps bolstered by the small sips of wine.

"A very high pleasure to be acquainted with you both. I am Khaleo. And, as I said, I consider Kwamada my home."

"Consider it your home, perhaps," Morvedraz began, "but where is it you were born, Khaleo? I don't recall seeing anyone in the City with such interesting facial features."

"Ah, good Bolim, that is a tale far more suited to lengthier, more leisurely discussions, and perhaps a pint or two of ale."

"So you *do* imbibe after all! I'd thought your dainty sensibilities would not permit it."

"Permit it, on occasion." Khaleo accepted the plate of cheese from Erib's outstretched hand, and placed two silver *zek* pieces on the counter.

"Please, keep your coins, Khaleo. These are remnants that I'd either donate or need to discard, yet still fine and tasty."

"Well, thanks to you, Erib! I will not forget your generosity."

Khaleo had noticed that, just after "Bolim" had introduced himself, Erib's face had taken on a distinct look of surprise: brows raised, eyes wide. The *Zhoryan* prince thought to press the Dwarv further, perhaps even to his potential acquaintanceship with Morvedraz.

"So, tell me, good Dwarv, what avenue toward your wealth have you pursued in the great City?"

"Oh, I broker goods from the farther reaches of Antra. Mostly agricultural—grains for bread and ales—grown a far distance away from the City and therefore quite expensive, but sought after by more well-to-do producers."

As he listened to "Bolim" describe his livelihood, Khaleo continued to scrutinize Erib's reaction to his friend's words, and what Khaleo saw drove his suspicions of the Dwarv further. Erib's demeanor had grown more and more tense—brow furrowed, a thin sheen of sweat visible now on his forehead despite the cool morning air—as "Bolim" continued to relate his tale. *This is not the easy reaction of a friend listening to his companion describing what should be nothing but familiar details,* Khaleo thought.

"Well, Bolim, it appears from your fine robes and well-groomed appearance that you've done quite well for yourself in your ventures."

"I've been most fortunate."

"So much so that you're able to partake of wine and cheese in the earliest hours of the day!"

"Well, this is certainly not my usual routine, but something of a special occasion."

"Really? And what occasion might that be?"

"My children are experienced enough to take on more responsibility in managing my ventures. My son, especially, shows keen ability in the more technical aspects of commerce, while my daughter's graces have softened the resolve of more than a few hard-bargaining clients. I've decided to let them take on the majority control of my business. I'll stay involved, of course, but consider myself, as of today, semi-retired."

"Well, hearty congratulations to you, Bolim. You are a Dwarv most fortunate and wise."

"But, that said, I must get back to my office to ensure that my children are not shirking on their duties! I wish you well, Khaleo, and hope that your sojourn in the great City proves beneficial to you, in whatever regard that might be."

"Thanks, Bolim. In fact, you may be able to help me toward that very beneficial end. I'm actually seeking a wine merchant, who happens to be *Dwarvani*. Surely you must be acquainted with Morvedraz?"

"Ah, yes! Morvedraz, of course."

"You know him, then?"

"Know *of* him, only. He is more legend, more enigma than acquaintance to most of the City's inhabitants. He deals with citizenry far, far above those who partake of my meager dealings. Legend has it that the Regent of the *Maj*—albeit not directly—has sent parties in dispute to call upon Morvedraz' services in matters requiring delicate arbitration, and that he has never failed to settle a grievance or negotiate a dispute in a manner suitable to all those involved."

"I see." Khaleo puzzled over this response, for, though detailed, it still sounded general enough to hold a tone of evasion. "But, he still runs a wine shop, does he not?"

"Oh. Yes."

"Could you tell me where it is?"

"I believe it's at the opposite end of Long Street."

Khaleo followed "Bolim's" outstretched hand toward the direction where his finger pointed.

"I don't suppose he'd be open at this early hour."

"I really have no idea. His wares are far beyond my means, my success notwithstanding."

"So, you've never been there?"

"Years ago, and only to appease the appetite of one of my most lucrative clients."

"You've met him, then."

"No, no...he was not in the tasting room at the time. His daughter usually runs it."

"That would be, Nore?"

At the mention of his daughter's name, Morvedraz could not help but widen his eyes and breathe heavily through his nose, his scowl deep and long. Khaleo noticed the reaction, yet determined not to act on it.

"Do me the favor of your company, Bolim. Walk with me to Morvedraz' shop. Perhaps we might encounter the famed Dwarv himself."

"Since your delicate constitution does not permit you much drink, why is it that you seek out a wine shop?"

"Oh, my interest in Morvedraz goes beyond wine. Actually, I seek his counsel."

"His counsel does not come cheaply," Morvedraz said and paused, then added, "so I am told."

"Yes, I'm aware of that. But, regardless, lead me to Morvedraz. I'd be most appreciative."

Khaleo said this and placed his arm casually across "Bolim's" shoulders, applied the slightest bit of pressure to coax him toward the direction of the wine shop. But when Khaleo felt the force of the stout Dwarv's resistance, he knew better than to press the issue and risk revealing the true urgency of his motives.

"Well, I see you're set on getting back to your own affairs, Bolim. I understand, of course. But thanks for pointing me in the right direction, and if I do encounter Morvedraz I'll be sure to put in a good word with him for you."

Khaleo smiled and waved at "Bolim" and Erib, but when he turned to begin toward the direction of the wine shop his eyes widened at the fierce figure of Nore in attack stance, dagger poised and pointed at Khaleo's throat.

"Ah!" Khaleo gasped and jumped backward away from the blade. *"Leonora! You almost scared the life out of me!"*

"Oh, please, Khaleo, don't lapse into *Zhoryan* for *my* sake. It sounds like your Antran has improved dramatically since you took your stealthy leave of Zhakar's."

"Nore, your stealth skills are most advanced, indeed. You're so close I should have been able to hear you breathe."

Khaleo glanced quickly to his right and left and found himself surrounded by the masked assassins who must have accompanied Nore from the Black Chalice. He had no intention of cowering in front of Zhakhar again, particularly since his deception had been at least partially discovered when Nore had overhead his perfect conversational Antran. He kept smiling, however, as if his actions were nothing more than some casual misunderstanding.

"You have no idea, Khaleo. Now, step away from my father and slowly, slowly begin your way in front of me back toward the Chalice. Zhakhar has a few more questions for you, and I'm sure he'll be quite pleased that this time I won't need to translate for him."

Father? That's what she said, wasn't it? Of course, it's as I'd suspected! And with the realization that he'd been in conversation with the renowned Morvedraz all along, Khaleo knew he had only one way of avoiding a second audience with Zhakhar. It would be dangerous—perhaps lethal—but he'd sworn to himself long ago that he would retake the amulet, and with its power return the *Zhorhai* Kingdom to its former glory, under pain of his own death.

"Actually, Nore, I have slightly different plans."

In one swift motion Khaleo swept the plate of cheese off of the counter in front of him, sending it sailing toward Nore's head. When she ducked to avoid it Khaleo pulled from within his tunic a concealed dagger, spun around to Morvedraz' back and, reaching around the stout Dwarv and pressing a hand onto his chest, brought the blade to his throat.

Nore, eyes wide and unblinking and face flushed with fury, stood poised to launch a killing throw with her own dagger, the assassin's surrounding Khaleo closing in to do the same.

"If you so much as scratch his cheek I will bury this dagger in your neck."

"*That, Leonora, I do not doubt. But then you will have lost a fa-ther, Antra will have lost its Arbiter, and I'll have died taking to my grave the secrets I conceal which you desire so desperately to know.*"

"*If you think my stealth is advanced, wait until you feel the speed with which I can throw a blade.*"

"*Recall that I possess some of the same skills do you, cousin.*"

"*I will give you until the count of five.*"

"*Fair enough.*"

"*One...*"

When Nore began the countdown, Khaleo bent his mouth toward Morvedraz' ear and whispered, "Where's the amulet?"

"What are you talking about?"

"Please! Don't take me for a fool."

"I have no idea what you mean."

"*...two...*"

"You'd be foolish to leave it at your shop, no matter how well you'd secured it. It's far too powerful, and you know this. And I'm sure that cursed old wizard warned you against ever leaving it out of your sight."

"*...three...*"

"So, then you'd have no other choice but to keep it on your person at all times." And when Khaleo uttered this deduction he realized that from where he pressed his hand against Morvedraz chest there protruded a hard, slightly raised and rounded area.

"...four..."

"Gods! You've got it around your neck!"

"...five!"

Khaleo saw the glint of Nore's blade fly toward his head, clutched hard at the amulet through the material of Morvedraz' robe and uttered the *Zhoryan* incantation. Just when the point of the dagger would have pierced his neck and buried itself in the upper tip of his spinal column, Khaleo vanished.

8

Nore stared astonished when the missile-like throw of her dagger sped far past its now-missing target, about a foot and half above and to the left of her father's head, where Khaleo's had been, only to continue its course until it lost velocity and clanked to a rolling stop against the cobblestones of Long Street. The surrounding emissaries bolted glances from side to side, up and down the wide boulevard for signs of Khaleo, but their gazes were met by no more than shopkeepers opening their doors to the day's business, and citizens of the great City hurrying toward work of their own.

Nore watched her father's rigid expression soften finally, and saw him slump onto the stool in front of Erib's stand, as if spent after a great journey. She ran toward him, kneeling and rapping both arms tightly around his shoulders and burying her head in his chest.

"I'd have *never* let him harm you," she managed, tears flowing free and hot down her cheeks.

"I know, my darling. I have full confidence in the skill of your blade. It's what he was after that worried me far more. And if I could just ask you to pry yourself from me for a moment, I really do need to check something."

Nore stood, her tears dropping onto the dark, cold cobblestones, watching as her father slowly unraveled the gold-laced twine that held his robes. He loosened his collar and reached within, and though the adrenaline rush of being held at knife-point had stolen his finer sensations his fingers found the cord around his neck intact, and still dangling at its end the elliptical stone that Khaleo had sought so desperately to possess.

"Oh, thank the gods," Morvedraz murmured.

"What is it, father?"

"Come, Nore. Let's hurry back to the shop. I'll explain when we're safely locked inside."

Nore motioned for two of Zhakhar's emissaries to accompany her and Morvedraz, while bidding the other two make haste toward the Black Chalice so that they might inform Zhakhar of the morning's astonishing events.

"Koloran!" Morvedraz bellowed when he and Nore burst through the front entry of the wine shop. No answer came. "If that Khaleo has harmed him I shall use the amulet in any way necessary to render the swine's doom! Koloran!"

Morvedraz listened, thought he'd heard faint footsteps from deep within the compound adjacent to the shop proper, growing louder and approaching the tasting room where he and Nore stood. Hearing the frantic steps nearing, Morvedraz stepped to the far side of the room while Nore prepared her dagger for a lethal throw. But when the door to the back of the shop opened, it was only Koloran's flushed, sweaty face that peered around the rough-hewn door.

"Gods..." Morvedraz murmured and let go a heavy sigh. He walked toward his son and embraced him.

"I thought I'd lost you, boy."

"I'm sorry, father. I was way down in the barrel room taking inventory. I could barely hear your hail from there." Morvedraz held Koloran at arm's length, then, and saw that his eyes widened at the sight of his armed sister.

"What's going on?"

"We have much to discuss, my son. All three of us."

"Father," Nore began, "you said something about using an amulet. What were you talking about?"

Morvedraz uttered an audible sigh, and in the force of time that rushed within his mind he silently debated, realizing the wizard's endless lessons, lamenting that under no circumstance should he ever, ever reveal the amulet's existence, but decided finally that his family should—must—be party to the knowledge, one they would need in order to progress the prosperity of the wine business, and, somehow, after Morvedraz' death, carry on the duties of Arbiter: "This."

Morvedraz pulled from within his robes the chain onto which he'd attached the amulet so many years before, held it close so that Nore could make out the etched writing on the stone's bluish face. He felt he'd second-guessed himself all these years, keeping the *majik* stone a secret from the one who could have helped him discover the depth of its purpose, and thought now to reveal all.

"Can you read it?"

"Yes. I can't translate it directly into Antran. It wouldn't make sense. Essentially it means, 'power'. But, not just *any* power. The implication is, *ultimate* power. Where in the world did you get this?"

"*Father wizard, what in the Gods' names did you place in my keeping?*" The old Dwarv murmured toward the ceiling, then uttered a low groan.

"Morvedraz..." Nore spoke his proper name, its emphasis compelling her. "What are you talking about?" She turned the amulet over in her hands.

"I'd hoped to never have to suffer this day, but it has arrived nonetheless. Come. Both of you. Let me brew up a large pot of blakwine and let us take refuge in the Arbiter's quarters above. Nore, direct Zhakhar's men inside and to guard the entrance upstairs with their lives."

"They'd do so without being commanded, Father."

Morvedraz only glanced at his daughter, now knowing full well that she'd developed a far deeper acquaintance with Zhakhar's assassins than Morvedraz ever had wished.

The emissaries in place, he bid his children up the narrow stairwell, barring the door behind, and trudged after them, wondering how he would begin to relate the tale of his origins, and the true nature of the stone he wore around his neck.

The three sat around the large, round table in the uppermost floor of the wine shop, in the room that contained no windows that would open, and only a vent in the ceiling to let escape the warm, stale air laced with *kororah* smoke that collected in the chamber when conflicting parties sat facing one another in binding negotiations, for all knew that when one invoked Morvedraz' skills and influence that the outcome of any such arbitration was final; there simply existed no higher authority—though his was technically unofficial—from whom disputing parties could seek relief.

Each had spent much time in this room: Morvedraz as Arbiter, Nore and Koloran preparing it for yet another lengthy session of their father's furtive work. But all three felt so out of place, never having sat around the table together, that they felt as if they'd entered into unfamiliar confines and odd company.

"I'd appreciate, before I begin my tale," Morvedraz directed toward Nore, "knowing exactly what *you* know about this Khaleo person, and what in the gods' names you were doing with him at the Black Chalice."

Nore sighed, her eyes directed at the tabletop. "Andara and I were just bored. So, we went to the Chalice because we knew it'd be more exciting than Flannah's or any of the other grubby pubs around here. Zhakhar takes special care of us there, Father—"

"Oh, I'm quite aware of the care that Zhakhar pays you, dear daughter. It's from what I pay to *him* that such service is secured."

"Oh." Nore paused, eyes wide now and trained on Morvedraz. She'd of course resolved that not only her beauty, but, more pleasing to her, her eagerly shrewd nature had actually drawn Zhakhar's attraction, and ultimately his good favor. "I didn't know that—"

"Of course you didn't know. Nor would you have, ever. But today is about the telling of truths, so let's begin there. Don't get me wrong. I like Zhakhar, and do respect him. He has quite a moral code for someone who deals in, shall we say, less than savory pursuits. And though I've forbade you set foot in the Chalice I know all too well that it is that which we're forbidden that we long for, always. In any case, I told him that if harm ever beset you or anyone close to you at his establishment that the consequences would be most grave. And he agreed that he'd take full responsibility for your well being whilst in his presence. For a fee, of course. We are businessmen, after all. He wouldn't have agreed to such terms if he didn't care about you, *and* his relationship to me. But, please continue your account of last night."

Morvedraz watched Nore squirm, unused to being scrutinized in this manner—her seemingly furtive dealings about the City revealed as her father's common knowledge—but she recouped her composure and began again to relate the events of the previous night.

"It was when the place was empty except for me, Andara and Zhakhar. Kor had secured the entry and extinguished the candles in the windows. Suddenly there was such a banging on the entrance that it seemed like the front door would explode. That's when Kor opened the door and began tossing Dwarvs like—well, like Dwarvs—onto the floor of the main lounge while Zhakhar towered over them. He was more than just angry, especially since it was so late, and it had been a particularly complicated night"

"Yes, I understand he was able to deal with that wretched Lethani whoremonger quite effectively."

Nore's eyes widened, never having considered that Morvedraz would be privy to such information with such ease.

"Uh...yeah. Anyway, the Dwarvs looked official, even had a scroll with the Dwarvani royal seal, stating their mission, so Zhakhar listened to them. They said they were pursuing a fugitive, wanted in their kingdom for murder and conspiracy, and that they'd watched him enter the Chalice. Zhakhar was weary of the night as it was, so he accepted their story, their apologies, and kicked them out. I went home because I worried that they might show up at the wine shop and pound the door down like they did at the Chalice."

"Why did you think they'd come here?"

"They asked Zhakhar for you. By name. He said he didn't know you."

"Go on."

"I was ready to head back into the house and go to bed when Andara came and told me I had to go back. That's when Khaleo had shown up there, speaking Antran as badly as you speak *Zhoryan*—"

"What is, '*Zhoryan*'?"

"It's what he says the language I speak is called. Since everyone agreed that his features were too similar to mine to be a coincidence, Andara tried a few words on him, and they all realized that he spoke it. Flawlessly. Now I'm anxious. I'm actually going to have a conversation in my own language! He gives us this story about being from Kwamada, and I'm thinking, right! This guy isn't from Kwamada. Anyway, Zhakhar tells us to just talk while everyone else goes to bed—"

"You mean, he left you alone with Khaleo?"

"Kor was just inside the hallway, Father. I was in no danger."

"Very well. Continue."

"So, that's when Khaleo tells me about what he says is my background."

"Which is?"

"I'm a hybrid race, bred between the *Zhorhai* and other races that lived near their kingdom. He said that he and I are related. Cousins, in fact. That I was an adopted part of the royal family. Oh, and that I'm actually about 250 years old."

"What?!"

"Yeah, it was a bit of a surprise to me, too."

Nore continued to relate the background of Khaleo's pursuit, the bloodless coup from within the Zhorhai royal family, the betrayal of the races that bordered the kingdom, the plot against the *Dwarvani.*

"Then he tells me he's travelled all the way here to approach me, wanting to take me back to *Zhorhai* to help him reunite the remnant groups of his...*our* people. To rebuild the kingdom again."

"And your response was...?"

"No! I told him that my life is here, in Antra. It doesn't matter what I look like, what skills I possess or what language I speak. And I said I wasn't going to travel thousands of miles back to a place that doesn't mean anything to me, which is when he started talking about an amulet. He said it came from his kingdom, that it could be used as a teleportation device, and he said that he thought you knew about it. Of course we all thought this was crazy. And I would have, still, until you showed me this."

"Yes. Clearly his true target was not you, but the stone."

"Do you know how he disappeared?"

"He pressed his hand against it, through my clothing, clutched it through my robes and uttered some words in your language. So, I suppose it *can* be used to transport oneself, whether you hold it directly or not. I mean, if it simply rendered Khaleo invisible your blade would have surely met with its target, seen or unseen."

"True. I wonder where he ended up? He wouldn't go through the trouble of teleporting back to his homeland without the amulet in his hands."

"He may have assumed that it *would* be in his hands. In which case, if he did transport successfully back to...what is it you called the place?"

"*Zhorhai.*"

"Yes. Well, if he did and has found himself empty handed, we should expect a repeat visit, though I've no idea how long it would take him to travel such a distance."

Koloran had listened to all that had been said so far with no small degree of wonder. But as he pondered the events that Nore had described and Morvedraz had augmented, a thought occurred to him.

"Father, would it not be unwise to assume that Khaleo has even left the City at all? He had no way of knowing whether the amulet would have been transported with him since it lay next to your skin, even though he was able to activate it."

"Excellent point, Koloran. So, we shall assume then that our perpetrator is still within striking distance and act accordingly."

Morvedraz paused, realizing that he had a decision to make, one that would change the relationship he had both with his children, and the amulet itself. He knew that the stone was his greatest weapon should Khaleo return to challenge him for its possession. But since it appeared that Khaleo knew more of how to invoke the stone's powers than did Morvedraz, he realized that it was time for him to finally yet reluctantly unlock the secrets that the tablets held.

"I need to show you both something extremely important that must be kept in utmost secrecy. And as the saying goes, a secret remains thus if it is known by only the one who holds it. That being said, please understand that, should you disclose any of what I'm about to tell you and show you, you put not only your own lives at risk, but mine."

Morvedraz poured both Nore and Koloran each a steaming mug of *blakwine* and, feeling it was his responsibility to tell the tale, began with the story he'd never before voiced.

"I didn't understand it at the time why we lived in the forest, so far from other *Dwarvani*. But I accepted it as normal, the way a child living in poverty simply accepts that he will eat only a scavenged meal, and sleep on a bare dirt floor; he knows no other reality. But the old wizard who found me in tatters on the forest floor eventually explained what had happened to my family, and why. My father had once sat on the *Dwarvani* High Council, and was considered an ambassador of sorts, which is why the wizard had approached him over any other Dwarv in the hierarchy. He knew that my father was used to intermingling with other races and might be more open to understanding the plans the wizard was to disclose and the actions he would propose the *Dwarvani* take to thwart them."

"But, Father," Koloran interjected, "why would a Humani wizard have any reason to approach a Dwarv, who'd be immediately suspicious and close-lipped?"

"Well, this wizard had discovered something that would be of very high interest to the *Dwarvani*. And it's taken me this long to put all the pieces together...unfortunately, what I've concluded I did so only through the details Nore has related about Khaleo, his tale of her origins, and the realization of his true motivations.

"You see," Morvedraz continued, turning toward his daughter, "I believe now that the old wizard, my adopted father, came from the kingdom of your origin."

"What?"

"I actually had no idea until just now. It took hearing you relate what Khaleo had alleged to confirm what I was beginning only to suspect. If you, Nore, are indeed

250 years old—and look nineteen—then the wizard must have been aged a thousand, perhaps several thousands of years, for his skin sagged with the great burden of time, his back was bent, his knees were weak and knobby. It was a struggle for him to rise in the mornings without the aid of spells and potions. And, while his hair was white as you'd expect someone of such advanced age, as opposed to yours that turns from flaxen to silver and back, his skin dulled while yours glows with a bronzed luminescence, his eyes remained true to what I'm assuming was his race. They looked like yours. Actually, they looked *exactly* like Khaleo's: smaller than yours, but almond shaped and in color a glowing amber. He spoke of a great kingdom where he'd come from that had all but vanished, crumbled from within by conspiracy and greed, and ultimately defeated for betraying the bordering races that had made them strong, and a ridiculous plot to overthrow the *Dwarvani* kingdom. This was the plot he'd warned my father of, and had attempted to convince him that war was not the answer, that an alliance could be established between the pure *Zhorhai* royals living in exile and the Dwarvani high council, that the renegade of the *Zhorhai* could be thwarted in the same manner with which they'd taken control, now having grown lazy and fat from their abundant, exploited wealth.

"This, so the wizard told me, was what my father had presented to a secret session of the High Council, convinced by the wizard's reasoning and resolve. It sounds almost ridiculous now—a Dwarv recommending his own kingdom put their trust in a practitioner of *majik*. And it was after not much deliberation that the same council rejected my father's proposal and voted unanimously for war. He objected hotly. With no regard for his experience or service to the Kingdom, they expelled him from the council and banished my family to the Dark Forest. But the old wizard kept watch over us, knowing that he'd asked my father to take a great risk, one I don't think he even realized how great. While the wizard was able to soften our experience in the wilderness, through *majik*—driving game in the direction of my father's bow; enriching the hard, craggy soil of the forest floor to grow vegetables and grains—what he'd never dreamed would come to pass did, most clandestinely and violently. You see, the Dwarvani high council had convinced themselves that my father had somehow colluded with these renegade *Zhorhai*, and they mistrusted the source of his assertions since they'd come from not only the strange race, but a wizard at that.

"On a cold night in midwinter, when the legions of *Dwarvani waryers* would march toward the *Zhorhai* king-dom to destroy it, they took a slight jog to the south, straight toward the humble thatch-roof hovel where we lived. When the torches hit our roof and lit it like a match struck to flint my father screamed for me to run."

Morvedraz had to pause, feeling the pressure and sting of tears held at bay behind his eyes. He took several deep breaths, then continued.

"I scrambled as fast I could out the rear door of our dwelling and made straight for the densest trees, knowing that Dwarvs would be reluctant to follow into the forest. There I hid in the hollow remnants of a rotted log until the Daystar pierced the green canopy. I crawled out and sat on the forest floor and listened. The only sounds were the morning song of birds and the rustle of leaves blown by the breeze. I crept back as silently as I could and found our dwelling burnt to the ground, my mother and father nowhere in sight. That's where I remained, waiting for my parents to return, not understanding that there was noth-ing left of them *to* return. I was six years old."

Morvedraz placed his head in his hands and closed his eyes. It was not until he felt the pressure of both Nore's and Koloran's hands on his shoulders, then their arms wrap around him, did he allow himself to weep. After he'd done so for several long minutes, he raised his head, wiped his face with his sleeve and continued.

"He found me after I'd given up our home site, having scrounged for every remaining scrap of something to eat, and taken to the forest where I could gather the berries and roots my father had taught me were edible, and hide from both *Humani* and beast. I'd assumed the Dwarvs would forget about me, sure that I'd perish in the forest from hunger, the elements, or a predator. After convincing me that we both could well perish without each other's help, I agreed to accompany the wizard on his journeys and attend to his waning years."

Morvedraz sat back and lifted his mug of *blakwine* to his lips, then paused, returned it to the table.

"I think this occasion warrants something a bit stronger."

From a compartment within the base of the table he pulled a bottle of Kwamadan brandy and three short, stout glasses, filled them two fingers full and pushed one each in front of Nore and Koloran.

"Let us remember my father, for wanting to do what he thought was right. The old wizard—"

"What was his name, Father?" The strain of real emotion was audible in Nore's voice.

"It's strange, but I don't know. At the time I was either too respectful or too afraid to inquire. I was only a small boy, after all. At first I simply called him Wizard. After awhile, and I don't even remember when, why, or if I'd thought about it at all, I began calling him Father. Since I called my own father Papa, it didn't feel strange, or seem like he was portraying himself as any kind of substitute. It just felt...natural.

"And let us drink to the lost lives of the two of you. Nore, now we know something of yours. Koloran, I'm sorry I don't have any insights into your background."

"The only insight I recall of my background, Father, is hunger, cold, and pain. As far as I'm concerned, my background began the day you found me in the alley of the Rough Zirkot."

"Thank you, my dear boy."

Morvedraz raised his glass, and his children followed suit, then each tipped the glass back and emptied its contents into their waiting mouths.

"Now that we are a bit fortified, I believe the time is appropriate for me to reveal what I'd promised. So, please follow me. I have something to show you that, with Nore's help, should reveal the entirety of what powers the amulet possesses."

Having learned the incantations that awoke the amulet only by ear, never having seen them actually written in *Zhoryan*, Khaleo's incomplete understanding had caused him to make several assumptions of the amulet's workings and his ability to manipulate them, both of which played to his distinct disadvantage. First, he'd assumed, having grasped the stone through the material of Morvedraz' clothing, that this tactile engagement would be sufficient for the amulet to bind itself to him, and thus materialize in his hand after the *majikal* transport. Second, he'd convinced himself that the incantation he'd learned hundreds of years ago would instantly cause the amulet to transform into a teleportation device that returned him to the site of the *Zhorhai* palace. He was wrong on both accounts.

When the rushed disorientation and churning queasiness of the *majikal* transport had subsided, Khaleo opened his eyes to discover two disturbing facts: first, that the amulet was no longer in his grasp, and second, that he sat cross-legged on the cold stones of a place he unfortunately knew far too well: the basement of the Black Chalice. Though the amulet did transport him away from the grave path of Nore's dagger, it had merely taken him back to the previous place he'd been prior to the Daystar's last full cycle, the actual purpose of the incantation he'd spoken.

"Blast! I must get my way back to that wretched Dwarv and find if he knows anything of the lost tablets. Only with them will I be able with certainty to invoke the amulet's power."

He stood and hurried toward the basement doorway, only to realize that the entirety of Morvedraz' cadre of protectors—Nore, Zhakhar's cohorts—would likely be scouring the City for him, and that the very place where he now sat would be the last in all of Antra they'd think to look.

He surmised his surroundings, felt with his hands in the dark and found that the tops of the barrels that stood stacked in the room all lay thick with a deep layer of dust; these were not full wine barrels, or even barrels aged for re-use, but simply extras that had likely sat for years undisturbed. Khaleo fished around in the darkness until he found a torch hanging from a wall sconce, and in a nook in the stone below it a flint. He pulled the torch from the wall, struck the flint against the stone until the sparks ignited the torch's tinder-dry cloth.

"Ah, much better." He spoke audibly to himself, sure as he was that the literal depth of his hiding place would suffice better than any other in the City to conceal him. Finding several other torches positioned apart on the walls of the room, he lit them all and was able to take stock of what remained at his disposal to use to whatever advantage he could muster. There was little, save the empty barrels, the flint, and the torches that would soon burn themselves out. He extinguished all but the first to conserve his sources of light. Despite knowing about the secret exit that led to the building's exterior he could not leave the Chalice, for without the amulet he'd have no way of returning to the basement. He'd need, then, to venture into the upper floors for food and water, and, not having the presence of mind to have eaten any of the cheese from

Erib's stand, nor having had a proper meal in nearly a day and a half, decided that exploring other rooms or floors would be an unfortunate yet fast-approaching necessity.

I've only been here for half an hour, at most, but likely that would be enough time for Nore and Zhakhar's men to have returned and warned him. Surely he'd have dispatched all available to search the city for my whereabouts.

And taking this assumption as his only advantage, Khaleo extinguished his torch, gently raised the latch on the heavy door, pulled it open and smelled the staleness and moldy scents of a hallway that had seen neither light nor passage in years. Feeling bolstered by this isolation, he struck light to the torch again, held it toward the hall and watched as door after door on either side stretched out in front of him and disappeared into the darkness past the flame's range. He took three silent steps forward to the first door on his right, pressed down on the entry lever, but it remained stiff in place. He did so to every remaining door in the hallway—twenty-four in all—with no different result, until the very last, one that opposed the one from which he'd originally emerged. When he pressed the lever he felt it give, catch, creak against the rust that coated it, but finally release. Khaleo heaved an audible sigh, but when he opened the door saw that what awaited him was a stairwell, narrow and curving sharply to the left, corkscrewing upward to the higher floors of the Chalice.

Alright, then. Up we go...

9

Zhakhar leaned against the table where he sat with Andara, looking glumly from side to side and hoping for some news—*any* news—from his emissaries, from Nore, but the cavernous lounge of the Black Chalice held nothing but the tired and frustrated worries of the two who sat in its silence, until the shuffle of soft-clad footsteps hurried up the main core of stairs and through the dark hallway that led to where Zhakhar and Andara waited.

"Master Zhakhar!"

Rising, Zhakhar met the captain of his emissaries with open arms.

"Malik, what news?"

"Only bad, I fear." Malik spoke slowly, his eyes downcast.

"As I'd presumed. Tell me all of it."

"Nore and our team sped toward Morvedraz' shop, taking the direct route down Long Street for haste. Suddenly there appeared a most strange site: the Arbiter himself, sitting at a cheese stand, nibbling contentedly and sipping at a small glass of wine."

"That *is* strange. I've known the Dwarv for more cycles of the Daystar than I can count, and I've never known him to imbibe before the Hour of the Drug."

"No, master Zhakhar, listen! What oddity befell our eyes was not Morvedraz and his wine and cheese, but that Khaleo sat next to him, and the two appeared in pleasant conversation!"

Zhakhar thought to explode with the thought of Morvedraz in any such peril, but kept himself in check not to quell the efforts of his emissary to describe what had transpired.

"Go on, Malik."

"We set upon them silently, observing the pair's interaction, which from a distance looked amiable, but when we neared and could overhear their conversation it was clear that Morvedraz' responses attempted to evade Khaleo's questioning. The Arbiter gave a false name, made up details of his life. Still, Khaleo pressed him for information about *Morvedraz!* Finally, when Khaleo placed an arm around the great Dwarv's shoulder, looking like he meant to coax him toward the wine shop, Nore would have no more. She sprang upon Khaleo, in deadly silence, and poised her dagger for a killing strike. At that very moment Khaleo turned, jumped back in obvious fear, but still pretended at innocence. When Nore bid that he begin the trek back to the Chalice, slowly and ahead of her and our team, Khaleo flung a plate at her, clutched the material of Morvedraz' robes, then disappeared! I watched Nore's blade sail past its target and land on the street. Clearly, he'd used some kind of *majik.* We lost him after this."

Malik punctuated the end of his statement again with downturned eyes, mouth and face drawn toward the floor. "Forgive us, Master Zhakhar. And please let full responsibility for losing the fugitive be mine." Malik bent to one knee before the master of the Chalice.

Zhakhar shook his head and let go a heavy sigh. Malik was his skilled and loyal emissary, clearly bested both by *majikal* evasion that no one could have anticipated.

"Raise yourself, Malik, my most trusted associate. And put at ease the minds of all who serve under you. There is no action that you've described that warrants punishment. Rather, I give you my hearty thanks for making haste to warn me of the morning's events. But, tell me, you said that Khaleo and Morvedraz conversed, easily, as they sat side by side?"

"Yes?"

"Tell me, in what language did Khaleo speak?"

Malik's brow wrinkled. "Why, in Antran, master Zhakhar."

"And, how would you describe his verbal abilities?"

"I'd say he sounded fluent."

Zhakhar nodded and scowled. *Damn you for your deceit that fooled even me.*

"Stand up, Malik, please." Zhakhar placed his hands on Malik's broad shoulders and shook him slightly. "You have brought me information that is *most* important. But do this with great haste: take a team of two dozen, and fan out in pairs throughout the City. Make the Chalice the apex of your search. Question all, but do so pleasantly, and instruct all never to separate from the line of sight of his partner. Make no direct inquiries. Merely, assert that it is I who seek information about any unusual sojourners who's been witnessed about. Don't give out any more information than that. Rather, let those questioned fill in the details. By this method we might learn of our friend Khaleo's path and destination yet."

With a nod, Malik lighted away from Zhakhar to assemble his team and thus scour the City for Khaleo. Which left the Master of the Black Chalice alone again with Andara, sitting at a table in the midst of the cavernous main room.

"Zhakhar, I really need to go to Morvedraz'. See if Nore's there. I hope she is." Andara could not contain her emotions any longer: "I'm worried about her," she said, and burst into tears, leaning forward and bowing her head toward the floor of the Chalice. Zhakhar caught her and lifter her into his arms.

"Of course, dear girl. But please let two of my emissaries accompany you."

Andara raised her tear-streaked face up toward the broad, dark palette of Zhakhar's. "Thank you."

"Now, now, let's dry up these tears of yours." He pulled a silken hanky from his robes and dabbed at Andara's damp cheeks, watched her finally smile up at him. "That's better. You know your girl is among the most skilled fighters in the City. And she has a team of my men with her as well. They'd run circles around any attacker, and it seems Khaleo knows that all too well, choosing to hide rather than confront."

"I know. It's just that...she wants *so* much to learn about her background. You should have seen the look on her face when I told her that Khaleo spoke her language. She wants nothing more than to be able to converse in it. She tries to teach me, but, it's so difficult, so hard to pronounce..."

Zhakhar watched Andara shake her head and bow her head toward the floor, her face slack with sadness.

"Get yourself to the wine shop and find your girl. Stay by her side. But don't let Khaleo worry you. Let me first find him and determine what he wants and why, then decide on his fate. Perhaps in the dungeons below the City, perhaps given over to a certain band of Dwarvs. But in any case, neither Nore, nor Morvedraz, nor I will be bested by whatever Khaleo's motives are. And there will be plenty of peaceful time for you to learn Nore's language in the future."

Zhakhar smiled a broad, warm smile down at Andara, called for two of his emissaries, and watched the trio light from the Chalice toward Long Street and the company of Nore and the Arbiter.

Morvedraz rose from the table and bid that Nore and Khaleo do the same.

"Follow me." He turned toward the rear wall of the chamber in which they stood, Nore and Koloran looking on quizzically while their father faced the blank, stacked stones.

"Follow you, where, father? This room is the apex of the entire compound."

Morvedraz turned and saw the curiosity in Koloran's eyes, gave him a wry smile, then placed his hand against the largest of the wall's stone blocks and pressed into its face. The block gave way, compressing an inch into the wall, and around its border beamed a blue luminescence. A line of the same light then ran up and down the jagged seam of the wall's center, and when the light ended simultaneously at floor and ceiling, the seam parted.

Morvedraz stepped into the bath of blue light, turned to watch Nore and Koloran follow, eyes wide. The chamber itself was not large, but the light bent the room's borders, lending the walls an opacity that made them look fluid, and the space appeared to extend forever. Morvedraz stepped forward slowly, allowing his children to absorb their new surroundings and revel at the ethereal quality of the light.

"Father," Nore began, "it smells...I don't know...different in here. No remnants of spilt wine, no lingering *kororah* smoke. The scent is almost sweet."

"Yes."

Morvedraz had noticed that when he'd taken the tablets outdoors with him on journeys that their luminescence had dimmed almost immediately, and though they retained their bluish hue, looked to be wrought of any common stone. Delivered inside, however, into the depths of the safe room he'd had built to house the precious tablets, and placed in their inlayed spaces on the hewn mantel, the stones beamed the same bluish light that Morvedraz had witnessed from the amulet, immediately after it had been used to reduce the *Dwarvani* party in the desert to burnt carcasses.

Morvedraz placed an arm around each his children's shoulders and urged them toward the tablets' beaming brilliance.

"Why do they glow, Father?" Koloran asked.

"I don't know. They only do it in here, when they're safely tucked away in their nook."

"I do." Nore spoke, the determined finality of her words surprising even herself.

"What do you mean?" Morvedraz stared at his adopted daughter.

"It's a signal. Like a beacon. They're trying to alert someone. They're trying to get home."

"But, how can you know this? You've never seen them, even known of their existence."

"I wish I could tell you, Father. I only know what I feel. But those feelings are very, very strong. The deeper you try to hide them, the more ardently they try to send a message to the one who was their keeper, that this is where they'd be found."

"The old wizard never mentioned anything about this..."

"He may not have known. They may be signaling to someone who had passed from life hundreds, maybe thousands of years ago. And, if you believe Khaleo's version of events about our origins, the tablets' beckoning would likely fall on the universe's deaf ears. Even though I sense strongly what the tablets are doing, I'd have never suspected their location, even here, above my head. I'm hoping Khaleo lacks the ability to sense them as well."

"Yes, yes..." Morvedraz murmured, gazing at the glowing tablets in front of him. "Nore, can you read them?"

"Of course."

"Please, then, tell us what they say."

Morvedraz watched with hopeful exuberance while Nore squinted and puzzled at the intricate inscriptions.

"They're like reading the words on the amulet. I know what the writing means, but I can't translate it into Antran."

"You said the words on the amulet had something to do with power. Can you interpret the tablets similarly?"

"I'll try."

Nore stared and stared at the tablets, certain that she could interpret them with precision, understand every nuance of the directions they conveyed, but when she tried to verbalize these indications in Antran, could neither form the most rudimentary phrase nor even utter a single translated word.

"I...I don't know what's wrong, Father. I can read them. Clearly. I understand them in my own language. But, I can't explain, can't even describe their meanings."

"Unlike with the amulet?"

"Yes."

"Something *majikal* clearly blocks your comprehension."

"Do you think so?"

"Oh, yes, daughter. But, try..."

Again Nore stared at the stones, focused her energy on one line at a time, could easily read the lines in her own mind, but when she tried to transfer them to the Antran portion of her lexicon, it was as if the words simply vanished from her consciousness.

"I'm sorry. I can't."

"But, can you read them in *your* language, aloud?"

"Let me see."

"Wait." Morvedraz took the amulet from around his neck and handed it to Nore. "Now."

Holding the amulet, Nore looked to the first incantation inscribed in the left hand column of the first tablet, concentrated on the *Zhoryan* text, uttered the phrase aloud in full voice, and watched as her father and Koloran dropped simultaneously to the floor, murmuring as if in a dream state and breathing evenly, both fully asleep.

"Oops."

When Nore bent to shake her father to consciousness she placed the amulet onto the floor and noticed that the stone glowed the same bluish light as beamed from the tablets.

"Father! Koloran! Wake up!"

The two rose, looking as groggy as those who'd been awakened from a long, deep slumber.

"What happened?" Morvedraz looked to Nore.

"As soon I spoke the phrase the amulet got warm in my hand, and you two passed out."

"Nore, let me see the amulet. Both of you. Sit. I want to try an experiment, and I don't want you falling down."

Morvedraz clutched the amulet as he would to ply influence onto parties in arbitration. "Nore, I'm going to utter a phrase that I use, very quietly, but see if it sounds similar to what you just said in *Zhoryan*."

Nore nodded, sitting on the floor next to Koloran, both their backs pressed to the chamber wall. When Morvedraz whispered the incantation, Koloran listed to his left, his eyes closed. Nore felt a swooning sensation, but retained consciousness.

"That's it, father! Those are the words I just spoke. Mispronounced, but obviously effective."

"Then the volume with which you spoke them must have intensified their effect. All right, since we can't interpret any of the other incantations we must find a way to counteract this locking spell and de-mystify the tablets so that you can translate them into Antran. And, quite frankly, I have not the slightest idea where to start."

"Couldn't we take them to the *Kolej* of Wizards? Someone there might have a spell to release the lock." Nore looked with hopeful eyes at the tablets, anxious now to reveal their secrets to her father.

"No, no, we can't risk divulging their existence to anyone else. Word would travel, and I'm sure Khaleo's persistence would eventually yield him the knowledge not only that the tablets exist, but where he could find them."

"He must know that already." Koloran spoke, his voice even but emphatic. "It's why he sought you out."

"True. He may know *of* them. He may know that I'm somehow associated with them. But he can't know where they are. He'd have no way. The old wizard had been in possession of the tablets for who knows how many centuries, far before even someone a few hundred years old would have been born. And the wizard protected the tablets with his very life."

"We can't know that." Koloran spoke with an authority in his voice that even he was unaccustomed to hearing. "At least, we can't assume that. We can't assume anything. We have to conduct ourselves with regard to the amulet and the tablets as if Khaleo knows we have them and is willing to do whatever necessary to possess them."

Morvedraz looked at Koloran and nodded slowly. "You're absolutely right, Koloran. But there still remains the issue of unlocking the tablets' meaning so that Nore might interpret them for us in Antran."

Koloran did not hesitate with his response: "I believe that I may be able to help with that, Father."

Koloran had felt more than mere concern of late about Morvedraz' decision-making prowess and its subsequent outcome. His father, in many subtle ways, seemed to be... slipping. In his younger years he wouldn't have needed reminding to assume his adversary had every advantage available to him. He would have never allowed himself to be so physically vulnerable so that an enemy might not only strike at him, but surprise him as had Khaleo. And, in all truth, the Morvedraz of old would have never, never allowed *anyone* knowledge of the amulet and tablets, not even his own children, but would have furtively and tirelessly discovered their secrets on his own.

Especially not his children, Koloran thought. *For now Nore and I are in as grave danger as is our father. But, maybe I'm being too harsh. He needs our help. He needs our protection. Perhaps he had no choice.*

"What is it that you mean, Koloran?"

"Come. Let's first secure the tablets behind the wall, then head to the library. I've been amassing quite a collection of rare and ancient volumes, some of which impart the most esoteric knowledge. I believe there is one in particular that may be of some use in abating any *majik* that might be cast upon the tablets."

"Amassing a collection? Esoteric knowledge? Koloran, you speak of *majik* most potent! Such books would be ancient, and near priceless! How on earth could you have the means to acquire them?"

"Let's just say that I've found a very effective means of mining. But, that's a story for another day. Come."

Koloran led Morvedraz and Nore down the narrow stairwell from the Arbiter's chamber, across the atrium and toward the rear of the main building of the compound that housed the library. When Koloran pulled back the great doors and beckoned his father and sister inside, he had to smile when he listened to Morvedraz' audible gasp of wonder upon seeing the carved shelves laden with so many ancient tomes that there appeared little room for more. Indeed, several stacks lay about the floor around Koloran's reading table.

"It's true I've not paid any attention to the library of late, but, Koloran... How on in the gods' names could you have built such a vast collection? You speak of mining. Is this what you do on these 'days off' of yours? Travel to the Garnet Desert with a pick and shovel? But you look no worse for wear when you return. Your shirt is not stained with sweat; your hands show no blisters. In fact, it's always as if you'd taken some rare spa treatment in an expensive resort, your skin glowing, face full."

"As I'd said, Father, that's a story unto itself. We must concentrate on the issues at hand. After we resolve the matter of the tablets, we must then concentrate our efforts on finding Khaleo, apprehending him, and turning him over to whatever authorities would be appropriate."

"I'd like to turn him over to Zhakhar." Nore broke in with a tone of contempt. "He'd have a fine cure for Khaleo's slow tongue."

"We haven't the luxury of such indulgences right now, Sister. Let's concentrate on our advantages: we have each others' strengths, we have the amulet, and we have the tablets. Once we can interpret them we can use the amulet to its full power, maybe use it to locate Khaleo, even bring him to us. But until we achieve this degree of success all other efforts are merely wasted energy."

Koloran watched Nore take a deep breath, tighten her lips and exhale audibly through her nose. "Yes, you're right, Brother."

"Very well. Sit. Both of you. Let me find the volume that may help us."

After his first successful venture into the Garnet Desert, Koloran had spent the better part of the remainder of the year journeying there on the "days off" that he'd turned into nearly weekly occurrences, now that Morvedraz had grown accustomed to Koloran's regular absences, and having plied onto a grudging Nore—who seemed to before take as many "days off" as she could before the concept had even been defined—the more mundane tasks of running the wine shop. Koloran still balanced the ledgers, completed inventory reports so that his father could replenish stock, and after a while Morvedraz hardly noticed Koloran's absences at all.

And when he grew weary of simply culling perfect garnets from the desert floor and taking them to exchange for *zeks* at the local gem broker, he began to experiment with other valuable items. For he'd realized from the very beginning that the instructions within *Ancient Spells for Suc-*

cess & Profit gave no specific requirement as to the nature of the object of value onto which to apply the incantations; Koloran had simply grown used to—and amazed by—the ease with which he could reap precious stones. So after a half dozen garnet expeditions, he found another hidden spot in the wilderness—a cave that may have once housed the family of an ancient race, but lay abandoned now—and within it cast the *majik* that drew garnets from the bare desert floor onto a new item: a single solid-gold twenty-*zek* piece. And with the yield from this new focal object, Koloran would soon halt his trips to the gem brokers and procure with far more frequency as many valuable volumes as the proprietor of Centhum could amass.

Koloran turned now toward the tall walls of laden shelves and ran his hands along each successive spine of the hundreds of volumes that crowded the library's stacks, searching for one that he'd purchased several months prior simply because he thought the binding especially fine, and enjoyed the intricate calligraphy of the text within, having no idea that he'd make practical use of it at any time in the future, especially so soon, and under such potentially dangerous circumstances. It had even slipped his mind where exactly on the tall shelves he'd placed it, and he searched first the lower rows, and then climbed the rolling ladder that allowed him to pore over the higher lines of volumes he'd had less interest in than those on the bottom. But at last he recognized it—the ruddy dragon-skin spine embossed with cerulean lettering—pulled it from its tucked place snug near the wainscoting that trimmed the library's ceiling, climbed down the ladder, and set the tome on the table before his father and sister.

He'd had no inkling as to what purpose or power the volume may hold, purchased it instead for its beauty alone. But after having studied ancient Antran on his own for quite some years, for no other purpose but to appreciate his civilization's formative texts in their original language,

Koloran felt surprised when he read this book's name, remembered puzzling over its meaning, then casting his curiosity aside and applying it to absorbing the contents of other works. But now the title enlivened his curiosity, as well as his hope.

"*Tiladu Tsonahzreds.*" Koloran pronounced the ancient words with proper inflection and accent, though these were lost on both his confounded father and sister.

"What in the name of the god's is this strange tongue, and how is it that you can read it?" Morvedraz winkled his brow and stared at the unfamiliar characters.

"It's Antran. Not as you'd know it, but the Antran that is not spoken anymore, and only scholars make use of it to study the old texts. Our most ancient volumes of literature and poetry were written it."

"It sounds harder to pronounce than *Zhoryhan.*" Nore shook her head.

"Than what?"

"Oh, sorry. Another story for another day."

"But, Koloran," Morvedraz interjected, "what does it *mean?*"

"Literally, it means, 'remove restraint'. But I'm really not sure what kind of restraint it's referring to. I'm not even sure the contents are *majikal.*"

"So, for all you know it could be a very old locksmith's manual." Morvedraz glowered from behind his voluminous beard.

"I don't think I'd have paid as much as I did for anything so...literal in nature."

"Well, then, since you're the only one who seems to be familiar with the origins of Antran, please spend some time with it and glean what may aid our purpose."

"I shall immediately, Father."

"Fine. Nore, please help me get the tasting room open for the day. Any more time taken from our normal routines may arouse suspicion. I want all to appear normal, as if we'd simply woken from a restive sleep and are hard about our usual affairs."

Nore nodded and, with unusual energy, dashed from the library and down the steps toward the first floor to open the wine shop. When she'd pulled back and tied the curtains away from the windows she looked up and gave a start, for there in front of her on the outside of the thick glass double-panes stood Andara, her hand poised to knock on the shop's wooden door. Nore flung the entry-way open and pulled her inside, slamming the door closed in one motion.

Andara burst into tears. "I was so worried!"

"Shh... Everything's fine. We're all safe here. Father and Koloran are upstairs. I'm just getting the shop opened for the day."

Nore held Andara tightly and rocked her slightly from side to side until she calmed finally and her tears subsided, then held her at arms' length and gazed into her reddened eyes before planting a long, soft kiss onto her lips. Andara smiled.

"Wanna hang out here today? Help me around the shop? I guarantee we'll be popular."

"I'd love to. But I'm supposed to be at the markets in an hour for security duty."

"I have an idea. Wait one second."

Nore opened the wine shop door and leaned into the street, cupped her hand around her mouth and whispered as loudly as she could without arousing curiosity from passersby.

"*Vhalor!*"

She had only to utter his name once, and Zhakhar's emissary peered from around the near corner of the wine shop's building.

"*Come here!*"

In two silent strides the armed young *Humani*, Zhakhar's newest emissary—yet deadly as them all, who would die not only for his master but for anyone in his care—stood before Nore with hands folded over the dagger he concealed beneath his leather jacket.

"I need you to do me a favor."

"It is *my* favor to do as you wish, Leonora. Only ask, and it shall be accomplished."

"Go to the slave market. Find the proprietor and explain that Andara has been summoned by Morvedraz for a task today. Tell him that the consequences will be more important and more profitable to all Antran business, certainly his own, than her presence in the security detail. Explain that she regrets the short notice, but knows that he would well understand that when the Arbiter makes a request, the invited hurries toward his presence."

"I will do this at once and will report back to you after to confirm the proprietor's response."

"Thank you, Vhalor." Nore grinned at the young man, who nodded, gave up the slightest of closed-lipped smiles, then bounded out the wine shop's door.

"See. Wasn't that easy?" Nore beamed toward Andara.

"Nore, I can't always call on your father's name as an excuse to shirk on my own life duties. I've heard that I may be in consideration for Security Lead on my shift, which would put me in direct line to attain Captaincy."

"Darling, do you *really* want to be in charge of slave market security as your life's vocation?"

"It's steady, honest work. And it serves the people. Look how I was able to help Melora. Think of how much more I could do if I had higher status. I could be part of Zhakhar's network, his arm at the market to ensure that no abuse ever befell—"

Nore placed the paired middle and index finger of her right hand gently onto Andara's lips. Then Nore shook her head.

"Andara, my Andara... Do you *really* not understand what I'm asking you?" Nore lowered her hand.

"No?" Andara spoke, her voice slightly tremulous.

"My dearest, I want you not just in my company, or my arms, or my bed. I want you in my *life*. I want us to be involved with each other, wholly. I want you to be my partner, beside me in all dealings, from today forward, until our souls leave this world. I will soon, along with Koloran, assume responsibility for our father's business. One of us will also, eventually, assume the title of Arbiter. I'd always hoped that my father would see me in the role, and I've tried hard to temper myself so that he'd consider me worthy. I'm not certain he does. But my brother has shown uncommon prowess lately in both his ability to assert himself and in the wisdom he's brought to help deal with our current problems. Should my father choose Koloran to inherit the Arbiter's responsibilities, I will resolve to run a very busy, very successful wine business. And I want you by my side to help me do it."

Nore watched Andara's eyes widen along with her smile.

"I...I don't know what to say. I mean, I do, but... Nore, I had no idea that you felt this way. We've only been together a year—"

"*Only* a year? Don't you think we've had enough time to grow accustomed to each others' strengths and shortcomings, to know and accept each other wholly despite our foibles and odd proclivities? I know you better than I've ever known anyone, and the more I know you the more I want to be with you. I know when you need me, and I know when you need to be alone. I *trust* you with everything that is precious to me. I know you'd do anything for my father and brother as well as for me. And now I want you here, with me, moving forward to build our life together. Andara, I love you, completely."

Nore smiled and wrapped her arms around Andara's shoulders and pulled her close.

"You've never said 'I love you' before." A single tear seeped from Andara's right eye and rolled down her cheek.

"It's about time I did."

"I love you, too. I don't think I realized how much until I thought there was a chance I'd somehow lose you over this Khaleo business."

"You will *never* lose me. And Khaleo, despite his deception and cleverness, has the distinct disadvantage of having not only Zhakhar against him, but the Arbiter of Antra. We have the advantage, Andara. There's no way he could possibly wield power over us."

"What about this amulet he kept talking about. What if he gets his hands on that?"

Nore averted her eyes momentarily from Andara's, and she noticed the slight hesitation.

"Khaleo has no amulet. And there's no way he'll get his hands on one. No chance."

"Ah, my darling, your *bravada* is showing."

"My *confidence*, you mean."

Nore watched Andara smile and shake her head. "Well, if you want me involved in the wine business, you'd better start showing me my way around this place."

Nore smiled. "Come on. Let's get some bottles open for today's tasting."

Koloran spent the better part of two hours poring over the first chapter of *Remove Restraint*, but the going proved tremendously slow. He'd never before encountered such a complex version of ancient Antran, and the florid calligraphy complicated his understanding. Finally, determined to glean what help the volume might provide, he concentrated solely on the ancient word for *majik*, and began to scan the pages for it instead of trying to comprehend the entirety of each chapter. After combing through the first five he finally hit upon the word, repeated several times in Chapter Six. Then he spent time discerning the words adjacent to *"majik"* and found that finally, near the section's end, he'd come upon a passage that might prove useful.

Next to *"majik"* was the verb "to secure." Examining further he found words for "spell", "text", and "comprehension." When he finally came upon "unlock" he knew he had the passage he'd hoped existed. Lighting his lamp—for day had turned to night as he'd labored—Koloran began the painstaking task of translating the entire chapter into modern Antran.

"Koloran?"

He started, so intent on completing the translation that he'd not heard his father's footsteps when he entered the library.

"Yes, Father?"

"How goes the work?"

"I believe I've come upon a section of the text that may prove useful."

"That's great news. But, would you take a break for a few moments? I've been wanting to have a word with you and time has lately proven short, what with all the commotion with this Khaleo person. Would you take a glass of wine with me in the veranda?"

Koloran's eyes widened; he himself drank very little, perhaps a single wine with dinner on a special occasion, and he'd never been invited to sit down over glass with his father.

"Of course, Father. My eyes do grow weary."

"Come, then. The evening is pleasant, and the Daystar's warmth still lingers outside."

Koloran followed his father out of the library and into the foyer of the building's second floor, across the atrium and toward the wide double-doors that opened onto the garden-laced veranda that overlooked the port on the Great River. He walked under the latticed enclosure dripping with grapevines and leaves. *Znub Naztar's* reflected light cast an almost opalescent tint about the veranda, and the river's rippled current shimmered as if upon it there floated thousands of silver *zeks*. Koloran watched his father unlock the wine cooler tucked behind the veranda's bar and bring forth a very old, very expensive-looking wine, the label he recognized as Kwamadan, deftly uncork the dusty bottle and pour two tall glasses of the black-red vintage.

Koloran lifted the crystal wine glass and held it up to the torchlight.

"Father, this wine is so dense I cannot see through it!"

"It is very old, and very rare, Koloran. The grape is called, 'Mourvedre.'"

"It sounds like your name, Father."

"It's the origin of my name; rendered in *Dwarvani* the wine would indeed be called, 'Morvedraz'. I chose it as a fitting symbol of the amulet and its powers, and for the role that the stone has allowed me to assume in this life-time. But, more importantly, and as a tying gesture to the purpose I see for you in the future, I wanted to open a bot-tle that would signify the rare opportunity you will have in your *own* lifetime, one that no other person, likely in the entirety of the City of Antra and beyond, will have.

Koloran followed his father to the round wooden ta-ble that stood in the center of the veranda, watched him pull back the curved wooden bench.

"Sit, my son."

"Thank you, Father."

"Koloran, our discourse has always circled the mun-dane pursuits of the wine shop. Inventory, accounts pay-able and receivable, procurement—"

"They are not mundane tasks to me, Father."

"Bless you, my boy, for they are."

Koloran watched his father give up a wry smile.

"We've spoken very little of my other vocation, that which has brought our family riches far beyond that which a mere wine shop might reap."

Koloran watched as his father tilted back the wine glass and brought it to his lips, then placed it back onto the table, the contents so viscose that the entire side of the vessel from which he'd sipped remained coated in red.

"Koloran."

"Yes, Father?"

"You have proven yourself most keenly of late. So much so that I regret not noticing sooner how you've developed into such a capable young man."

"Thank you, Father."

He watched his father pause, take a deep, cleansing breath, and felt the calloused strength of Morvedraz' hands on his shoulders.

"You will be Arbiter, my son."

Koloran stared unblinkingly at his father's stern face, the resolute eyes the color of worn granite, the creased, leather-like skin of his face, the downward curve of his scowl; suddenly, all the weight of what would become Koloran's responsibility fell upon his shoulders, and he had to reach out to his father for support.

"My boy, what's wrong?"

"Father... Forgive me. I had no idea, no thought at all that you'd choose me for a role so full of incredible and auspicious responsibility. I thought that Nore's strength would surely—"

"Nore's strength is her charm, and her passion, and the swiftness of her blade, Koloran. Her intellect is as sharp as that blade, I know, but I'm afraid that in the role of Arbiter her passion mingled with her obstinacy might spark a bloodbath the likes the City has never seen. And, despite her constant shirking and taking advantage of your dedicated nature, she has nonetheless faithfully achieved two accomplishments I'd hoped she would, and that will serve you well: she has learned the wine business expertly, and she has grown in love for you so much so that she would die to protect you. Of this I am certain. And when you assume the role of Arbiter you will need all the protection you can muster."

Koloran took a deep breath and exhaled audibly.

"But, why me, Father?"

"You have shown uncommon wisdom, Koloran. Wisdom that I'm sure has resided in your being for far longer than it has shown itself. Perhaps these 'days off' of yours have allowed you to flourish in more ways than you'd had opportunity to in the past, in ways beyond which you'd even expected. Perhaps this garnet hunting has brought about in you a confidence that had remained untapped. I do not know. But I do know this: the manner in which you've conducted yourself with regard to your family, our current issues, and your contribution to them both, have shown themselves as more than admirable. You've bested me in your responses to both, and I'm sure you must have realized that."

Koloran blushed at his prior thoughts about his father's recent shortcomings, and cast his gaze toward the veranda's stone-tiled floor.

"Come now, my boy. I may be an old Dwarv, but I still have a few wits about me. Surely you'd conceived that in years past there'd have been no way that Khaleo could have gotten close to me, let alone shoulder to shoulder. I saw it in your eyes when you spoke of our necessary reaction to him. That was when I knew. It's time for me to retire. And time for someone young, strong, and capable—time for *you*—to assume the role. And, so, now I give you this."

Koloran watched his father open his robes, lift the gold-laced cord from which hung the amulet over his head, and place the stone onto the table before their bottle of wine.

"Take it. For it is now yours."

"Drape it onto my neck, Father. As a gesture of passage."

"Very well."

And with the weight of the stone around his neck, Koloran felt both the pressure of responsibility and the charge of power that he knew followed.

"But, Father, how shall I learn the facets of arbitration? The amulet may be powerful, but certainly I cannot assume total responsibility for—"

"Fret not, my boy. I'm not dying any time soon."

Koloran smiled embarrassedly at his father's dark humor.

"I will, of course, remain as your counselor. We will sit in tandem for your first interactions. In fact, we will do so tonight, for I have two parties scheduled to bargain over—"

"Tonight? But, Father, our trouble with Khaleo must be our main purpose! And dealing with how to unlock the tablets is surely the best hope in—"

"Koloran." Morvedraz spoke and raised his open palm. "One thing you'll learn, not only as Arbiter, but simply as your life progresses, is that circumstances notwithstanding, life goes on. Must we deal with Khaleo? Of course. Must we discern the tablets? Doing so would be most helpful. But, despite all of those priorities, we must conduct ourselves within the manner that the gods have prescribed for us. For if we fail at that, we truly fail our lives in this world."

Koloran nodded, never having heard such calm wisdom from his father's words. *Or perhaps*, he thought, *never having listened closely enough.*

"I will do my best, Father."

"You will do better than that, I am certain, my son. I'd not have chosen you otherwise."

10

"Okay, so, the racks are organized first by varietal, then by region, and finally by vintage."

Andara watched Nore hold the torch high, but not so close as to set flame to the dry, wooden racking that held the hundreds of bottles staged to supply the wine shop's tasting counter. Andara clung to Nore, keeping a safe distance from the open flame, listening to her explain how the wines should be brought out beginning with the lighter whites and progressing toward the deep, rich reds, but all the while marveling at her lover's knowledge, a side of her Andara had not yet experienced. Nore often scoffed at her role in the wine shop, preferring self-deprecating humor to describe the responsibilities she so often shrugged upon her brother. But it was now obvious to Andara that Nore's abilities to manage the business ran far deeper in her being than the cursory comments and flighty shrugs with which she'd always described her role; obviously, her knowledge was not only sound, but expert.

"I've never seen you like this."

"Like what?"

"Going on and on about the wine business. You speak it as fluently as you do your other languages." Andara smiled and pressed herself against Nore, who held the torch high and away of Andara's hair.

"Whoa, wait a second." Nore slipped the torch into the narrow sleeve of a wall sconce and took Andara in her arms.

"It's quite alluring, hearing you speak so eloquently and...intimately about wine."

"Alluring? You *have* to be kidding me. This can't be any more boring. I'm surprised you haven't run screaming already."

"The only direction I'm running is toward you."

Andara held Nore tightly and <u>kissed her full on the lips, opening her mouth and intertwining Nore's tongue with her own</u>. But just as she reached to caress her lover's shoulder and allow her hand to trace Nore's torso, a muffled yet nearby hail caused both young women to start and pull away from one another.

"Nore! Where are you? There are customers at the counter!"

"Uh-oh." Andara blushed.

"Don't worry. We'll charm the *zeks* out of them in no time."

The door to the bottle storage room opened, and Morvedraz himself strode inside.

"Oh, hello, Andara. I didn't know you'd come to visit. You are, as always, most welcome."

"Thank you, Morvedraz." Andara stepped toward Morvedraz, lifted his calloused hand to her lips and planted a light kiss onto his knuckles.

"My dear, that is not at all necessary."

"Of course it is." Andara smiled.

"You are most charming, indeed. Nore, please, attend to the folks at the counter. They're looking quite thirsty."

"Actually, Father, I was hoping to give Andara a chance to run the tasting counter with me today. We've gone over all the details, and I'm sure she's more than capable."

"Really? Very well, then. Andara, your efforts would be most appreciated."

Andara nodded and smiled at Morvedraz, squeezed Nore's arm, then bounded toward the shop's counter to assist her first customers.

"She is as bright a young woman as she is lovely, Nore. I hope you're not considering your time with her as lightly as you do your wine shop duties."

Nore blushed and looked toward the storage room floor. "No, Father, not at all. In fact, I asked Andara to run the wine shop with me today because I have a very serious proposal for her."

"And what is that, my dear?"

"Father, I love Andara. Wholly and completely. I want us to be partners in all our dealings. And I'd like your blessing that we would be joined."

Nore watched her father's weathered face widen into a bright smile.

"That's certainly the best news I've heard this cycle of the Daystar, my daughter. Of course you have my blessing. If you would like, you are more than welcome to make your home here. You may occupy the entire third floor, so you might feel that you have privacy. But, if you should wish to seek a house of your own I would of course understand—"

"Father. You hurt me." Nore smiled as she chided Mor-vedraz. "Of course we'd love to make our life here, nearest you and Koloran. Andara would do anything for you both. And...if we could have the whole upper floor to ourselves that would be more than generous of you. It would be... amazing" Nore beamed.

"Come here." Nore accepted her father's embrace, then bounded out of the storage room and toward Anda-ra's bright presence behind the tasting counter.

"Ready to give notice at the slave market?"

"What do you mean?"

"I asked my father for his blessing, and he'd not only given it happily, he's invited us to live together on the uppermost floor. Andara, we'll have our own place that's ten times bigger than anywhere we'd be able to live in the City, and our business will be but a few steps below us!"

Andara's eyes widened with her smile. Then she saw that the Arbiter himself approached, his arms open toward her. "Congratulations, dear girl. Please know that this is now your home, and you are as near to me as my children."

"Oh, Morvedraz, thank you!"

"Only tell me if Nore is not treating you with the care you deserve, and I shall make certain to admonish her." Morvedraz smiled.

Andara shook her head. "I will do my best to contribute to your family."

"My family is now yours, daughter."

Morvedraz patted Andara's cheek, then retired upstairs.

"Wow, you've certainly charmed my father. Now let's see if you can charm a few *zeks* out of our tasters." Nore winked.

Word traveled at the speed of the Daystar's rays, and soon the full length of the shop counter stood three deep with wealthy citizens clamoring for a taste in the company of the Arbiter's delightful daughter and companion. The *zeks* flowed as copiously as did the wine, with many patrons leaving with multiple cases, and when Nore tallied up the shop's earnings in the evening she discovered that she and Andara had, indeed, set a sales record the likes they'd seen only during times of preparation for high holidays, or when Zhakhar needed to replenish the Chalice's broad inventory.

"My father will be most pleased! Look at our final numbers for the day."

"I should think that with such a sum we'd be earning our rent quite handsomely."

"Come. Let's lock up and go upstairs to tell him"

"Wait. We have glasses to wash, and the bottle racks should be replenished tonight so we won't have to worry about rushing in the morning."

Nore grimaced and shook her head. "We'll let Koloran deal with that. Come on."

"*Nore.*" Andara squinted chidingly. "It was *our* counter for the day. It should be our responsibility to take care of it properly, not foist the drudgery onto your poor brother.

He has enough to do behind the scenes as it is. And, since you and I have just received your father's blessing that we should be partners—in all dealings—I think it would be an excellent example to set that no task is beneath us."

Nore sighed. "You're right."

"So, I'll start on these glasses if you want to take a hand truck and bring a few new cases from downstairs."

"Ugh, I *hate* bringing wine up those stairs."

"Alright, fine. *I'll* go lug some wine upstairs. You can wash." Andara paused, then added: "Still want to join with me now that you know what a task mistress I am? Now's your only chance to get out."

"Silly..."

Nore watched Andara's smirk widen, then gazed after her when she disappeared down the stairs toward the storage cellar. Sighing once more, she donned an apron and began filing the sink behind the tasting counter with hot water and soap. She was arm's- deep in suds when Morvedraz and Koloran walked through the door from the main part of the building. Nore looked over her shoulder and paused, watching the two stop and stare with open mouths.

"What?" Nore puzzled.

"Sister, you're washing glasses."

"Yeah?"

"You *never* wash glasses."

"Well, like Andara said, it was our room for the day, so it's our responsibility to maintain it."

"Ha!" Koloran exclaimed. "I think I am going to enjoy having Andara here with us. And, congratulations, Sister. I wish you both much happiness." Koloran smiled broadly.

"Thank you, Brother." Nore shook her head but smiled, and continued to wash.

"Koloran," Morvedraz began, "our first clients will arrive shortly. Please greet them while I prepare the Arbiter's chambers."

"Father, *I* should prepare the room. You do me too much honor too soon."

"Nonsense. The sooner you're seen in the position, the sooner clients will become accustomed to you, and word will spread that the shift has taken place."

Nore noticed that Morvedraz spoke quickly, and with confidence, but puzzled over the conversation.

"Nore," Morvedraz spoke and motioned toward his daughter. "Come here, please."

Nore dried her hands and walked to the other side of the counter to stand before her father and brother.

"I know you'd hoped to assume the role, but I have chosen otherwise. I hope that you will understand—if not now, then in time—why Koloran will be Arbiter. He shall sit tonight in the role, I beside him as counselor."

Nore sighed slightly and glanced downward, then nodded and placed her hand on Koloran's arm and looked directly into his eyes. "You will succeed. My heart is with you." Then she placed her arms around his narrow yet muscled shoulders and embraced him, felt only a little surprise that her formerly shy and retiring brother returned the embrace full on.

"Father, you have made the best choice. I will support Koloran always, in any way I'm able."

"I know you will, Daughter."

"I will prepare the Arbiter's chamber," Nore insisted. "It's only fitting that you should greet those arriving together."

"Thank you, Leonora."

Nore nodded once more, then bounded upstairs to tidy the space and replenish the *blakwine* and *kororah* sticks that always accompanied such dealings.

Morvedraz saw the creases of concern that were visible on the faces of the two parties—one a wealthy building owner, the other the tenant who'd proposed to lease space to start a business importing goods from lands near and far; they were some of the farther lands—and the goods they offered—that had given the owner sufficient trepidation to cause him to deny the use for which his tenant had already proposed—at least he'd indicated thusly in his indictment against the tenant. The problem was that the lengthy lease had already been signed by both parties.

But further confusion shone clearly on the face of both landlord and tenant, for they'd each heard of Koloran, had seen him silently serving the wine shop's function, yet had experienced only of his attendant nature, and that he was never known to have accompanied the Arbiter during any negotiations.

"Gentlemen, welcome. You know of my son, Koloran. I have most important news to share with you regarding his role in our dealings tonight, and in all future dealings, such as they may be. But let us take up residence in the Arbiter's chamber and I will explain."

Morvedraz stepped aside, as did Koloran, and held a wide, welcoming arm toward the staircase that led to the chamber above the wine shop. Each noticed that both landlord and tenant gave one another a quizzical look and even shrugged, slightly yet visibly, before one followed the other up the narrow stairwell.

Morvedraz felt that this first arbitration would be as trying for Koloran as for the disputing parties, perhaps more so. But he judged that this particular disagreement was founded more on the conceit of a very conservative owner versus the young and brash entrepreneur wishing to light out and make his fortune: the former, a certain Marcaldo of a patrician *Humani* family that had dwelt in the City for generations—and had collected as much amassed wealth—and the latter, a young Za-Zhirazani who'd purported to be a distant relative of Zhakhar of the Black Chalice himself, though this remained as yet unsubstantiated, who'd only resided in the City a scant six months before approaching Marcaldo with the lease proposition.

True, the property had lain empty on the market for quite some time, located in a lesser part of one of the waterfront districts more akin to dead warehouse space than active commerce. But, as they said in Antran real estate, the deal closed as the Great River's current flowed. Marcaldo, it was well known, held so many properties in the City that he'd become more of an absentee landlord, collecting the tens of thousands of monthly *zeks* from dozens of leases and conducting himself more often to the wine shop and the pleasure districts than to his family's offices. So, it was a surprise to many in commercial dealings why he'd made such a fuss about young Ankhar's use of the space.

Morvedraz had made discreet inquiries, of course, and had discovered what he believed to be Marcaldo's true motive; it seemed that Ankhar's youth did not belie his skill at negotiating a commercial lease, and that in doing so had convinced the somewhat inebriated Marcaldo to sign over a term that included a lengthy duration of free rent, ten thousand *zeks* space improvement allowance, and, while agreeing to yearly rent escalators, the deal would not cost Ankhar more than what he'd saved with rent waiver. Marcaldo remained, so Morvedraz had discovered, embarrassed by the bungled deal and wished to somehow save face. And Morvedraz felt certain that a few points of finer details of the lease that spelled out specificities required of each party, bandied back and forth, along with the slightest invocation of the amulet, would leave each pliant toward some kind of mutual agreement in no time.

Morvedraz watched as first Marcaldo, then Ankhar, then Koloran bowed to enter the chamber room, for each had to, the entry more befitting *Dwarvani* stature. And when Morvedraz himself moved into the soothing light he felt his heart swell with love for his daughter, who had not only shown her maturity of late in choosing Andara, but in affirming her devotion to Koloran, as both sister and protector. She'd spent only a swift few moments before the chamber would be occupied by the negotiating parties, but had managed to transform the space into such a welcoming and warm room that Morvedraz saw a look of comfortable ease play even upon crusty old Marcaldo's face. The wall sconces all shined with fresh, long and elegant tapers; the wine and *blakwine* racks were stocked and the bottles properly dusted and glinting in the candlelight; the table, that often saw the rougher part of debates, sparkled clean and reflected each who sat around its perimeter; even the receptacle that held the spent *kororah* ashes had been emptied and polished.

"First, thank you for the aid of your services, Arbiter. I'm sure that Marcaldo is as appreciative of your expertise as am I. And must I say that your chamber bespeaks the success and honor that precede you." Ankhar spoke with voice both bright and swift, as soon as the parties had seated themselves around the wide, round table, attempting to assert his presence that his graciousness not to be bested.

"The Arbiter would no soon as doubt my gratitude any more than I would his probity," Marcaldo countered, "since I have sat many times in his presence within the small confines of this very chamber in negotiations both lengthy and heated. However, it does look quite well appointed this evening."

"Yes, yes, please be it noted for the record that both the gracious gentlemen have paid me tribute in the grandest fashion and that their sentiments are most appreciated in kind." Morvedraz spoke with casual yet happy disregard for both Ankhar's obsequious ambition and Marcaldo's grumpy arrogance. "But tonight is not only an important night for your business partnership, but for mine as well. Great changes are coming, both for me, and for the City in its entirety, and you two shall sit as witness to a monumental shift in Antran commerce."

"What are you saying, Morvedraz?" Marcaldo grumbled.

"What I am saying, old friend Marcaldo, is that tonight, as of this moment, I retire as Arbiter of Antra."

Morvedraz watched the smiles, then the color, fade from both Marcaldo's and Ankhar's faces, and he had to admit a sense of satisfaction for catching them both so visibly off guard. At the same time, what he'd feared to find in Koloran's face—some flushed shade of apprehension—he saw shone of nothing of the sort. Instead, Koloran beamed a fitting, confident smile and looked coolly yet agreeably on both the shocked faces across from him.

"What do you mean, *retire*?" Marcaldo glowered. "You don't retire from being Arbiter! That's like retiring from being Regent of the *Maj*! Like...retiring from *life*!"

"And what of our negotiations?" Ankhar's voice had suddenly taken on a tight, high-pitched tone that had not shown in the previous moment, and his eyes darted unchecked between Morvedraz and Koloran.

"The role of Arbiter is not only my responsibility, but my creation. I decide its boundaries. Your negotiations shall proceed. And I will be present. Yet they will be led by my son, Koloran. The new Arbiter of Antra."

Morvedraz gazed at the shocked, petrified faces of each negotiating party and waited for who would lodge the first protest. Fittingly, it would be Marcaldo.

"Why, this is unacceptable! It's *outrageous*! How can serious businessmen sit and expect, in front of their very faces, that a mere shop keeper's son should not only be unceremoniously anointed Arbiter, but that he—having demonstrated no prior experience or training—should be fit to preside over complex and lengthy negotiations!"

"Yes," piped Ankhar, in the same fitful squeak as before, his brow now beaded in sweat. "I must say that I, too, protest."

Morvedraz laughed under his breath and waved a dismissive hand at each offended party. "First, *ceremony* beyond those that have taken place in the confines of this room have never graced the role of Arbiter, I can assure you utterly; the title is rarely voiced, and then only in tones hushed and furtive and safely behind the high walls of very wealthy compounds. Secondly, yes, of course, your reservations are noted. But your case, Marcaldo, is neither complex, nor should it take much time to resolve."

Ankhar's drawn facial features perked for a moment, sensing some advantage in Morvedraz' admonition to Marcaldo.

"Don't get your hopes too terribly high, Ankhar. You've had a significant part to play in this little farce as well."

Both Marcaldo and Ankhar now squirmed in the soft, padded velvet on which they sat, both glancing as mistrustfully at one another as they each did toward Morvedraz, who simply sat and stared resolutely at the two. Hoping that Koloran would understand this silent indication as a segue for his participation, Morvedraz screwed up his craggy Dwarvani face and glared at each party with an equally distasteful look in his eyes. And as he'd wished, Koloran understood the cue perfectly. He stood, arms wide, his voice deeply magnanimous.

"Gentlemen. Respected Marcaldo, ambitious Ankhar. First, let *me* say to *you* that you are *most* welcome in these chambers: Marcaldo, certainly as you have always been, a worthy and trusted associate of Morvedraz; and Ankhar as a new acquaintance, and, I hope, prosperous client who will return as your ventures multiply. And let me also say this: I am both honored and humbled simply to sit in your presence as you negotiate a fitting settlement to your agreement, however, taking part and allowing that arrangement to succeed and flourish for you both is my most cherished ambition."

Morvedraz glanced up at Koloran, whose presence had clearly affected both the disputing parties, for they each now clung to hear the young man's next words.

"You are both absolutely correct—technically, and morally—to question the appointment of a new Arbiter prior to your negotiations, and, indeed, in your very presence, with no warning, no hint that any such distraction might detract from the gravity of your arguments. But, let me assure you that my appointment was neither a furtive deception nor a hastily-wrought decision. And, if you might hear me out, I believe I will be able to convince you that my father's intention in bringing me to bear on your case will prove not only invaluable experience to me, but, given the freshness of my insight, might prove an advantage to each of you."

Morvedraz watched Koloran pause, motion to sit, then, as if a flash of inspiration materialized into thought, stand again:

"I will go so far to say that, if you all would allow—Father, you included—if you hear me out, I will assure each of you that while the origin of my role as Arbiter might appear momentary to you, my preparation has been as lengthy as my instruction has been expert. Wise Marcaldo, strong Ankhar, I vow to you this: that someday those who would cross wits in this chamber and leave with equal satisfaction on all sides will envy the likes of the two who *first* sat in counsel before the second Arbiter of Antra."

Morvedraz did all he could to contain a broad smile, indeed had to literally bite his own tongue lest he give up a laugh with the swelling pride and joyful satisfaction it brought him, listening not only to Koloran's shrewd strategy, but his convincing oratory, watching his deft movement. Where had his skill come from? With whom had he practiced? Truly, Morvedraz had felt himself slipping as Koloran had observed, yet far, far longer ago than over these recent troubles. He knew that to continue as Arbiter would put himself in danger, and that if he did not appoint a successor, might well put Koloran and Nore at risk as well. What would happen if, disadvantaged by his lessening faculties and now palpable fear of the amulet, he let a negotiation get out of control, turn business adversaries into violent enemies? Warring factions could well take revenge on him, his business, his family. No, it was time to quit. Immediately. And, while he'd lately been astounded at Koloran's stature of personality, he'd decided to forego any such lengthy apprenticeship that the duties of Arbiter might wisely require, but, simply, having chosen Koloran, throw him into the role as Morvedraz had thrown himself so many years before.

What Morvedraz could not have expected was that Koloran would not simply inhabit the role with force, grace and aplomb, but that he would embrace it.

Morvedraz watched the now vastly subdued Marcaldo and Ankhar settle into their cushions and await the new Arbiter's direction, wondering how Koloran had invoked the amulet to cast onto the parties this obvious pliancy. He'd not watched his son's hand disappear for even a moment beneath his robe, had not seen him clutch nor even apply the slightest pressure to the front of the material to engage the stone around his neck in the slightest degree. Yet, Marcaldo and Ankhar sat, the prior tension visible in their faces receded, now quietly listening.

"Gentleman, I have reviewed, under my father's scrupulous guidance, the entirety of your lease agreement for the harbor-front property. Marcaldo, the paragraph that spells out the legal use of the space clearly and generally states that 'warehousing, office work, trade, and/or any other legal use' are appropriate activities under the agreed-upon lease. Would you disagree with that in any way?"

The now somewhat groggy-looking Marcaldo squinted, shook his head slightly, and said simply, "No."

"And would you further agree that Ankhar's proposed purpose for the space—to participate in the trade of imported goods, all of legal status under the requirements of the Regent of the *Maj*—is an appropriate use, as spelled out in the lease?"

"I would."

Morvedraz noticed that the subdued yet still frenetic-looking Ankhar could not contain his excitement over the exchange.

"Now, Ankhar," Koloran continued, "clearly it is within your right to conduct your business under the terms of this lease. However, there remains, shall we say, a question regarding the *circumstances* under which these terms were negotiated."

The ferret-like Ankhar now squirmed anew. "What is it that you mean?"

"Ankhar, is Marcaldo not only a respected but *proven* businessman?"

"Why, yes. One of the most honored in the City."

"Of course. And would such a seasoned and skilled negotiator have agreed to such terms of rent and allowances so that the balance of the entire lease would yield to him a negative return?"

Morvedraz watched as Ankhar only stared wide-eyed at Koloran, his mouth closed, the sweat that had gathered on his brow now trailing its way, bead by bead, down his face.

"It would be...unusual," Ankhar gave up after a long pause.

"*Most* unusual, indeed," Koloran responded immediately, clipping the end of Ankhar's final word. "So unusual, in fact, that in all the trade records kept since such accounting has been performed, never once has one party, their adversary's negotiating acumen notwithstanding, *ever* agreed to such terms."

Morvedraz stared intently at Koloran, saw the graceful features of his face transform, until the visage that shone its hot anger toward Ankhar hardly resembled Morvedraz' gentle son at all.

"Ankhar," Koloran, continued, leaning now toward and towering over the young Za-Zhirazani with never-before demonstrated power, "do you realize how many thousands of agreements that would be?"

"I would imagine—"

"*Tens* of thousands."

"But, would not a sound negotiator use any method that might bring him advantage...?"

Koloran's indirect assertion was all that it took, for Ankhar now knew implicitly that his deception had been discovered, despite his futile attempt to influence the new Arbiter.

"*Nearly* any, yes. But to lace the wine glass of he with whom you negotiate to dull his senses even more than the fermented grape essence is not only unfair, it is, in the City of Antra, a criminal act."

"Oh, my," Ankhar attempted weakly, "I am, of course, still unfamiliar with many of the laws of the great City..."

Upon hearing the assertion that he'd been drugged into agreeing upon the lease, Marcaldo stood, albeit uneasily, having to hold onto the edge of the table to steady himself, and growled at Ankhar.

"Why, you little snake! I should have listened to the Board of Commerce when they recommended that I reject your bid for my property!"

"Now, now, Marcaldo." Koloran spoke with force yet with a soothing lilt to his voice that subdued the old *Humani* and rendered him back into his seat. "Let us not invoke the ire of the Gods by turning their wild creatures into pejorative metaphors and thus insulting their creators. For once we have edited the obviously, shall we say, *mistakenly* written sections of the lease, not only will you realize a small profit, but your adjacent properties' values will be well enhanced by the simple virtue that Ankhar's business will attract a physical clientele, not merely horses and carts to load and unload goods. He will, indeed, generate active commerce, to his benefit, and thus to yours. His success will be yours in kind.

"Now, gentlemen, I have, with my father's explicit guidance, drawn up a new lease. Here is a copy for you both. Please review the section that spells out Rent, the revised addendum that defines the allowance for improvements, initial in the bottom right-hand corner of each page, and sign and date the last where indicated."

Morvedraz tried as best he could to contain the surprise that his wide eyes and raised brows gave up, and felt glad that both Marcaldo and Ankhar pored scrupulously over the lease documents in their hands and paid no attention to the former Arbiter. For Morvedraz had not in the least sense given Koloran any general instruction in the writing of a commercial lease agreement, let alone the specificities of terms.

Each party read the revised paragraph, that permitted *three* months free rent instead of *thirty*, on a term of five years; the ten thousand *zek* allowance for building improvements had been reduced to five thousand.

"As for you, Ankhar, I'm sure that the honorable Marcaldo would be more than willing to attribute his prior agreement of thirty month's free rent to a misplaced zero that had been, quite obviously, a significant yet simply undetected error. And, Marcaldo, having now a fittingly modest yet enforceable lease for your property, a suitable profit, and the benefit that Ankhar's success will surely bring you both, I don't imagine that signing the new agreement will be a problem."

Both Marcaldo and Ankhar signed the new lease without hesitation, and while they glanced at each other with still mistrustful gazes, they each looked thankfully upon the new Arbiter of Antra.

Koloran continued: "The details of all other discoveries that have been discussed in this chamber will never leave these walls. Now, if you please, gentlemen, the original leases."

Each party willingly handed to Koloran the original lease documents, which he immediately tossed into the flames of the chamber's stoked fireplace.

"As you both know, gentlemen, the arrangement reached in this room is ultimately binding. There exists no higher council of arbitration. So, go forward in agreement, and may you both prosper in kind."

Koloran held his hand out, first to Marcaldo, then to Ankhar; each took the open palm into his own and quietly uttered in thanks, "Arbiter," each giving both Koloran and Morvedraz a respectful bow as they exited the chambers.

"Ha! My boy! You have no idea the pride I feel at this moment!" Morvedraz beamed at Koloran, lifting the open bottle of Kwamadan brandy and tipping it toward the not-quite-empty snifter that sat neglected in front of him. Koloran raised his hand and placed it flat onto the glass's orifice.

"Please, Father, I'm not nearly done with my first pour. And I'm afraid that another will only go straight to my head."

"Ah, very well. Forgive my indulgence. And, while we must deal with our troubles in the morning, tonight we celebrate your performance! Koloran, I do not believe that I, myself, could have dealt as swiftly and deftly as you did with those two. Your powers of perception are high, indeed. And, while we had the basic information from our sources, the manner in which you presented it was masterful beyond my skill."

"Thank you, Father. Indeed, it felt almost—how should I say—*natural* to engage both Marcaldo and Ankhar. I felt no trepidation whatsoever. It felt as if the words I spoke to them simply manifested in my mind, as if placed there by some beneficent force. In fact, engaging them felt...*easy*."

"Easy! My boy, you have no idea the benefits this negotiation will reap you, simple as it was. Satisfying Marcaldo would have been reward enough, but taming Ankhar as well! Each will relate long tales of your wisdom and judiciousness to all who will listen. Koloran, your power as Arbiter will rise swiftly, indeed."

Koloran feigned a smile and lifted his brandy, felt the sweet, hot liquid only touch his lips, and placed the snifter back onto the table, staring at the glass's swirling golden liquid. All he'd said to his father was true: he'd felt complete ease, eloquence, total control over the two men whose combined prowess and experience should have vastly overshadowed Koloran's. He only felt unease because he had no idea from whence this ability had come.

"But, Koloran, please, tell me something."

"Yes, Father?"

"How is it that you invoked the amulet?"

Koloran wrinkled his brow and looked at his father with widened eyes.

"What do you mean, Father?"

"The amulet! When I watched both surly old Marcaldo and brash young Ankhar swoon in their places I *knew* you'd somehow secretly and skillfully applied the amulet's power of pliancy onto them!"

Koloran glanced about the interior of the chamber, at the candles that had almost burned completely down, at the wooden walls that tapered upward toward the vent through which he could gaze upon the small circle of stars shimmering in the Antran night. He looked at his brandy glass on the table, placed his hand around it to ensure himself that it—as well as the surroundings of the chamber—were, indeed, real, then responded to his father's assertion.

"Father, I did not engage the amulet."

Koloran watched Morvedraz' face wrinkle.

"What in the Gods' names are you saying?"

"The amulet. I didn't use it. In fact, I wasn't even wearing it." Saying so, Koloran opened the wrapped seam of his robes and displayed to his father his smooth bare chest and empty neck.

"But, where is it? You could not have left it in your room—"

"Certainly not, Father. I placed it in the hidden alcove, on the platform next to the tablets themselves."

Koloran watched his father rise from the table to the rear wall of the chamber, never shifting his gaze from his son, depress the stone that sent the lines of blue light streaming toward floor and ceiling to outline the seam of the passage. Morvedraz waited until the hidden doors had parted completely before stepping inside. Koloran then rose and followed his father into the alcove, the blue opalescent light now swirling all around, and stepped forward to stand next to his father in the room's deepest space; there, just to the left of the recessed tablets, and glowing the mild blue light like them, sat the amulet, its golden-laced cord still attached to it and wrapped concentrically around where it had been placed, just how Koloran had left it.

Wait. Koloran thought, then suddenly remembered: *I didn't loop the cord around it like that. I just set it on the counter without paying any mind to how the cord lay. Could I have placed it so and simply not remembered?*

"Oh, thank the Gods..." Koloran heard his father say, then felt the weight of hand on shoulder.

"Thank you for using proper judgment to store the amulet securely. But, Koloran, we must discuss the abilities you displayed at length, and how you have plied them without any *majikal* assistance."

"I did not use the amulet, Father." Koloran spoke with resolute volume and strength. "However, I'm not convinced that, somehow, *it* did not use *me*."

The Great River had coursed its way around the City of Antra for tens of thousands of the Daystar's cycles, the swift, frigid current carving the deep canyon that guarded the metropolis's southern border. Stepping into the river's strength meant danger to most, even those who could swim with expertise, unaccustomed to both the water's speed and its brutal cold. The combination of these two elements forced onto one who would be *thrown* into the river from the high cliffs, his limbs bound so that he had not even the chance to flail toward the shore, should prove fatal. But there began the series of contradictions that saved the otherwise doomed Valthan of Leth: the cold woke him from his beaten unconsciousness; the fast water carried him away from the City toward more friendly confines; the carpet into which he'd been bound prevented him from loosing his strength in a vain attempt to swim against the river's force.

Zhakhar's emissaries had, of course, assumed that, once plunged into the frigid water, the carpet would become saturated and, after only moments of allowing the disgraced Lethani to ponder his tortuously shortened life, sink into the river's freezing depths, drowning Valthan in the process. What the emissaries did not know was that the carpet's material—a highly-prized wool from a province near the Dwarvani kingdom—repelled water with such effectiveness that the carpet might as well have been as impervious as the stone of the cliffs towering over the river. Instead of encasing him in his tomb as they'd intended, the emissaries had unwittingly provided Valthan with the most suitable flotation device he could have ever fashioned. And it was this very rug, meant to drag him to his death, that ultimately saved his life.

The rags they'd stuffed into Valthan's mouth to silence his moaning had served to staunch the heavy bleeding that had poured from the base of his severed tongue. Though his blood loss had been profuse the combination of the pressure from the rags and the cold of the water had eventually stopped the flow of blood. Valthan's own semi-conscious condition aided him in that it calmed him sufficiently so that his heart had slowed to a rate near death, further allowing the wound to curtail its bleeding but still maintaining just enough flow to oxygenate his brain.

When the river's rush subsided many miles from the City of Antra, the carpet that carried Valthan finally stalled its progress in a relatively calm pool that jutted into the right bank. There the carpet floated for many hours while its inhabitant suffered fatigue and grievous thirst despite lying inches from the cold, fresh water. This should have been Valthan's end, indeed, were it not for the most unlikely of circumstances. A party of barbarian thieves, wanted as criminals throughout the kingdom, had side-stepped the more widely travelled roads and lit out into the barren wilderness to avoid confrontation from those who sought their capture. Searching for a suitable place to camp for the night, they scanned the horizon and saw through the telescope's lense what looked like an outcropping of rock that appeared to border the Great River. A half-hour's ride toward the site offered them more than they'd hoped for: a shield against the elements, a calm pool from which to drink and water their horses, and—

But, what was that? A tubular object, some eight feet in length, lapping at the shoreline. It's crimson color shone brightly against the tan mud of the bank and blackish-green water. They examined the item up close, determining that it was, indeed, a rolled up carpet, and that it looked to be extremely well-made, so much so that they'd decided to extract it from the shallows, dry it out with hopes that they could sell it, or trade for it. When they heard the rolled carpet groan, they dropped it onto the sandy bank, cut the cords that held it closed and unfurled its length. The barbarian leader did not at first recognize the *Humani*, still and pale, waterlogged and gaunt, breathing shallowly. But after they'd stripped his soaked clothes, wrapped him in a clean blanket and propped him next to their fire, the leader realized two things: one, that the ruined clothes the *Humani* had worn were made of some of the most expensive silk the leader had ever seen; and, two, that the *Humani's* features, despite their bloated look, having been saturated in water for many hours, appeared familiar.

When they pulled away the rags the wound that had sealed against the course cloth reopened, and blood now poured again from Valthan's mouth. The barbarian leader knew that there was only one way to stop the bleeding for good and thus give the *Humani* a chance: the wound must be cauterized.

"I'm sorry in advance, my friend, for having to do this. But, as I believe you *are* a friend, I fear it's the only way to save your life."

Four barbarians held Valthan's limbs and torso against the ground, two secured his head from moving while another plugged his nose to force open him mouth, then the leader pressed the white-hot metal against the bleeding wound. Valthan let out a ragged scream that only subsided when he lost consciousness. But the bleeding had stopped.

He slept for an entire cycle of the Daystar, awoke only when the barbarian leader had decided that they could no longer afford to tarry by the river. Jerking awake from the nudge of the leader's boot, Valthan at first tried to crawl away. Then, realizing in front of whom he sat, attempted to speak.

"Do not lose your strength over that which you have no control, friend. I fear your ability to speak has been, shall we say, severed. But, do this. Nod once if the answer to my question is affirmative, twice if negative."

Taking the barbarian's direction, Valthan nodded once in acknowledgement.

"Are you of the region of Leth?"

Valthan nodded once.

"Would you be acquainted with raider Loknar?"

Again, Valthan gave one nod.

"Were you not the *Humani* that first struck a trading partnership with Loknar, giving him his start in business?"

Once more, and now with wide, hopefully eyes, Valthan nodded once.

"Very well. Despite your distorted condition I thought I recognized you, if from nothing but the robes you'd worn. You would then be Valthan of Leth."

Tears streamed down Valthan's eyes, and he slumped forward and hugged the barbarian's boots.

"Enough of that. We are acquainted with each other, this much is true. Loknar is my cousin, once removed, and has spoken highly of you and your sponsorship. He has grown quite well-to-do from your association. I recall seeing a painting of the two of you in his manor. He holds you in very high regard. So, I hope that you will hold me and my company in equal light if we would help you to mend yourself and get you back home away from whatever trouble has befallen you."

Valthan righted himself and wiped the tears away from his swollen face. He tried to speak, then, realizing that speech would not serve him again, simply gave the barbarian one affirmative nod.

Another of Valthan's advantages that had served him over the years, despite the trouble he had encountered in conducting business, was that he had grown, simply, extraordinarily wealthy. However, his liquid wealth remained secured at his home city in Leth, and cast into the wilderness he had no resources whatsoever with which to repay the barbarian leader. But after several hours of pains-taking negotiation—the barbarian posing questions and offers, Valthan nodding until his neck hurt—the two came to an arrangement that would not only deliver Valthan back home, but would restore his power of speech.

"The method is as expensive as it is delicate, but I know of one apothecary who has performed the procedure before with a good margin of success. I will take you to him after having secured payment for your transport."

Thus the barbarians nursed Valthan as best they could so that he could be placed onto horseback without falling off, and began the long, hot journey through the open desert toward Leth. After many days of avoiding both man and beast, under the sweltering sun of the Antran wilderness, the party finally pulled into the long, tree-lined gravel path that led to Valthan's estate. Upon seeing their master supported on the shoulders of two barbarians, Valthan's servants ran from the house to take him into their care. They washed him and clothed him in silken robes, then tucked him into bed. The barbarians were safe at the remote estate, and Valthan indicated to his servants with the aid of quill and parchment that the visitors should be well cared for. For three days the barbarians ate and drank their fill from the estate's vast stocks, the servants hurrying to fulfill their every request. By the fourth day Valthan had gained enough strength for the next leg of the journey.

After three days' ride the barbarians, with Valthan in tow, road into a small town on the outskirts of Leth. There appeared little activity, and few inhabitants, but there, in the middle of a narrow dead-end street was a storefront, and above its bay window the Lethani word for 'Apothecary.'

The procedure took the better part of the next day, for the surgery was as intricate as it was costly. But for ten thousand gold *zeks* Valthan of Leth had purchased not simply a prosthetic, but an actual live replacement tongue;

from whom it had been harvested no one mentioned, and Valthan did not ask. The barbarians again accompanied Valthan to his estate and partook of his generosity at will. For the barbarian's troubles, Valthan parted with another ten thousand *zeks*, and after several more days of healing finally tried out his new muscle. He thought it felt familiar—though longer than his original—and while his speech sounded somewhat thicker it was more than intelligible.

"I cannot thank you enough. Please, consider my home an outpost when you are in the area, whether I am here or not. I will instruct my servants to welcome you in kind."

"My thanks to you, Valthan. You've made my path toward early retirement all the shorter. Enjoy your new-found gift of speech. And may you avoid the circumstances that took it from you in the first place."

Valthan nodded once—a commemorating gesture to the Barbarian leader's help—then waved as he watched the horde disappear into the rising desert dust. Retiring to his study, Valthan took a mug of *blakwine* and sat at the broad desk that overlooked the orchards and verdant grassland of his estate, and began the careful planning for exacting grievous revenge on Zhakhar of the City of Antra.

Up the steps we go. What we'll find, nobody knows.
Khaleo felt far less fear than perhaps he should, silently ascending the circular steps from the bowels of the Black Chalice in hopes to find an equally deserted level, yet stocked with far more than the empty wine barrels he'd discovered below. When he came to the stairs' end at yet another closed doorway he placed his hand on the lever and applied pressure to it as slowly and evenly as he could. The latch raised in the same slow care with which it had been engaged, and Khaleo pushed until the door gave way. Darkness met him on the other side, for which he felt most thankful; perhaps this floor had been neglected as had the

lower. But the air in this corridor smelled fresher, as if it had been replenished from above more recently than the lower, and there lingered no mildewed smell of neglect. He struck the flint against the stone wall and lit his torch and saw to his dismay that yet another long hall of opposing doorways met his beleaguered gaze.

He sighed. *Very well. Perhaps this search will yield more useful discoveries.*

And, indeed, his search proved far more fruitful on this level of the Chalice. Behind the first door he found row upon row of stacked, pre-made torches and pallets of the materials required to make even more, and buckets full of flints. Clearly, Zhakhar would not be allowing the Chalice to dim in the slightest, and Khaleo shook his head at the thought of the poor sod who'd sit in this dank room for hour upon hour, wrapping cloth around lengths of pole and binding the cloth with kerosene-soaked twine.

Now that Khaleo's lighting needs were solved, he continued onto the next room, where blankets and bedding lay stacked in racking around the room's perimeter. In yet another he found tools and hardware of various sorts, and while he could not immediately think of a need for most of the items therein, he spied in a corner one loan wooden bucket with a wide opening and looped handle; though the thought of what he'd use it for made him grimace, he knew he'd no other option for the time being. He continued to explore the storerooms, hoping for items as exotic as weaponry or armor, but finding none. What he did find, however, made him feel as thankful as he did ravenous for both food and drink: in one room, barrel after barrel stenciled with the Antran block lettering for, 'potable water,' and in yet another dried, spiced meat hung to cure. There remained still a dozen-odd doors yet to open, but the site of the food and water made Khaleo grasp for as many strands of the jerked meat as he could stuff into the burlap bag he'd found. He filled three leather water flasks, grabbed blankets and a few extra torches, and made his way back toward the stairwell downward.

His timing could not have been better, for just as he'd almost closed the door that sealed the stairs, he heard the muffled yet exuberant voices of what could only be two of Zhakhar's henchmen entering the hallway from the opposite end. Of course, because the length of the hallway made the darkness stretch before them, they'd be unable to see to the opposing side where Khaleo paused to eavesdrop on their conversation, and thus stood ready to receive what he considered at the time quite good news.

"Ha! Ehrg, why does Zhakhar insist on keeping our stores at such a depth within the Chalice? My knees ache simply getting here let alone hauling the stuff back up."

"He used to keep it on the same floor as the main room, but then caught a number of employees helping themselves to food and wine in a very deliberate and organized manner, and nearly at will. The employees were 'terminated,' shall we say, and the stores were plunged into the depths beyond easy grasp."

"Well, better those fools than you and me. Let's get our pull and be gone."

"Aye, Dhelorth."

"Say, have you heard news of this Khaleo person? I understand that the search for him produced not a shred of a lead. How could someone simply vanish into a city in which some of the less-than-savory citizens would sell their own cousins for a copper *zek* or two?"

"I can't imagine. I heard that Malik himself offered his resignation to Zhakhar for failing to apprehend the fugitive. Of course the master would hear none of it and only thanked Malik for his efforts. But it is strange, that our cohorts could not come up with even a single person who'd seen so much as a glimpse of one with shifting-colored hair and golden eyes."

"It leads you to believe one thing, does it not?"

"What's that?"

"That either this Khaleo has mastered the *majik* of invisibility, or he has discovered a hiding place so effective that he eludes even the skillful emissaries of the most shrewd and ruthless merchant in the City."

"If he has made such a discovery, he'd do best to maintain it with all his strength. For I cringe at what will befall the stranger should Zhakhar succeed in uncovering his whereabouts."

"Indeed, Ehrg. Indeed."

Khaleo shuddered, then pulled the stairwell door secure and descended to his *almost* perfect hiding place.

Khaleo, despite his derisive feelings toward Zhakhar and his entire network of cohorts, still held high regard for the sheer skill of the master of the Black Chalice. How could he have maintained such prowess in a City known for so high degrees of competition in the less-than-spoken avenues of commerce? What Khaleo did not realize was that one of Zhakhar's traits that guarded his status was that, for as expert as he was at the practice and execution of his more visible and flashy areas of expertise—commanding the small army of deadly emissaries who fought at his will, the ability to deal with criminals as wealthy and powerful as Valthan of Leth in such swift and lethal circumstances—he remained just as scrupulous in the far more mundane details required in running an establishment like the Black Chalice.

To guard against internal "shrinkage" of inventory, Zhakhar bid a wall-to-wall count be conducted of the Chalice's entire contents once a month, with specific employees assigned to specific goods and areas within the general stores of the Chalice; he kept the areas small, staggered their count frequency, and assigned at least two counters to each, such that, to complete an entire inventory of all goods counting would take place almost every day of the month. And Zhakhar wasn't concerned only with the food, wine and spirits or high-dollar goods, but the stores of absolutely every item under the Chalice's roof, furniture included. Items valued at over the 500 *zek*-level of worth carried asset tags, but all items were coded by hand with their location and their number in series; you could pick up any random torch jutting from a wall sconce along the most remote corridor in the Chalice and see from its tag that it was torch #572 of 700, 5th floor, storeroom 24.

He gave scrupulous instructions to all conducting the inventory that should even the slightest variance be noted from the reams of reconciliation scrolls, that this should be highlighted and brought to Zhakhar's attention as soon as the discrepancy had been discovered, no waiting until the inventory had concluded. So, when Ehrg and Delorth, the two whom Khaleo had listened to from the dark end of the hallway, had completed their task—that of not only fetching provisions for the tavern proper, but completing the monthly inventory in their assigned level—what they presented to Zhakhar raised not only his eyebrows, but his ire.

Zhakhar immediately sent for Malik, captain of his emissaries, to assist in analyzing the discrepancies. Inventory levels on only the fifth lower level of the Chalice—the building's second deepest level—had came up short in several odd categories, and then only in minute amounts, almost as a miscreant child would abscond a few random items from a store's shelves for the mere thrill of doing so. But the fifth level below the Chalice was no retail shop, barely accessible to the few in Zhakhar's employ who had clearance to enter the lower floors, and was certainly not reachable by a random stranger.

"What do you make of these shortages, Malik?"

"They are, I would say, curiously insignificant. Perhaps a faulty count by one of the inventory clerks after stocking the rooms?"

"Perhaps. But all the clerks understand the importance of accuracy, and that I suffer no poor arithmeticians."

"That is true. And, frankly, the staff has been most consistent all year. I recall no other discrepancies to date."

"Correct. Therefore, what may we deduce from the *type* of items that we're short?"

Zhakhar watched Malik puzzle over the question.

"They seem random at best."

"Really? I think not. In fact, I feel they were taken very deliberately."

"How would that be possible?"

"Alright, let me put it this way: torches, blankets, food, water. And in small quantities. Who might such a lowly take benefit?"

"I'm sorry, master Zhakhar. I don't follow you."

"Oh, and here's another detail to consider: from which rooms were the items missing?"

"Why, the ones at the very end of the hallway."

"Right. And which goods are stored in the rooms nearer the entry from the upper floors?"

"There is silverware, crystal and porcelain, fine lace, woolen and silken guest robes—"

"In other words, items that could be sold, that to a thief would be far more valuable."

"Yes, of course."

"And to whom might the shorted items be far more valuable than any of those fineries?"

Zhakhar watched Malik strain in thought, then saw the glimmer of realization flash in his eyes.

"One who would need such items for mere survival!"

"Correct, Malik."

"But, Zakhar, who would possess the ability to infiltrate our stores, and then only in order to provide himself with only provisions enough for a few days and nights?"

Zhakhar smiled at Malik. "I can answer that question, I believe, most definitely, Malik. But first, let me put it to you this way. If, indeed, a thief had made away with these few items that might sustain him, why do you think he'd have taken a heavy wooden bucket from the hardware room?"

"As a means of transport?"

"There are lighter sacks stacked in ample supply in each of the rooms. What other use would a bucket provide? Transport is correct, by the way. But what might a person, say, stranded in a remote place without proper 'services', need to attend to in a most urgent manner?"

"He'd need a waste bucket."

"Exactly!"

"But, Zhakhar, where would such a thief be thusly trapped? And, how in the names of the gods would he have infiltrated perhaps the most secure storeroom in the City?"

"Think about what you've just asked, Malik."

Again Zhakhar watched the lines of concentration on Malik's face as he pondered the information from all angles. After several long, pained moments, Malik's face relaxed and he scowled soberly before answering.

"Because the thief hides within the very rooms from which he has stolen."

"Malik, my most trusted captain, I believe that the Chalice has an unaccounted for border."

"But how could he have penetrated the lower floors of the Chalice? There is but one way, and that is from above."

"If I had to bet, I'd say that the means were *majikal*, and if I'd have to guess I'd say that our old friend Khaleo would be the source. Please assemble a team at once, and, ever so silently, extract him from the depths of our establishment. And, please, send word to Morvedraz that the fugitive that endangered him and his daughter has been found, and that his capture is imminent."

It could not have amounted to a more inelegant position in which Khaleo found himself, squatting in severely needed relief over the wooden bucket after having stuffed every rope of absconded meat jerky into his mouth, swallowed after chewing just barely enough to render the meat digestible, and, after several uneasy minutes in which his stomach and lower extremities grumbled audibly, found himself expelling his too-fast meal, almost in the same shape in which it had been devoured. What he had not taken into consideration was that, having travelled to Antra with provisions raised of his own hand, from is own land, that his constitution would be unable to absorb the rich and spicy fare of the City, and its hidden parasites. And just as the final hot stream of relief splattered into the officially christened chamber-bucket, just as Khaleo himself groaned in ease, the door to the sixth level of the Black Chalice's dead storage room burst open, and the heat of a half dozen blazing torches lit the dim interior to discover a very shocked *Humani* caught in a very shocking position.

The stench of Khaleo's excretions was prominent, and the emissaries' grimaced collectively before rushing forward and dragging the stranger—his pants still around his ankles—up the stairwell and until they'd reached the second floor. A half dozen buckets of water tossed onto him and a rough toweling with burlap made his appearance—and smell—suitable enough for an audience with Zhakhar.

"Friend, Khaleo!" Zhakhar boomed, seeing the fugitive presented, two dagger-wielding emissaries flanking him on either side. Zhakhar sat in his favorite alcove above the main floor the Black Chalice, but when he noticed that Khaleo's garments looked in less than fine condition—in no such condition worthy to press upon the silken pillows of the alcove—Zhakhar scowled and bid the company to the main Chalice floor. When all sat on the rough-hewn benches around a large circular table, Zhakhar bid forth wine and brandy, plates of cheeses and cured meats, of bread and fruit.

"Come, Khaleo, you must be famished after subsiding below on nothing but dust and darkness. Please, help yourself!"

Zhakhar filled a goblet with wine and pushed it toward where Khaleo sat, flanked by armed emissaries.

"Thank you, no. I'm afraid that my stomach is still in a bit of distress."

"Oh, and I see that your Antran has improved vastly! You must have taken advantage of some sort of crash course. A wonder that you've found the time!"

Zhakhar watched Khaleo grimace, and look down though his eyes still trained dagger-like at the master of the Chalice.

"I, um, apologize for my prior deceit. I thought that to speak to you in Antran would have left my goals vulnerable to misinterpretation, and thus undeserved danger."

"On what grounds? That your 'goals' may serve only you and no altruistic advancement of your supposed exiled race?"

"It was only when I slumped at this very table and gazed across the room at the one whom I'd searched for, for years! My own race and blood but a few feet from me! How could I know the reaction I'd cause? Not only from you, but from Leonora herself. Subversion was my only ally. I beg your forgiveness."

"Forgiveness is not my lot to bequeath. Seek that from the Regent of the *Maj*, whom you will have audience with surely."

"You must not turn me over to authorities! I need to speak to Morvedraz and discover..."

"Discover, what?"

But Zhakhar only looked on a now silent and sullen Khaleo, his eyes as downcast as his face. Zhakhar bid him secured within a guest room, a giant Kuzhani emissary tasked to entertain Khaleo within the locked quarters until such time that his transport would be secured to the Regent of the *Maj*.

12

Nore and Andara lazed in bed, warm in each others' embrace, bathed in the Daystar's early rays streaming through the skylight in the far end of their spacious suite atop Morvedraz' family compound after spending their first night together as a true couple, the languid glow of lovemaking still radiating from each their bodies. Koloran, as a gesture of thanks for Nore's support as well as her and Andara's newly established joining, had offered to take over wine counter duties for the day and afford the ladies some time alone to celebrate their union, time that each knew would be short and far between in the near future.

"That was sweet of your brother to give us the day together. He didn't have to do that." Andara whispered into Nore's ear and kissed her shoulder.

"He is a good guy, so kind and genuine. And I think my change of attitude of late has inspired him so much that his gratitude comes easily. You should have seen his face when he saw me with my arms elbows-deep in the wash sink behind the tasting counter yesterday."

"That must have been a shock."

"A very pleasant one, yes. And of course I attributed my new-found dedication to your influence."

"Uh-oh. I have a reputation to uphold now. I'd better be on my best behavior."

"Andara, Koloran *really* likes you. He always has. I mean, you're not his sister, so that's a big advantage right there. But you've always treated him so much better than the clients of the wine shop, who only paid him any attention when they needed a fresh tasting glass, or to pull their wine order from the cellar. You always spoke to him, asked him how he was doing, treated him like a friend, not the help."

"Well, he *is* your brother, after all. Of course I'd want him to like me."

"Yeah, but it's more than that. You *remind* me of him. You treat people with kindness and respect not because you have to, but because it's your *nature* to. Look how you shed tears over Melora at the slave market. The other security people would have probably not paid her more attention than any of the other poor souls on the block that day. But you saw her not as a commodity, but as a person. And I know you've always looked at those who are cast into those roles like that. They've always affected you. That's another reason I didn't want you dedicating your life to the market. It goes against your very essence as a person."

"Wow." Andara propped herself up on her right elbow and looked into the amber of Nore's eyes. "I honestly never knew you paid such close attention to me."

"Well, I *do* love you for more than your looks."

Andara smiled and planted a light kiss onto Nore's lips. "I've been paying pretty close attention to you, too, my love. The wild, brash, headstrong girl I met a little more than a year ago wouldn't have had the attention span to make such observations."

"Well, when my attention is drawn to someone so amazing I can't help but start to look beyond her silken skin and brilliant smile."

The two relaxed again into a soft embrace and dozed. They'd have remained so for the entire morning had not three rapid knocks on their bedroom door jolted them to full consciousness. They then listened to Morvedraz' strained, muffled voice from beyond the closed door.

"Nore, Andara, I apologize for the intrusion, but I must ask for your attendance in my office as soon as possible."

"What's wrong, Father?" Nore called, sitting straight up now.

"Please, it'll be far easier to explain with you two and Koloran assembled together. Come as soon as you can."

Nore and Andara hurried to pull on their leather tunics and boots, then made their way into the office area behind the wine shop proper. There Morvedraz sat at his wide, ornately carved desk with Koloran seated across from his father. Morvedraz motioned toward the chairs around the conference table, and Nore and Andara each took a seat.

"What's happened, Father?"

"One of Zhakhar's emissaries has just left. He brought news that they've found Khaleo."

"What?" Nore's eyes widened. "Where had he been in hiding?"

"In the last place in all of the City that anyone would have thought to look for him: the basement of the Black Chalice itself."

"How in the gods' names could he have found a way into the Chalice? Zhakhar's security is as tight as his accounting."

"Yes, my daughter, I'm well aware of that. Unless he suffers from a security breach of which he is as yet unaware."

"I can't imagine that. He treats is people well, better than any other tavern owner in the City."

"Yes that's true. Such a betrayal of his trust would be most unusual."

"Father." Koloran spoke, his voice full of calm yet firm authority. "Since the last time anyone has seen Khaleo he stood behind you clutching the amulet in his hand through your robe, I'm going to venture that his sudden disappearance may have transported him back from whence he'd come. And, sister, you'd said that he'd spent at least part of the previous night in the Chalice's chambers. It's the only other possible way I can think of how he'd gain access. Since we know that Khaleo at least *partially* understands the amulet's powers—or, at least we must assume so—it's perhaps more reasonable that he'd used it to teleport back to his last safe place."

"In whatever manner he made it into the Chalice, I want to be there to see the look on his face." Nore spoke quickly and stood. "Andara, come with me. Father, Koloran, we'll find out what's going on at the Chalice and report back to you."

"Go with haste and return in kind, Daughter."

Nore nodded toward father and brother, her face stern in determination, then took Andara's hand and the two bolted from the office and out the wine shop's front door.

It felt more than unusual for Nore and Andara to approach the entrance to the Black Chalice in the relatively early hour of the Dagger, even stranger to see that Kor's molten eyes burned in the outline of the tiny chalice-shaped portal, the door itself, as usual, devoid of any other adornment. The two young women approached and saw the huge eyes widen, then the wide expanse of the Chalice's door open and the great Kuzhani stride forward to usher Nore and Andara inside.

"Leonora, Daughter of Morvedraz, and Andara, welcome. Zhakhar awaits you."

They smiled small, polite smiles and nodded at Kor, who never allowed his sober demeanor to falter, and watched as his huge arm swept behind when they entered, an arm that would have thwarted any attack and that would have been severed voluntarily if the end would have meant protecting the Arbiter's daughter and her companion.

The Chalice stood empty and silent. No wall sconces burned, no crowd abounded. Nore had never been inside her infamous hangout other than during times of either high traffic or at least high intrigue. Seeing the empty tables, the long bar abandon of occupants, not even any staff save Kor in his huge yet silent presence, felt more than awkward.

"Um, Kor? Is Zhakhar nearby?" Nore gazed into the huge Kuzhani's red eyes.

"Yes. Come."

Kor led the way toward the familiar alcove that Nore had enjoyed so many times, so many she'd thought gleaned from none but her own charms, that had brought her such priceless fair—the sparkling wines, rich reds, and brandies of Kwamada; the pastries and succulents of the finest producers; the doting company of some of the most charming and dangerous clientele of any other tavern in the City, all in the unwitting yet handsomely compensated care of none other but Zhakhar, master of the Black Chalice. Walking now toward the chamber, Andara at her side, Nore felt an aura of taint, that the warm privilege she'd been afforded in the past had transformed into nothing more than the byproduct of another deal, struck between the powerful, and that Nore mattered not at all but that she was daughter of the Arbiter of Antra.

Nore parted the thin veil that separated Zhakhar's alcove from the view of the Chalice interior and saw him seated, as Kor had said, though in no apparent state of anxiousness whatsoever.

"So, am I as welcome as when my father was Arbiter?" Nore spoke boldly and in full voice. Andara squeezed her partner's arm.

"You are as welcome as you've always been, Leonora, daughter of Morvedraz, and as you will continue to be until which time you do not wish to grace my chamber with your lovely presence." Zhakhar intoned languidly, his girth resting against the alcove's satin pillows, a great goblet of ale poised in his left hand.

"But what's this you speak, when your father *was* Arbiter? Last I heard there'd been no change in the company leadership. Hahahaha..."

Nore watched as Zhakhar, obviously very pleased with himself, waved toward the head of the alcove. "Come. You've never been shy before. Why start now? May I offer you ladies some sparkling wine to celebrate our reunion with friend Khaleo?"

Nore looked into Andara's eyes, saw them narrow, and her head shake just slightly.

"No, thank you, though, Zhakhar. We promised to report back to my father and Koloran once we determined how things were going here with Khaleo and all. Is he being guarded nearby?"

"He is, indeed. This time one of Kor's cousins has volunteered to chaperon our guest. Lok is even bigger than Kor!"

"But, Zhakhar, haven't you interrogated Khaleo yet?"

"Oh, yes, for hours. His statements are as pathetic as they are ludicrous: swearing that hiding his Antran language skills served only to protect him from a fate he could not have known under my roof; that his original act of fleeing the Dwarvani was because he feared for his life over unfounded accusations; that seeking out your father was done to warn him of the Dwarvani *waryers*; that taking your father by the neck was done out of fear and desperation...etc., etc."

"But has he spoken of the amulet?"

Nore watched Zhakhar's eyes widen. "No, actually. He's not mentioned it again."

"Zhakhar, may I question him? I'd like to do so in *Zhoryhan*."

"Be my guest, Leonora. I've already alerted the authorities of the Regent of the *Maj* as to Khaleo's actions and subsequent deceptions. I've spent far too many resources of time and personnel on him, and I can see in him no advantage toward my general profit no matter in whose charge he's left. I only wanted to ensure that your father and you were kept away from harm. Emissaries from the

Regent will arrive later today. Until then, you may engage him as you like."

"Thank you."

"Of course. But, before you push Khaleo to his last breath, what's the meaning of this strange expression you'd used, '*when my father was Arbiter*?'"

"It is no expression. It is literal fact. My father has retired. Effective night before last. My brother, Koloran, has assumed the responsibilities in full."

Nore watched as Zhakhar's eyes widened, then his smile, and continued to gaze upon him dispassionately while the usually stern, sober master of the Chalice doubled over in laughter.

"*Koloran! Arbiter*?! Daughter, you've always had a way of getting a rise out of me, but that's just the most preposterous thing I've heard in quite some time from you."

"The 'thing' is an assertion, and after you've met with my brother you'll realize that his ascending to the role of Arbiter is as wise a decision as it is deserved."

"Your brother. The mute tasting-counter clerk. Whose eyes remain downcast no matter any attempt at interaction. Who could no sooner hold a conversation with someone of my stature than—"

"Be careful whose stature you question, Zhakhar. For you have not spoken to my brother for well over a year, and I would say that he is as anxious to meet you as he is on equal footing to do so."

"*Really*? Koloran seeks an audience with *me*?"

"Oh, yes. He bid me expressly to inquire of your schedule over the next few nights."

Again, Nore held back her ire while Zhakhar guffawed into his pillows, nearly spilling his ale.

"Leonora, my schedule is *open* to the new Arbiter of Antra! Please bid him visit at his leisure. I am *most* interested in engaging him. But, now, please make your way to Khaleo, for I'm afraid that your time with him grows short."

"I will inform Koloran of your accommodating schedule, Zhakhar. But, please, should he show up seeking an audience, treat him with the same respect as you'd have treated my father, or, at least, as how you've treated me."

"Your request is moot, my dear girl. Koloran is welcome and in the same honored manner as your entire family."

Nore's face remained impassive, but softened somewhat, and she nodded in thanks to Zhakhar, then guided Andara away and, under Kor's direction, toward the room that held Khaleo.

Khaleo slumped in a crude wooden chair while Lok, standing at attention next to the doorway—barred from the *outside*—and with vibrant concentration gazed at the fugitive from his station, arms crossed and eyes wide. After Kor had first sealed the two in, Khaleo had looked up periodically and attempted to engage Lok in conversation, which had proven as futile as speaking to the very stone walls that surrounded them. Now Khaleo attempted to doze and, perhaps by the power of suggestion, induce some semblance of inattention in Lok, though the chance was fleeting.

Then, suddenly, he heard the grate of wood against metal—the beam that barred the door sliding away from its iron locks—and then the door creak slowly open. Lok turned to engage the entrants, but Khaleo saw that the huge Kuzhani never let his attention stray from his charge for more than a brief moment. Khaleo watched Kor enter—his face dour, eyes stern—look toward his cousin and nod; Lok stepped into the hallway, assumedly to guard the door from without, and Khaleo's eyes widened at the sight of Leonora and Andara entering the dim chamber.

"What a pleasant surprise! I'd thought to never see the likes of either of you. Please excuse my appearance. I was plucked rather hastily from my abode, and in none the most, um, appropriate of conditions—"

"Silence, beast. Speak when you are spoken to."

Nore's *Zhoryhan* sounded harsh and guttural, and Khaleo's eyes widened upon hearing himself referred to in the very colloquial, very crude term.

"I'm impressed, cousin. I'd not thought you to retain such base words in your vocabulary. Surely, your subconscious must contain even fowler language, still."

"My subconscious is none of your concern. Why did you target my father?"

"My, my...your conversational skills would improved vastly if only you might take a bit more warm-up time to—"

But Khaleo's weak attempt at subduing Nore's resolve only resulted in the toe of her boot connecting quite squarely with his chin, sprawling him onto the cold stone of the chamber floor, then gasping as her right hand gripped tightly—far tighter than he'd thought her able— at the full sack of his crotch, while a dagger poised in her left, pointed at his throat.

"Ah, I see that the Zhorhai anatomy is at least comparable to Humani males. Please trust that I've had much experience inflicting retribution in this region."

Khaleo attempted a smirk, sweat pouring down his face. *"Yes, I feel the pressure of your sincerity."*

"Now, answer the question: why did you target my father? And please don't waste my time or yours with trivial answers. Zhakhar cares nothing for you. The Regent of the Maj will care less. I care of nothing but my father's safety, and I will have no problem dispatching you. Now. Unless you'd like to end your long, glorious life bleeding out on the stone floor, answer the question."

Khaleo sneered and glowered at Nore, glanced at Kor and Andara, who both simply stood, looking rather disinterested, arms folded in front of them and leaning against the stone wall, then trained his gaze into Nore's own.

"I know he has the amulet! He has to! I know of the old Zhoryhan wizard who'd taken a Dwarvani orphan into his care. It is legend among the remnants of the Zhorhai! It is said that the two eventually made their way to the City of Antra, where the wizard passed on, but bequeathed to the Dwarv the Amulet of ultimate strength, and that here he made his fortune from it. What other Dwarv in the City approaches Morvedraz stature and wealth? It is unheard of! And I need the amulet, Leonora. I need its power to bolster the remaining few who await me—our—return. Please, consider it again! Approach your father about the amulet. Convince him to allow you to take possession of it. Only you or I would be able to invoke its full strength—"

"Enough. Clearly, you seek power you have no means to possess, your ability to manipulate it notwithstanding. My father is a skilled negotiator and expert businessman, and has built his reputation in kind. He has no knowledge of an amulet, or any other such majikal device. He's a Dwarv, for the gods' sake. Now, when I release you, lie prone until I am clear of you, then back yourself against the wall."

"But, the floor is cold, and I wait for how long I do not know..." He thought this his only chance, to soften his demeanor, his eyes, his mouth, the lilt of his voice, and as soon as he felt Nore's grip slacken the slightest degree, Khaleo struck, wrenching his body sideways and lashing a brutal backhand toward Nore's head.

What Khaleo did not know was that the glove Nore wore—the same that held his crotch tightly—was embedded with steel barbs that pierced the skin more deeply as the hand the applied pressure. When Khaleo jerked to the side, Nore clamped down, and the barbs cut through the leather pants and into Khaleo's most tender flesh. The pain was searing, which caused his ill-timed swipe at the skilled fighter to flail miserably. And then, her barbed claw buried in Khaleo's now-inflamed groin, Nore plunged the dagger in her left hand into the fleshy outer base of the fugitive's thigh, snapping the handle off to bury the blade.

Khaleo screamed accordingly, and while the wound was deep, it was far less grave as it was excruciating. Nore then tore her grip from his groin—equally excruciating—and rose.

"I'll leave you to the Regent of the Maj, cousin. I'm sure he'll have about as much patience with you as I have. But, if for some reason you escape his grip and find yourself again in the great City, seeking out amulets or whatever such devices that interest you, know that the next time my blade penetrates your skin it will be through your soft temple."

Kor lifted the still-writhing Khaleo and planted him onto the rough cot that stood against the back wall of the small chamber, tied a rag around the wound on his leg, then with one stride stood in front of the chamber door and gave one clenched knock against it. Lok unbarred the door and swung it opened, changing places with Kor while Nore and Andara followed the trusted Kuzhani toward the main floor of the Chalice, back toward Zhakhar's alcove.

When Zhakhar saw the sweat that both beaded on Nore's head and had soaked through the leather of her tunic, he widened his eyes.

"I trust you've left something of Khaleo for the Regent's emissary to question, Daughter?"

"He's all in one piece, though some of those pieces smart quite a bit at the moment."

"Very well. And what truths did your tactics extract from our acquaintance?"

"Talk of Dwarvs who cavort with wizards who bequeath to them *majikal* amulets used to enrich themselves."

"Indeed. Fantastic tales from a fantastically foolish visitor. I trust his time spent in the Regent's care will yield him more of that he's already experienced if his stories prove consistent. Well, go now, Leonora, and ensure your father—and the new Arbiter—that their safety is secure, and that all is well again in the great City. At least until such time that Khaleo might escape the Regent's dungeons, which may not be for a very, very long time."

"Thank you, Zhakhar. I will never forget your kindness and loyalty."

"Nonsense. Such distractions are bad for business. I was merely acting to protect my investments."

Nore smiled. "Very well. Until next time."

"Take care, Leonora. Oh, and if the word that travels as fast as the Daystar's rays is true, I believe I owe you and Andara hearty congratulations. Please return during more pleasant times and do me the honor of helping you celebrate your union."

The two smiled at Zhakhar—even looked a tad sheepish—nodded their goodbyes and were soon striding down Long Street and toward the Merchant Zirkot, toward Morvedraz and Koloran, to assure them that Khaleo had been apprehended, and that all was, indeed, well in the great City. But as they marched Nore felt a strange sense, an intuition she'd never before experienced, and a thought struck her that had seemed not to materialize from her own mind, as if placed there by some unseen force. And, strangely enough, the thought manifested in *Zhoryan: this is not the last time you will meet with your cousin.*

When they passed the Temple of Uchila—protector of all right souls—Nore slowed, placed her hand around Andara's arm, and turned her toward the temple doors.

"What's wrong?"

"I'd like to stop and ask a blessing."

She watched Andara's eyes widen. "I'll wait here for you."

Nore nodded and walked toward the entrance, pulled open the heavy doors and strode slowly into the cool, dark antechamber. She passed the pillared walls that separated the entry from the temple's main sanctuary, bowed in respect toward the altar and made her way toward the small alcoves that flanked the sides of the great room. There she knelt in front of an icon and bowed her head, listened to the low chanting of the priests in a distant chamber, smelled the incense that floated in the temple's atmosphere. Then she struck a match and lit two incense sticks—one for her father, one for her brother—and murmured the essential invocations that would beg protection for both the former and the new Arbiter of Antra.